THE OCTAGONAL KNIGHT

by
Eric Carlton Neperud

For Saundra,
Wife, Partner in Adventure

By Eric Carlton Neperud

THE LIMBO CHRONICLES
  Trees And Weeds
  Limbo
  The Octagonal Knight
  Dragons And Golems
  The Brotherhood Of Giants
  Wizards And Druids

THE YELLOWSONE TRILOGY
  Wonders Of The Wilderness
  Fleas Upon Snow
  The Periphery Of Sorrow

ISBN: 0-9983838-2-1
ISBN-13: 978-0-9983838-2-8
Published by Valhalla Books

Cover Illustration by Eric Carlton Neperud
Map on back cover by Eric Carlton Neperud
Map on page 237 by Eric Carlton Neperud

My name is Will Amette, or it was before I was reborn. I'm now called Stick Bluewood. I'm not proud of my life of crime, but if I didn't steal I wouldn't have been incarcerated. Sometimes criminals are truly rehabilitated. I was one of them. I became an Octagonal Knight, but I'm getting ahead of myself.

I was given a one-way ticket to Dartmoor, a high security penitentiary world. Most people sentenced to life are murders, but a few, like myself, are habitual offenders. Brave is the word we use to describe people too stupid to be scared. I should know. I've never been scared, not until I heard where I was being sent. I've immersed myself in physicality, but not violence. Would I have to fight to stay alive? My concern was premature. There were things on Dartmoor more dangerous than inmates. A pact was formed to not harm one another. If we united there was a possibility we MIGHT survive.

It was so dangerous on Dartmoor I was molecularly transported there instead of taken by spacecraft. Why put pilots and prison guards at risk unless it was absolutely necessary.

Chapter 1

STICKMAN

I walked out of the teleport portal into in a dim coniferous forest. I turned around, expecting to see the fleeting link to freedom one last time. All I saw were trees. Of course. What merit was there in a two-way portal? The floor was open, with most of the lower branches either dead or broken. The canopy was dense. Light penetrated sporadically, creating irregular shadows, my imagination transfiguring them into feral animals. I may not be too far off---the magnitude of their ferocity and peculiarity being impossible to predict. On a terra-formed world mutations occur more often, and more extremely. The strong are particularly adept at surviving in a hostile environment. If a bunny happened to hop from behind a bush it likely had 10 sim fangs.

My jailors intended to challenge me. I wasn't provided with a weapon, a tool, or even clothes. I wasn't a particularly modest person, but when insects are buzzing around you, biting and stinging, one feels more comfortable when their delicates are protected. I got poison oak on my crotch when I was a child. I didn't care to repeat that excruciating, tenacious experience.

I began looking for something to make clothes out of. I was interrupted by my stomach growling. One would think that a prisoner scheduled to be sent to a dangerous, unfamiliar world would gorge himself. There was a strong possibility that my food supply, initially anyway, would be limited. Whenever I become nervous I don't eat. Why couldn't I be one of those people who ate to console themselves?

Should I just eat the first berry I find, or nut, or mushroom, or should I wait until I find someone who knows what's safe to eat? Would my jailors go through the trouble of constructing Dartmoor if they wished to kill me the first day? I wouldn't put it past them to poison me enough to make me miserable.

My potential meal was delayed when it became dark, unexpectedly and suddenly. When I say suddenly I don't mean the time it takes for sunset to transition into dusk then into darkness. Within a couple of minutes it went from midday brightness to nearly pitch black. There was a full moon, but it was concealed---most of it---by the forest. The few moon rays that did penetrate the canopy, in contrast, made the darkness even darker.

My objective was no longer food, but shelter. Considering there was no suggestion of a city nearby that meant climbing a tree.

There are some things that return to you from your childhood, like riding a bike. Climbing a tree wasn't one of them. Not only was it harder to pull myself up than I remembered, some of the branches broke this time. Through much sweat, scratches, and curses I reached a height I perceived to be safe. It may have been only three meters up, but it felt like twenty.

The sensible thing would have been to try to get some sleep. It wasn't healthy to be weak from hunger AND a lack of sleep, and I was going to have to retain as much of my health as possible in order to survive alone---temporally, preferably. The nocturnal din prevented drowsiness. The sounds were both loud and unfamiliar, in the way city sounds are perceived to be by someone living in the country, and vice-versa. I was also kept up by the discomfort of awkwardly straddling a branch without the protection of pants. Adam wore clothes less from modesty than from the chaffing. It wasn't surprising Eve was the one who snagged the apple. Men became hunters instead of gatherers due to their exposed genitalia.

Daylight occurred as spontaneously as the night. I survived. I promised myself that I wouldn't spend another night that way. After I found food I would find a cave, or build a crude hut out of sticks. The best solution would be to find a settlement, but it could be days for that to happen, and I was apprehensive meeting other criminals, most being more treacherous than I.

I found a few red berries and ate them. They were more appetizer than belly filler. I had to eat something more substantial---protein---MEAT! But how? Hunters used lazar rifles, with tracking projectiles. Kills weren't guaranteed, but the projectiles at least prevented people from being struck inadvertently.

What could I construct from the elements that was a poor substitute for a rifle, but still a substitute? A bow and arrows? Even if I could find a vine of proper length and elasticity to string a piece of wood, it would be difficult to make arrows---good ones---with stone arrowheads and feather stabilizers. That left flinging stones, either in a sling, or by hand. Or a spear. Stones were adequate for small game. Anything larger was likely to become more upset than

5

damaged. I wasn't skilled enough to hit an agile, petite beast. So a spear it had to be.

Another benefit of sharpening a stick was its reusability. I'll only have to make one. All I needed was a jagged stone to sharpen the end of a straight tree limb. The limb couldn't be too thick---making it too difficult to throw---or too narrow---not providing enough bulk to cause significant damage or overcome wind resistance. It also couldn't be sitting on the ground too long, the decay set in weakening it enough for minor pressure to fracture it. Best would be for me to break a branch from a tree, but if it came away that easily it would probably be too brittle to use. I needed a saw if I was going to procure a limb of any quality. I could use a stone as an axe if I had to, but it would take time.

It took me just minutes to find that perfect piece of downed wood. The stick was two meters long and straight as a dowel. Its circumference was narrow enough that I could completely wrap a hand around it, creating a good grip. There was a rough place on the stick about halfway down, not substantial enough to cause the stick to diverge from its flight path, but sufficient to prevent it from slipping.

What didn't take minutes was sharpening the spear. Not only did the piece of rock I used refuse to modify the wood in the manner I intended, it had a tendency to slip, causing it to scrape away as much of my hand as the wood. After a frustrating quarter of whittling I rejected perfection. A fire was required to harden the point. That wasn't going to happen---not today.

My first target was a squirrel. To say my throw was off was to boost my ego. I was fortunate I didn't skewer my foot. The attempts that followed were slightly more accurate, but just as fruitful. I came within a meter of the target---once. I examined the spear point. It was perfect---for playing billiards. I re-sharpened it, cutting myself again.

I used a nearby creek as first a sink, then as a fountain. I was told there weren't any harmful micro-organisms on Dartmoor---there was plenty of things larger to make up for it. I didn't put it past my jailors to lie, but I was willing to risk getting diarrhea. It would keep my mind off my hunger.

As I cupped my hands around my second helping of water, something colorful swooshed past me in the water. Then another. They were orange and red and yellow, with splotches of black and white. I lunged for my spear on the creek's bank, my feet causing a brief chaotic fury in the water. Please, don't scare away the fish. As the water cleared I saw the rainbow scales again. I threw the spear. Water splashed upward as it penetrated the liquid. It floated up to the surface and was swiftly carried away by the current. I madly followed it, scraping my feet on the irregular, sharp rocks below. Around the first bend I found my spear---snagged by a debris cluster. Becoming elated that I wouldn't have to find another sick and modify it, I didn't watch where I was going. I slammed my knee into a boulder. Not only did it look like a vegetable peeler accident, it stiffened and swelled. The cold water eased the pain. An unexpected benefit of the free-flowing blood was it acting as a fish attractor.

Instead of throwing the spear this time I used it as a skewer. I hit something with my first attempt, reinforcing the gifts and limitations of my athleticism. I was extremely agile, but not very accurate. I could chase down a ball, but not throw it. Defeat an opponent in wrestling, but not in darts. I was successful one out of every two attempts at spearing a fish. A dozen of them were thrashing on the bank before I realized I had more than enough to last me several days.

Before I was able to climb out of the creek with my bad knee, something else began to investigate the blood trail. It was a frog, larger than what I was accustomed to seeing, but not substantially---more animal than monster. It swam towards me, with bulging red eyes in front, and slimy, rubbery legs kicking behind. When it was three meters away it leapt at me, its hind legs behaving as powerful springs. I put myself into a defensive stance, attempting to deflect it with my body. In that brief instant when one's instincts and reflexes engage prior to a calamity, I noticed a florescent green hour glass on its back. I reached for the spear, a

7

fish still skewered. As a continuation of the motion I swung it in front of me. The frog fell, landing chest first onto the point. It slid down, settling on top of the fish, creating an ungainly, bizarre shish-kabob. The momentum from the contact pushed me back. I stumbled on my bad knee, the impulse of my fall causing the spear to jolt from my hand.

I lay there for an indefinite amount of time, completely immobile, reeling in pain. But feeling pain meant I was still alive. After recovering enough to move, I glanced briefly at my spear and what enveloped it. The slimy secretion on its skin glistened. Maybe it was okay to touch the frog, and even to eat it, but I wasn't going to risk it. I could make another spear, and there were other things---already caught---to eat.

I contemplated---very briefly---rubbing two sticks together to make a fire. It was supposed to take a long time to generate enough heat to create an ember. Be it my affinity to physicality, or an attention deficit, I wasn't a patient man. I've eaten sushi before---paying substantially for it---so I wasn't going to begin complaining now. I never liked sushi. I ate it as a lark, a test of my manhood, my ability to endure discomfort. Raw fish was a taste I never acquired. But if I didn't start acquiring it I wouldn't be around long enough to devour the things I truly enjoy. People got weaker the longer they went without food. Weaker meant less strength, less endurance, a poorer immune system---and poorer reflexes. If I was a fraction of a second slower with the spear I would likely be dead already.

The raw fish didn't feel too great going down, but I felt much better a quarter later, after it had time to digest. My strength returned. If it wasn't for my knee I would have felt wonderful. I found a straight, strong stick to replace the contaminated spear. I didn't take the time to sharpen it, my immediate use for it being storage for my fish, and, concurrently, as a cane.

I still hadn't found a good place to sleep, so that was my priority now. I had no idea when it would get dark. The sun hadn't changed position since morning, so I wasn't able to even approximate. There were some worlds that rotated so slowly daylight was measured in weeks, not hours. Others so fast the sun soaring above made you dizzy. Moderate temperatures---and vegetation---indicated a standard length. Then why did the sun not move? With my bum knee, shelter was now limited to ground level.

Caves were often found in canyons, so I followed the stream bed downstream. Streams eventually flow into rivers, and rivers into seas. People settled beside large bodies of water. I was dreading interacting with inmates, but it was the best opportunity for me to survive for the duration. I found a few small openings in the banks of the shallow canyon that cradled the creek, but none of them were large enough to sustain a man. Being reluctant to walk in or beside the creek, I scanned for potential shelter from above. The desire to not come into contact with another of those large, probably poisonous, frogs---green widows, I called them--- outweighed the potential missed opportunity.

Dusk arrived before I could find my shelter. The dimming of light lasted a handful of minutes, but to someone frantic it felt like seconds. I strongly considered hiding in a bush.

I saw a man. It was difficult to distinguish his features. The moon provided some illumination. Like the night before, the forest blocked most of it. If it wasn't for the opening the creek created I probably wouldn't had seen him at all.

"Hello," I said weakly, not certain if I wanted to make contact. He didn't respond. I walked closer to him. He didn't move. "Hello," I repeated, stronger than before. I was committed now, either to the benefit, or detriment, that would come from it. Still no response. I moved even closer. Then I discovered why he hadn't moved. He wasn't alive, or had ever been. He was a doll constructed from sticks, green trousers and a tan shirt covering the rudimentary facade. Above the clothing was a watermelon, with two ovals cut out of it. Below them was a narrow, parabolic opening, twisted awkwardly. The stick man was supported by legs thrust into the ground.

Stickmen were constructed to scare away birds or other animals, usually within a crop field. That meant a farm with people and food was nearby. But where? All I saw was forest.

A light flickered into existence, but it didn't come from a farmhouse. It came from within the watermelon. Maybe it was programmed to come on at night, but on Dartmoor, a primitive planet?

When the stickman moved I dropped my walking stick, which may have been the stupidest thing I have done since being incarcerated. It's been said how a man reacts during calm, relatively good times isn't a valid examination of his character. How a man reacts during stress that's the true test. I reacted well during the green widow altercation. Let's see if past behavior is an indicator of future performance.

The stickman pulled up one soil encrusted leg out of the ground, then the other. It walked towards me methodically. I was too dazed to react. It swung its arms at me, pummeling my head and upper torso. I fell. The only thing that kept me conscious---a temporary condition---was the throbbing pain in my knee, where most of my weight seemed to be.

I woke up with a dreadful decaying odor blowing in my face. The stickman must have moved me, because I was no longer near the creek. And I must have been unconscious for quite awhile, because it was light again.

Something incredibly large and excessively furry straddled me. It looked like it was doing pushups and I just happened to be beneath it. Its fur was loose on its belly, dangling far enough down to brush against me. It tickled, in an irritating, non-playful manner. I had to focus on not reacting to my discomfort. Playing dead was prudent when escape wasn't imminent. Something dead doesn't grunt.

Colored light burst around us. There are rumors of a bright light at the end of a tunnel when one dies. Colored lights are more festive. But others aren't supposed to see the light, and this furry monster above me certainly did. It leaped off me and ran, its back legs together, then its front legs. I heard it briefly after I no longer saw it, the crunching of branches and the cracking of leaves dissipating a few seconds later.

"What do we have here?" asked a mellow, deep voice.

"It looks like an infant," responded a whiny, higher pitched voice. "It better be worth what we spent to save it."

Chapter 2

COR, MIN, FAS

I didn't grow up wanting to be a criminal. Believe it or not, I wanted to be a priest. I wasn't being altruistic. They were powerful. People looked up to them. They followed their advice. I grew up in a religious family, so when I made my desire known to join the priesthood it was well-received. The Amettes were Cors from way back, with records confirming their assistance in the foundation of the religion, and its dispersal through the masses.

Religions can be either metaphysical or philosophical. Being egocentric, most consider themselves to be all-encompassing. A majority of the ancient religions, Christianity and Buddhism the most prominent, are metaphysical---Confucianism being one of the few exceptions. Most modern religions, in contrast, primarily adhere to philosophies. As the Garden Planet began to disperse its masses into space, religious beliefs became more convoluted. Dogma created on one world didn't necessarily apply to those living on another---or in the void in between.

The role of the philosopher and the scientist is to explain the world---or worlds---around them. Through their mutual disdain for one another they developed---together---an understanding of the modern universe. Not the entire universe, and not every aspect of it, but they were able to create a schema for how people functioned, singly and in clusters. It was an arduous, frustrating expedition to discovery. Whenever a scientist or a philosopher made some headway in their explanation of the universe they came to a road block. The scientists, being unemotionally impartial, hadn't a clue how organisms reacted to one another. Philosophers, in contrast, were only able to express their ideas and intuitions using ethereal terminology. Originally they came together to flaunt their superiority. They ended up in bed together---figuratively, and literally. Opposites do attract. Through interactions---the ying complementing the yang---they developed the EMBODIED TRINITY. Christians weren't pleased with the name, in particular after people began to truncate it to the TRINITY. They demanded legislation to be passed to forbid other groups from using that term. The point became moot when someone reminded them that most tenets of Christianity were borrowed from other religions.

The Embodied Trinity broke all aspects of human existence into three classifications: physical, mental, and spiritual/emotional. It was so simple, yet so encompassing. Everything could be explained as combinations of their characteristics. Each cluster of classification constructed its own philosophy, its own religion. Names had to be assigned---and that was nearly of as great a debate as the creation of the Trinity. References from the Garden Planet were eventually agreed upon, with Cor, Min, and Fas representing the physical, mental, and spiritual/emotional aspects. As the religions became more established, churches began to form around them: Temples of Cor, Min, and Fas. Within a generation the philosophical religions had more influence than the metaphysical ones.

Genetic material is retained within a family, passed down from mother and father to son and daughter. Individuals with strong Cor traits generally had children with strong Cor traits. People today are more liberal about inter-aspect marriages, but for many years it was taboo to marry someone not of your Temple. Potential suitors were often tested to insure the sustained purity of a Temple. Inbreeding---within a Temple---caused certain characteristics to be emphasized, resulting in the creation of new races. Purity within a Temple identified a person as much as their height and weight.

I was 55-10-35, meaning I was 55% Cor, 10% Min, and 35% Fas. To become a priest I had to be at least 50% Cor, so I barely qualified. I was one of those borderline seminary students the other kids made fun of. Not all the kids taunted me, just the ones with slightly more Cor than me, those with insecurities that THEY didn't measure up.

With my secondary trait being more than 33% I was influenced almost as much by emotion as I was by physicality. Sometimes that got me into trouble, my emotions dictating what I did and how I reacted. Being only 10% Min, I didn't have much common sense. I often challenged people bigger and stronger than me, over minor slights, or just to test myself. I had to be the best, my insecurities in the foreground. Most of my friends thought I was crazy going to seminary school. Those already there thought it a waste of time---mine and theirs.

I was eventually kicked out. If I was able to focus I think I would have been able to cut it. I did believe in most of the physical philosophies. I couldn't return home. My family disowned me. Generation upon generation of Amettes loyal to Cor, only to have this headstrong spawn disgrace them. One heathen ruining the entire pew.

I rebelled after leaving school. My activities were anything but pious. I only stole from the rich, if that mattered. I did it as much for the challenge as for financial reward. My downfall was my fondness for socialization. No, a woman didn't turn me in. I thought it might be more fun---and more profitable---to be part of a group. I didn't count on incompetence. I made the assumption everyone was dedicated as I in committing a crime in as perfect an execution as possible.

I was sentenced to life on Dartmoor, the jury determining the accumulated value of my crimes exceeded the maximum allowed to sustain my citizenship. Being caught bothered me, but not the idea of spending the rest of my life on a penal colony. I was becoming bored with my existence. This eternal imprisonment would give me a new start. By the time I passed through the transport portal I was actually feeling excited.

Chapter 3

STICK

"The first thing we need to do," spoke my deep-voiced rescuer, "is name you."

"I'm Will Amette."

"No you aren't," countered his whiny-voiced companion. "Not anymore. Well, Centaur, what should we name this infant?"

"Anyone ever tell you it's not nice to call people names?"

"INFANT isn't really an insult," the bigger guy replied. Centaur was it? Now that's a strange name. "Everyone new to Limbo---still green---is called that." He looked at his friend. "It has to be something representative of his first day here, Pebble."

"Scarecrow?

"Scare?"

"Bear bait

"Bear?"

"Bait?"

"How about BAD LUCK? Who ever heard of an infant getting himself killed twice in the same day?"

"Almost getting himself killed twice. We prevented him from dying that second time."

"Don't I get some say in what I'm called?" I pleaded.

"Not really," said Pebble. "The first person, or persons, who find you, gets to name you."

"But it would be prudent to take suggestions," added Centaur. "He might keep the name for a hundred years."

It's odd how we organize information. Hearing one strange thing spoken reminds us of others. "Did you say I died?"

"From your description of your encounter what other conclusion could we reach?" Pebble questioned.

"Don't I look like I'm live? Now?"

"NOW is a modifier," stated Centaur. "And your state of being has been modified. You were re-created. The same process that terra-formed Limbo brought you back to life. The planet is in flux---including the things on it."

"So, I can die, repeatedly, and always be...re-created?"

"Don't be so gleeful, infant," said Pebble. "Every time we are re-created we are modified, more often detrimental than beneficial."

"Think of what happens when something is copied," Centaur explained. "A copy is usually not an exact replica of the original. It's close, but there are some minute flaws. If that copy is copied, even more flaws occur."

"So what happens after a dozen re-creations?"

"You are so severely mutated that you are no longer human," Centaur answered.

"Sometimes it takes fewer re-creations than that," added Pebble.

"So try not to die."

"We need you to retain your humanity long enough to pay off your debt." Great.

"How does one earn a living here?" I asked. "Or do we? Has Dartmoor become more a commune than a prison? Where everyone shares happily with his neighbor?"

"Hardly," said Centaur. "That's not to say many don't abandon their life of crime. Being sentenced here was the breaking point for many---their epiphany. There are entire cities of merchants, and healers, and builders---even police officers."

15

"We have the HUMAN PACT," stated Pebble. "There are enough dangers on Limbo to survive without us also having to survive each other. I used to commit every crime imaginable, including murder. Now I even have trouble hunting animals for food."

"We don't know if that deer was always a deer. It could have been human a year ago."

"So I could mutate into an animal instead of a monster?" I asked.

"Anything is possible," said Centaur. "You might even mutate into a plant or a rock."

"How about CREEK?" Pebble suggested. "He followed that creek for quite awhile."

"He does seem to be wet behind the ears."

A mosquito began circling me, spiraling in closer. In the state of mind I was in even the slightest irritation set me off. That high-pitched buzzing was torture, boring into my brain. I snatched a stick from beside me and struck the insect, killing it.

"STICK?" Centaur and Pebble suggested simultaneously. The connection was to the stick I now held, but it reminded me of the stickman.

"Do you agree?" asked Centaur. I nodded. Savior and curse. It was too perfect.

Something was wrong. "DID I JUST KILL SOMEONE?!"

"Probably not," said Centaur.

"PROBABLY?!"

"I'm confident our jailors added mosquitoes to the indigenous fauna, to torment us."

"And even if it was once human, didn't it deserve to die, having been mutated into a mosquito?" asked Pebble. "It was either intentionally a nuisance---deserving our wrath. Or a mutant of circumstance---deserving to be put out of its misery."

"Being a mosquito wouldn't be that bad. All that food for the taking, in the form of a protein-rich smoothie. Not just humans to snack upon, but horses, and cows, and deer: a perpetual

16

smorgasbord."

Chapter 4

PENTA

In addition to STICK, I was given the name BLUEWOOD, same as the forest I found myself in when I entered Limbo: the name the locals gave their world---never living a real existence, being given a life sentence on a prison planet, but never dying. So Stick Bluewood I had become, Will Amette an anonymous memory: a character from a book, or a holograph, or someone I once met.

I became a quasi indentured servant. I had this debt to repay. Whatever Centaur and Pebble used to scare away that bear apparently cost a lot of money. They were entrepreneurs, doing a little bit of this and a little bit of that. Nothing amounting to much: no security, no guaranteed minimal profit.

I was provided with clothes to wear and rudimentary provisions, all deducted from my share of whatever windfall we may accumulate. That windfall was usually in someplace remote--- and well guarded.

Criminals often took the easy route, which meant doing anything that earned them an easy buck. Washing dishes, serving meals, making beds, were beneath them. Dying in the wilderness beneath the paws, claws, or fangs of a feral mutant was nearly as disdainful, but better than starving.

Salvagers, seekers of discarded fortune, were gamblers. Would the big score come before the mutation? Most salvagers were infants: too naïve, and too desperate. They too became respectable citizens of a city, if they were lucky enough not to become too mutated, continuing their lifestyles, but now as foes of humanity. Every mutation wasn't negative, but most modified them enough that the unchanged were squeamish in their prescience. Those significantly mutated were, at best, outcasts, some living isolated, others grouped together.

From the earliest days of Limbo's occupation adventurers sought encounters with monsters for the thrill, or for the occasional reward given by respectable humans for their destruction. As monsters became stronger---mutations stacking---adventurers were more easily defeated. Their possessions became treasures. Monsters recruited monsters to create mutation conglomerates. Treasures became concentrated and grew. Adventuring became more profitable, but also more deadly.

"Where are we heading?" I asked. We've been walking constantly since daylight, northwest relative to the sun being due north---which it wasn't. The sun was stationery above the center of Limbo. You'll probably thinking the center of a planet is its interior. It is, but although the planet is often referred to as Limbo, Limbo is actually that part of the planet occupied by the penal colony. And no, I can't just walk out of the prison. There's supposed to be some kind of energy shield keeping the inmates in. What's behind the shield? No one knows. Why do we have a stationary sun, that dims at night? We're likely on an artificial world, at least one that's no longer orbiting a sun, or too far away from it to receive much heat or light.

Before we began walking I got a good look at Centaur's map. It was very confusing. Instead of having north, south, east, and west on it, it had ORDER, CHAOS, POSITIVE, and NEGATIVE. Mountains and rivers and seas were scattered across the circular map---and cities. The only one I remembered was Gulag, in the center---the bull's eye. I had no clue where we were. If the angle of the sun was any indicator, we weren't that close to Gulag, but that depended on the relative height of the sun to the size of the penal colony.

"Three Rivers," said Centaur. I don't remember seeing that

18

on the map, but there was only so much I could take in at a glance.

"If we were heading to Bluewood City we would already be there," Pebble stated.

"Bluewood City has a limited supply of stones. I would like at least one defensive penta with us in case of emergencies."

Pebble turned around to look at me. "I hope you're worth ten gold."

I hoped so too. I felt guilty that Centaur and Pebble had to spend so much saving me. A gold coin could be exchanged for ten silvers coins, or 100 coppers. A copper could buy a basic good: a loaf of bread, or a beer. How long would it take for me to earn the equivalent of 1000 loaves of bread?

Half-an-hour into our walk we left the forest. The remainder of the morning we traveled through a grassland, disrupted intermittently by a solitary shrub or tree. Midday we intersected a wide trail, which we followed the remainder of the day.

Time was supposed to pass more quickly when one is distracted, so I brought up something that had been on my mind since Centaur and Pebble scared the bear away. "What was that thing you threw at the bear? A flare? Fireworks? Dynamite?"

"Penta," Centaur replied.

I looked confused.

Pebble sighed loudly. "Don't infants know anything anymore?"

"That's why they're called infants, Pebble. Think of penta as a kind of energy that is created when five elem bond. What is elem? Elemental energy. There are four varieties, paired with the primal elements: earth, air, fire, and water."

"It sounds medieval to me. Pre-medieval. Do you expect me to believe in wizards in pointy hats making alchemist potions?"

"Is it any less believable than people coming back to life? Limbo does have its wizards, but they're more penta peddler than sorcerer."

"Very powerful penta peddlers," Pebble added.

"Yes. Definitely people you don't want to make angry. That's why we like to keep our distance. They rarely leave their tower, so unless we enter an emporium, a Wizard sanctioned penta shop, it's extremely unlikely we'll see one."

"Is there some special way to combine earth, wind, fire, and water together? If anyone can do it they'll be explosions everywhere"

"Elem is rare, a handful of particles per square kay. There are people who make a living finding it. There are devices that assist them, but they still have to be in the right place at the right time. To be a good elem prospector you have to be intuitive and conversant."

"Accidents must happen when combining elem."

"To those who bind their own: witches and warlocks. Derogatory terms for dangerous people who might get you killed if you're too close to one of their miscues. There is a relatively safe alternative. The Wizards not only peddle penta, they package it. The most common method of packaging is in capsules. Walls separate the individual elem until the penta is needed."

"And this happens when these walls are corrupted when some trauma is induced? How much force is required? It must be significant or accidents would occur, frequently. That penta capsule couldn't have made significant impact against that bear's fur. Did you throw it on the ground beside it?"

"I swallowed it?"

"You….? How is that possible? You survived. Unless you also died. Did those bright lights just shoot out of your ass? Shouldn't you and your clothes be burnt to a crisp?"

"It depends on how well I manipulate the penta. There ARE many accidents. An infant should never swallow a stone---what the capsules are more commonly called. We can control where the energy is released. Unless I want my body to be affected, I release it many meters away."

"Aren't there safer methods to release penta?"

"If you apply enough force to a stone it will activate, but you won't have any control over it. Rods and rings are safer. Their external triggers retain contact, so you maintain control. They're more expensive. A ten charge rod costs a 90 gold. A ring, at least a 1000. You'll only see wizards and the superfluously affluent wear one. The accumulative energy in a ring is supposedly so great that it attracts elem, like metal shavings to a magnet."

"Is there some book I can buy, or class I can take?"

"If you want easy---and safe---stay away from penta, in all its forms. If you find any, sell it."

"But you used penta---to save me."

"I'm not saying there aren't uses for it. Penta are tools, and sometimes tools can be dangerous. A saw can help build a house, but it can also cut off a finger.

"There are a few safeguards. Each stone and rod and ring is labeled with runes, symbols of the four elements. The combinations of the elem can be learned, the actions of the released penta, predicted. That doesn't prevent the same penta sometimes experiencing drastically different results. Different people manipulate penta differently. There is as much an art to it as a science.

Chapter 5

DEMI-HUMAN

We arrived at Three Rivers at sundim. It had too small a population---and tax base---to afford being walled, but it was still well protected. In addition to being nestled within the confluence of two mighty rivers---the Neutral and the West Fork---a deep gorge was dug below the city's exposed south side, and filled with seepage from the two rivers. Three narrow causeways connected the city to the land south of it, the east and west causeways bordering a river. Archers and catapults relentlessly patrolled them.

To enter the town we first had to cross the Neutral River. A ferry was provided, but not the fare. We also had to pay to enter the town. Supplying safety was expensive. Instead of repaying my debt it continued to grow.

"Let's see if we can replace that penta we consumed saving you, infant," Pebble commented.

We couldn't. Three River's penta shop---only Wizard owned outlets were called emporiums---was closed. The hours it was open for business were so restrictive to render bankers generous.

"I guess we'll have to rent a room," said Centaur without much enthusiasm. We had planned to re-provision and escape, camping on the way back to the Bluewoods. It wasn't practical to leave the city to return tomorrow morning. More debt for me.

The innkeeper insisted he managed a quality establishment. "The beds are pest free." Like he was going to tell us if they weren't. "You planning to eat supper here, tonight? A twenty percent discount for those who room AND board."

We took him up on his offer. The bowls of stew were hearty. The meat---whatever species it came from---was abundant. The bread, fresh. The ale was extra, but as plentiful as the meat--- and just as gamey.

This sick feeling---no, it wasn't from the food---suddenly overwhelmed me. "You don't think the meat in this stew might be closely related to us, do you?" I spoke softly to my companions, not wishing the innkeeper to overhear.

"Unlikely." Centaur took another bite of his stew, putting emphasis on his lack of concern.

"Unlikely? Can't you be a bit more positive than that?"

"Some people do resort to cannibalism. Most of them live in the Negative Frontier."

"They're not entirely human," added Pebble.

"MY GOD!"

"My Gaea. You're on Limbo now, infant."

22

"So you're saying there are actual restaurants that serve HUMAN?"

"Those mutated enough to no longer be considered human usually abandon cities," said Centaur. "I think there are a few places that serve DEMI-HUMAN. I've never been to one myself."

"How far detached from humanity would something have to be for me to eat it?" I questioned, introspectively, not expecting a reply.

"Infinitists believe the more distantly related to something we are the less immoral it is to consume it. Eating birds being more moral than eating cows. Vegetarians being more moral than omnivores."

"To an ogre, eating a human may seem no more immoral than us eating pork," Pebble commented. "What do you think they call human meat? Meat of an animal is usually called something different. Pork from swine. Beef from cows. Venison from deer."

"Only you."

"A person thinking isn't the same thing as a person doing."

"You have been re-created more often than I. Maybe being that much closer to becoming a monster brings those thoughts to the surface."

"No. I had thoughts like before I came to Limbo. Few perfectly adjusted people are sentenced to Limbo."

I used to think about dying. It's been replaced with fears of mutation. With dying there was a possibility of going to heaven. What positive spin could I put on becoming grotesquely deformed? And I wasn't just going to change physically. I would come to think of myself as a goblin or an ogre. I would no longer think about having a physical relationship with that woman in the distance. The curves would retain their attractiveness---but now as a precursor to a hearty meal. I suddenly wasn't very hungry---a rarity for me, someone with a perpetual, voracious appetite.

The straw mattress was scratchy, but I got used to it. Walking 30 kays was a great sedative. I fell asleep immediately.

Chapter 6

GOBLIN UNIT

After breaking our fast we bought provisions for our return to the Bluewoods, a majority of it food. I also bought a rusty sword---another advance on my potential income. If nothing else I could give someone---or thing---tetanus. The better swords were more expensive than penta. It might be years before I could afford one of those.

The penta shop was small but sturdy---with a hint of elegance. Poor people couldn't afford to manipulate elem. Those who could wanted to be reminded of it. The shop was constructed of stone. Most of the city's structures were a hodgepodge of wood and stucco. The proprietor shared half of his profits with the Wizards. He didn't dare short-change them. A person cheated the Wizards ONCE.

Centaur and Pebble perused the penta shop like kids in a candy store. Once a person used penta his life was forever changed: nothing was ever as sweet. No rings were displayed. Three Rivers was either too small to justify an inventory, or being a franchise, couldn't be trusted with any. Or maybe they were just stored in a safer location. My companions finally settled on a stone. I was curious what the symbols on it represented, but I didn't ask. Not contributing to its purchase I didn't deserve to know.

Before we left Three Rivers we walked across the street to the Town Hall. It was a simple building, remarkably so in contrast to the elegant penta shop. The simplicity was intentional, to thwart accusations of overspending. Ex-criminals were acutely aware of abuse and corruption. Centaur and Pebble found what they were looking for without having to enter the building. BOUNTY was engraved on a slate billboard attached to the structure. In chalk, was written:

Termite Infestation Terminated	364 G
Flies Swatted	26 G
Water Elemental Dried	400 G
Octocat Ostracized	143 G

"Somebody is willing to pay 400 gold to destroy a water elemental?" I asked.

"The upper case **G** means goblin units, not gold coins," Centaur clarified. "Goblins are the most abundant mutational pest. Most are found in the Frontier, but sometimes a few wander into Neutrality. The value of a goblin unit is dependent upon supply and demand: how many monsters that need to be terminated in an area versus the number of adventurers willing to exterminate them."

"The going rate for Three Rivers is **.23**," Pebble added. "Up a hundredth from the last time we were here. The population of undesirables must be increasing."

"Or maybe too many adventurers are dying," countered Centaur.

"So there are really goblins here?" I questioned. I didn't entirely rule the dead coming back to life---cloning and gene therapy provided a foothold---but fairy tale monsters?

"And ogres and ghouls. People like to attach familiar names to things. Why not connect the severely mutated to monsters of legend? Those gnarled and animal-like we call goblins. Those overgrown and brute-like: ogres."

After a moment to digest what was said---there was going to be a lot of that the next couple of weeks---I asked, "Which bounty are we going after?"

Pebble's response: "So an infant that has already died once, almost twice, thinks he can collect a bounty? Didn't you have your hands full with a fluffy teddy bear?"

"Give Stick a break," said Centaur. "The bounty on an Ursus Major is **40 G**."

"I don't like being in debt," I said. "What would we have to kill in order for me to pay you guys back---completely?"

Centaur did some quick calculations in his head. "Either the termites or the water elemental. Your share will come to about 30 gold, leaving you 15 after paying us back."

"That's quite a windfall for an infant," said Pebble. "Don't forget, the bounty is proportional to the difficulty in receiving it."

"Let's make a deal. If I get killed you don't have to rescue me," I responded. "If I mutate into a monster I promise I won't eat you. Now, what's going to be easier, the water elemental or the termites?"

"The water elemental is a single creature, but it'll be very difficult, verging on impossible, to subdue it with just the three of us. One blow from it will likely kill us. Think of a thousand liters of water falling on you, instantaneously. And one strike by us would feel like a pin prick. Many pinpricks can kill, but not just three."

"There could be dozens of termites in the infestation," stated Pebble. "But...we can handle them, if we attack just a few at a time."

"Can't we just stomp on them?" I suggested. "They're just bugs."

"Nothing on Limbo is what we're accustomed to," Centaur retorted. "These termites will be the size of large rats, some as large as a cat or a small dog."

Talking to the officials inside the City Hall we learned the location of the house infested, and that any treasure we found within was ours: scavenger rights going into effect because the house was condemned. The concern was for the infestation spreading. The owners of the house hadn't been seen in days and are assumed to be consumed.

Chapter 7

INFESTATION

The house was atop a bluff overlooking the West Fork River. The word HOUSE didn't do it justice. It was a mansion---one of the larger ones. It looked reasonably intact from the outside, with just one large hole where the front door likely once existed. The exterior of the house was stucco, a major contributor to its preservation. Another was the termites not consuming the support beams. In addition to being larger than their mundane cousins, they were more intelligent.

"We need to make sure we kill the king and queen," said Centaur. "They are usually hidden away somewhere. If they survive they'll produce another brood."

"But not for a few days," said Pebble. "We'll be able to collect our reward and leave town before that happens. No one will know the next infestation is from the same breeders."

"I'll know. We must be professional. I must believe we are doing something more noble than just being bounty hunters. How can we remain sane for a hundred years without a higher calling?"

Did I hear right? "A hundred years?"

"In one form or another. Re-creations are indefinite as far as we know. There doesn't appear to be a limit."

"What might a person be able to accomplish if they live forever?"

"Not all accomplishments are beneficial," said Pebble.

"Pebble ought to know. He used to work for one of Limbo's most notorious shadow bosses."

Those simple words from Centaur---about him believing in something more important than the daily grind---influenced me

27

more than anything else. That and Pebble's loyalty. Without either, I never would have become an Octagonal Knight, but I'm getting ahead of myself, again.

Centaur scrutinized the termite-infested mansion, intently. "The key to our success---and survival---is surprise. We can't overwhelm the enemy, so we need a strategy. We need to be sneaky. No one is sneakier than Pebble."

"Thank you."

"Pebble is a skilled recon-neur. He'll investigate the termites while we devise a plan."

Pebble slinked, in the direction of the mansion, making no sounds. He hid in the shadows, becoming almost invisible.

"Insects see better in the dark than humans," stated Centaur. "So we'll attack during daylight. These termites might be smarter than typical termites, but they aren't that smart. The shadows within the house will confuse them. Unless Pebble reveals himself completely, he'll stay safe."

"Why don't we force them out of the house?" I suggested. "They'll have to come out of that opening---just one or two at a time. Smack, smack. Crunch, crunch. Easy. And entertaining."

"Entertaining? I should have saved the bear. I don't want to die, infant. I'm willing to pay for my indiscretions, but not with my humanity. Not the little of it I have left. You have a point, though, about attacking them out here instead of room to room. We could easily become trapped in that house. They may even collapse the roof on us if they become desperate."

Pebble slinked back to us. He didn't appear pleased. "They're all over the place. The interior walls are eaten away, creating one cavernous chamber. The first and second floors have been consumed, everything but the supports. The king and queen are in the basement, in a structure their progeny has built for them. Its roof rises above what was once the first floor."

"Stick suggests we force them out."

"I suggest we do the same. There's no way we can attack them individually in that large open area. Get on opposite sides of

28

the opening. Given enough time I can irritate anything, enough for them to want to come after me."

"Pebble definitely has a gift."

I unwrapped my rusty sword from the rag I kept it in. I was more concerned with the stained, flaky metal ruining my possessions than it being sharp enough to cut me. Centaur detached a large axe from his belt. We walked quietly toward the opening of the house, approaching at an extreme angle, to conceal us from those looking out. When we were in position Pebble noisily sauntered up to the opening, using words that I've read but never spoken. When he was within a meter of it he threw stones at the structure the termites built. A rumbling could be heard inside. I was concerned the mansion might collapse. Pebble walked away from it, at an angle that maintained line of sight. He was determined that the termites only focus on him, exclusively.

The termites rushed through the aperture so abruptly, and so swiftly, we missed the first two. They headed straight for Pebble. We handled the next two, my rusty sword making a scrunching sound as it cracked an exoskeleton. Centaur's axe completely split his opponent's back. Another two termites were upon us before we were able to react. Centaur recovered nicely, but when I brought my sword back up it caught on my initial opponent's carapace. With all my might I pulled up on the sword, lifting the 10 kilo termite 50 sims off the ground. As Centaur killed his second termite, all I could do was knock the carcass of my first opponent into my second. The second termite stumbled. It was almost enough time for me to recover and escape. Not quite. I was clipped, then attacked by not only termite number two, but by two others. Assessing I was the weaker foe, I became the focus of their aggression. Centaur came to my rescue, but not before he was squirted with a stringent amber liquid by the next two termites leaving the mansion. He screamed as his eyes squinted and watered. He swung his axe madly, sweeping his perimeter. If any of the termites had been within range their exoskeletons would have become splinters. They kept their distance, their exceptional intelligence saving them. Just when I thought I was a goner---one step closer to becoming a mutated monster---an arrow pierced the shell of one of my attackers, making first a crunching sound, then a squish. A second termite was pierced by an arrow. Then a third. The remaining termites fled back into the mansion. Two small hands grabbed my jerkin and pulled me away.

"I'll help you too, Centaur," Pebble uttered beside me, "when you stop swinging that axe."

"I CAN'T SEE!"

"They're back in their lair, except for the ones we killed."

As soon as Centaur lowered his axe Pebble rushed up to him. He led him by an arm to where I lay. In addition to my wrist being sprained---or broken---I had a few plugs of flesh bit out of me, one from each leg, and one from my side. None were deep enough to need immediate attention.

"I thought you weren't going to save me," I commented.

"I'm a damn liar," Pebble responded. "One of the many bad habits I have. You stuck your neck out, like the rest of us. You're one of us now. I don't leave one of my own behind."

"Are your eyes going to be okay?" I asked Centaur.

"Probably. We heal quickly on Limbo. Consider it a down payment for future re-creations."

We spent another night at the inn. It provided hot baths--- for a fee. "It's foolish to spend an extra three coppers for...water," Centaur complained.

"I insist," said Pebble. "And if you don't want to do it for yourself, do it for us. YOU STINK!"

"I don't smell anything---nothing at all."

"That's because your scent glands have melted. The stuff the termites sprayed on you smells like it's combustible. I get light headed just being near you."

"It just might work," I said to myself, but it was loud enough for the others to hear.

"So the infant is beginning to grow up. What have you come up with?"

"Let me just think about it some more. There has to be

something I haven't thought of. It can't be that easy."

After Centaur's bath and supper I told them of my plan.
"Why don't we just burn the house down with the termites in it?
It's condemned, so the town authorities wouldn't mind too much as
long as the fire doesn't spread."

"I believe the infant has become a toddler," stated Pebble.

"It might not sound like it, but coming from Pebble, that's a
compliment," said Centaur.

"There is a downside. Whatever treasure is in the house will
also be destroyed."

"Did you see any treasure?"

"No, but that doesn't mean there isn't any. The termites
might be storing it in that structure they built."

It felt good to be able to contribute. Being rewarded---
respected as a peer---for my first suggestion, I felt more confident
expressing myself. "If the owners of the mansion had any penta
don't you think they would have used it already, to protect
themselves? Anything else of value, like gold, will probably survive
a fire."

"Stick's right," said Centaur. "As soon as I can see again,
make that bonfire. I can already see some light. Nothing is in focus
yet, but I'm confident I'll be fully healed after a good night's sleep."

"If that stuff they sprayed at you is as flammable as it smells
that house will become an inferno," stated Pebble.

"Maybe I should wait to take that bath, then? Seems like a
waste to wash myself to only smell like smoke."

"You're taking a bath. Either in a tub or the river. Your
choice. With you not being able to see you're at a disadvantage."

"I'll eventually be able to see."

"Not if I can help it."

There were some advantages being a loner, like not relying
on others. Eliminating playful banter wasn't one of them.
Interacting with other people made life more interesting. The order
within one's self had to be balanced with the chaos of others.
That's something the extremes---people with an extremely high
percentage of one of the clusters of attributes---will never

31

understand. Maybe it was a good idea I was expelled from seminary. Was being exceptional or balanced better?

Chapter 8

OCTAGONAL

In the morning, Centaur's eyes were still sore, but he could see.

"We should barricade that opening," Centaur suggested. "We don't want any termites to escape."

"Before we do this, we need to bond," said Pebble.

"Becoming blood brothers?" I hypothesized. "Cutting our hands and clasping them? Something like that?"

"I don't think we can afford to lose any more blood," said Centaur. "I left about half of mine outside that house."

"I have another idea," said Pebble. "Follow me."

He took us to the inn's municipal bathroom. Only the finest inns had individual facilities. "Take your pants down."

"I'm your friend," said Centaur, "but I don't want to be that kind of friend."

"Shut up. Both of you pee on my stream." We did. "Be careful. This is a bond, not a bath. Symbolic, don't you think, the modest streams combining to form a more powerful river?"

"I don't think we need to make this event common knowledge," I said.

"Blood and urine are both bodily liquids," said Pebble. "What's the difference?"

Burning down the house was surprisingly easy. We notified

the town authorities what we were doing. We didn't want the fire brigade to put out the fire. When the remains of the house had finally cooled enough for us to search through them the only two termites we found that still resembled termites were the king and queen. Their subjects surrounded them. The sacrifice prevented charring, but not enough of the heat. What loyalty and devotion. It almost makes a person want to become a termite. How many mutations would that take?

Nothing of value was found. Maybe the owners of the house did flee before it was too late. The reward was collected: about 27 gold each. I repaid my debt and I still had enough left over to buy a new sword: utilitarian, but rust free.

We remained a trio for a year, until Hornet joined us. Sometimes a group needed to become larger. Not enough manpower meant a direction unwatched: north, south, east....and now west. Hornet's tenure was tenuous. Infants were death-prone. If he survived, he might get discouraged---salvaging was feast or famine---persuading him to settle into a more sedentary lifestyle. Hornet developed a knack for staying alive---an unnatural one. The GRACE OF GAEA we called it. Some of his luck carried over to us. Other times we got the brunt of the strikes that were intended for him.

Weeks after Hornet joined us we extricated an emerald pearl from arbols: a gibbon-like tree dwelling race. Viewing it up close we discovered it was more than a gem. It was part of a transport portal. If we could find the other pieces and connect them we might be able to escape our prison.

During our quest for the Emerald Pearl, Pebble died twice, the second time hurling his soul to the Frontier, to the fringes of civilization where the most extreme mutants resided. We eventually found him, on our journey to acquire the next piece of the portal. As feared he had been mutated---into a terran: a mole-like borrower. He was content with his new life, his mind and emotions mutating as substantially as his body.

Being just three again we passively recruited. Dinga was a

raven changeling. Having arrived on Limbo at the same time and place as Hornet the two formed a bond. Dinga's protector was a gent named Pulp. Most gents looked human---from a distance. Their size varied, from fractionally taller than a human to three times their height.

Prior to finding that first piece of the portal we met an innkeeper who had once been more. Octagonal Knights were the ultimate neutralizers. They were centralists, believing the universe functioned better balanced. Limbo being populated by criminals---a majority not yet rehabilitated---most balancing consisted of righting wrongs, defending the defenseless, thinning the herd of ill-repute.

I was determined to become an Octagonal Knight. As determined as I was to attend seminary school---without the power affixed to religious elitism. There was power associated with Octagonal Knights, immense power, but that wasn't what drew me in this time---not entirely. I could finally attach some meaning to my life. The problem, the Octagonal Order numbered just eight: symbolic of the quantity of moral dualities, but also preemptive, to thwart the dilution of power. To become one of those elite eight I had to defeat a reigning Knight in a battle of his choosing. If an Octagonal Knight dies in a battle that isn't a sanctioned duel his soul is transported to the Octagonal Prism in Gulag where his body is regenerated around it. Instead of being re-created he is regenerated. An Octagonal Knight must remain pure, never having been touched by the hand of Gaea, the spiritual embodiment of Limbo. My dreams defeated, for I had been re-created, just once, but once too many to retain my purity.

A week later I met another Octagonal Knight. I challenged him. If I couldn't become a Knight I could at least see if I could better one. I had always been cocky, but since I developed my swordsmanship---I considered myself the best swordsman in Limbo---I turned brashness into an art form. Looking back on it, it should have been obvious our meeting wasn't coincidental. He sought me out as much as I him. With much concentration, effort, and skill, I defeated him. To him it seemed to be just a formality. He fought with skill, but with no passion. My final blow knocked him down, broke and bleeding. His body disappeared in a rupturing of atoms. His sword, shield, and armor lay on the forest floor. I put on the armor. It fit like it had been made for me. I immediately became more attuned to my surroundings---and to seven others---and to the Octagonal Prism in the center of Limbo.

The innkeeper had spoken of a weariness. One couldn't be a proponent for balance for eternity. He became semi-retired. But he was beginning to feel guilty. The Knight I defeated had also wished for his demise, to free himself of his obligation? Was I worthy? Was it a mistake? I had led a less than moral life, and I had been re-created, allowing my genes to mingle with Gaea's. I was determined to become worthy, to overcome my past deficiencies.

So off to rebuild the transport portal we went. And if we are successful, do I choose to return to civilization or remain within the Octagonal Order? Shall I choose freedom or purpose?

Bringing the second piece of the portal to the first a miraculous thing happened. Force of attraction melded them, about a meter apart. They lunged east, towards the Chaotic Frontier. We now had a means of finding the other pieces.

What's the Chaotic Frontier? When someone is re-created their appearance isn't the only thing that mutates. Their mind also changes: their intellect, their emotions---even their morals. Gaea protected the less-mutated from the extremes by banishing them to the Frontiers. There is some truth to the legend. The most feral, the most chaotic, the most evil do live near the boundary shield, but is that due to divine decree or a fondness to maintain company with your own?

Chapter 9

GELATINOUS

We were on the road again, just a day after claiming the second sphere. It was going to take a full day to pass through the northern fringes of the Copper Forest. After that? It was still under discussion.

"Hiring a ship will save us a week," I insisted. Being physically inclined, I was impatient. I was always moving: walking or running, or pacing, leaping, throwing, gesturing. When I sat, my leg rocked. Disconcerting for others, but it kept me sane.

"I can't....I just can't." Dinga became distraught. Instead of distracting from her beauty, it intensified it. Contortions of face and body embellished. What became hideous on a plain woman were called beauty marks on an attractive one. And Dinga was stunning: raven black hair, an exotic countenance, and a fit feminine frame. Flaws humanized perfection, transforming art into the attainable.

"It might take longer to walk, but will cost considerably less." Centaur didn't consider himself cheap. He was practical. He had to be the adult. The one that said no. Having fun was fine, but it didn't pay the bills. A sacrifice made today meant more comfort in the future.

"It will only cost less if we don't have too many delays," I countered.

"I thought you enjoyed these delays?"

"In the West?" The Western Frontier was where the Positive mutants lived, the ones that were more likely to help than hinder. Meaning it was going to be boring. No challenges. Nobody to fight.

"We'll also be passing through parts of Neutrality."

Dinga didn't appear as stressed, but she was still agitated, her breathing elevated, and her body pulsating. Hornet came to her rescue. Their relationship wasn't entirely ambiguous. They were definitely a couple. The intensity of it was the mystery. They had just met---technically they had known each other longer, but as acquaintances---even less than that, more an awareness of the other, a mutual distant observation. At times they behaved like they're known each other forever. Other times, as if they were strangers. And the intensity between them---it was simultaneously uncomfortable and wondrous. "Dinga can't bear another voyage. The last two ships she was on sank."

Agitation turned into annoyance. "I can speak for myself."

Hornet looked confused---and hurt.

It took a moment for Dinga to realize what affect her words had on Hornet. She comforted him, initially in a manner a mother might a child, then more intimately. Before things got out of control, they led each other into the woods.

I turned towards Pulp. "What do you think?"

"They didn't enter the forest to have a private conversation."

"I mean about taking a ship or going around."

"I have no opinion. It's been many years since I've been on a boat. And I haven't left the Copper Forest except to visit my brothers for nearly as long. Either adventure will be enthralling. I do have a suggestion. If a consensus can't be reached, we may wish to balance the intensity of emotions."

"Dinga was vehemently opposed to travelling by ship."

"One thing I learned about women from being married," said Centaur, "their happiness will dictate the happiness of those around them."

"She cheated on you."

"She was happy while doing it. Which made me happy--- until I found out about it."

"Then you killed both her and her lover."

37

"And I haven't been happy since."

"Should we check the spheres again, to confirm the location of the third?"

"You think it could have moved since this morning?"

"The spheres had to have been moved at least once for them to become so scattered."

"Can we at least wait until we camp tonight?"

"Do you really think the next sphere could be in the Negative Frontier?"

"We'll know more in a few days. If the pull doesn't increase much, that probably means we're still far away."

"Does that concern you, Pulp, us heading East?"

"It will be...different."

"Is that all you got to say? Aren't Negative mutants your arch enemies?"

"It's difficult to have much animosity for someone you don't know. A majority of my siblings view the world differently than I, but...we're family. We have our disagreements, but they aren't malicious enough to break our bond, our shared history. I wouldn't call it affection. Mutual protection, perhaps, but as much for our emotional wellbeing as for our safety."

Hornet and Dinga appeared...disheveled...when they returned. Uncomfortable for all for the minutes it took them to pull themselves together. It was going to take a substantial distraction to alleviate the peripheral focus on what occurred in the woods. It was the third time they did that. Once after they were reunited. Then early the following day: yesterday. They glowed afterwards. Not like a light bulb. More a cluster of sparkles, like light reflecting off mica.

Being in the Positive part of the frontier, that distraction didn't happen. The subject had to be changed repeatedly, grasps for a potential foothold. With my transformation into an Octagonal Knight, thoughts of morality and the organization of the universe returned, but to a degree my young psyche wasn't capable of. Seminary was a means towards an end. Spirituality and dogma were necessary evils to acquire potential power. My views changed after being incarcerated, living on Limbo, and most importantly, after becoming an Octagonal Knight. Greatness could be measured in relation to a group, but it was limiting. There was a ceiling. Achieving for self-growth was infinite. I could run faster, throw farther, strike more accurately, help more people….

"I wish this armor came with an instruction manual," I remarked midway between Hornet and Dinga's interaction and where we intended to camp. "How am I able to encourage balance in such an unbalanced world? I am compelled to right every wrong, but something restrains me."

"It's the conflict between your past and future," Pulp hypothesized. "Current is the boundary---the front---the warzone. Morality is relative, and you're viewing it as absolute."

"It can't be completely arbitrary. Some people are blatantly evil, others are saints."

"True, but most of us are somewhere in between."

"Even those living in the Positive Frontier?"

"Too many confuse Positive with good and Negative with evil. Positives act to benefit. Negatives, to harm. Killing the person beside me to protect my family may be beneficial, but it isn't kind. Vandalizing a wall with graffiti may be rude, but it won't physically harm anyone."

"So killing my wife and her lover was Positive?" Centaur questioned.

"If you considered it a means to improve your environment."

"Everything is truly relative, then?" Hornet questioned. "Morality. Behavior. Do what you like if you can rationalize it?"

"Rationalization doesn't circumvent consequence---the harshest being internal. Being a Southerner I'm better adapted to diversity. Up North perceptions are more absolute."

"Are there really large groups of people that live together because they're chaotic or orderly?" asked Dinga.

"Who would you rather hang out with, someone like yourself, or someone who was different?"

39

"You spend more time with people with common interests. But it gets boring if they're the only people you socialize with."

"Why I volunteered my services."

"What do you believe?" I asked the giant...uh, gent. To deemphasize the negative stereotypes, or to adorn with a title? Insecurity or pomp? "Your view of the world?"

"Me as an individual, or a gent, or a Southwesterner?" I wasn't sure. Before I was able to muddle a response, Pulp continued. "I already spoke of what Positives believe. I'm also a proponent of Chaos. That doesn't mean I'm an anarchist. Without some Order there isn't a framework for Chaos. I believe rules are too confining. Whims must be followed. Some people believe the Chaotic to be unfaithful, even untrustworthy. But for that to occur they must lie, to others, and to themselves. Living within the moment there is no need to be deceitful. Actions and words are never insincere, just mercurial. AGREEMENT and APPOINTMENT are words never used. Something later in the day will come up, superseding prior plans, voiding all others. It's true that gents feel empowered, but some of us don't pursue those urges. Whatever superiority I suffer will be harnessed to protect you on our journey."

"Any hobbies?" asked Dinga.

"Archery. Women. I never get tired of frolicking. Arbols are extraordinarily playful. Sometimes they play hard-to-get, but the inevitable acquiescence is guaranteed."

"Urchin spoke of women being attracted to him."

"Gents definitely reek masculinity: large, strong, powerful. Being mutants, there is also the illicitness of a relationship with one of us. Being a Westerner, that type of attraction doesn't stimulate me. I do things that make me feel good, not dirty."

At camp we confirmed the location of the next sphere. It was definitely to the east, but how far? The Central Peninsula? Perhaps. All the way to the Liver? That didn't necessary mean the Negative Frontier. That was some relief. I was ready to right wrongs---as long as it encouraged balance---even eager to do so---but in an incremental manner. Initially, nothing too much larger than me. Definitely not something that discharged fire or acid.

"Have we decided on a route yet?" I asked.

"Not by sea," Hornet reminded us.

Centaur unrolled his map. "That still leaves us deciding whether to go around to the north or to the south."

"It will be quicker south," I stated.

"But that means backtracking," Hornet complained.

"I'd would rather not spend any more time in the Copper Forest," Dinga added. "Parts of it are beautiful, but I need some sunshine."

"Pulp?" Centaur wasn't indecisive, but he preferred everyone's input. There could have been something he overlooked, and if everyone contributed they would feel more bound to the decision.

"It doesn't matter to me. Time and distance are inconsequential. I'm here for the journey, not the destination."

Centaur thought for a minute. "We can wait to decide. We'll need to replenish our provisions. Gertrude is closer than Marsh Bay, but it's smaller. I'm not sure we can purchase everything we need there."

"So to the north," I stated.

"For now. We can reevaluate after we restock."

The evening passed peacefully. How could it not in the Positive Frontier.

"How many more hours in the forest?" asked Dinga.

Centaur unrolled his map, then took a moment to study it. "If this map is accurate, we'll leave it about noon."

"And how far is it to Marsh Bay?"

Centaur looked back at the map. "Seventy kays from the edge of the Copper Forest."

"And to the Northern Sea?"

"You must have been a joy to be around as a child."

"I was, but not for the reason you think."

41

"Why so interested?"

"Shouldn't a person want to know where they're going?"

"Destination, yes, but a detailed itinerary?"

"It takes the fun out of an adventure if you know what's about to happen," Pulp remarked.

"Are you saying you allow circumstance to dictate how much fun you're going to have? You're not able to have any fun in the rain?"

"Okay. I'll probably always find some way to have fun, but it'll be more fun if I can make most of it up as I go."

"Why do I like details? I feel more comfortable if I have some sense of control. Where? Why? What? When? Who? aren't bleats of curiosity, but of necessity."

Our pace picked up once we left the woods. Initially, fewer turns and obstacles, then a wider path after intersecting a coastal highway. This far from civilization the road was packed earth. Being exposed to sunlight, most of it was dry, but there were pockets---depressions and runoffs---that varied from being slightly muddy to boggy.

We didn't spot the sea until mid-afternoon. Dinga became giddy.

"I thought you hated the water?" I remarked.

"I hate boats---travelling in them. I LOVE the water. Playing in it. Soaking in a tub. Which reminds me. How much longer, today?"

"At least an hour," Centaur responded without looking at his map. "It's safer---and more efficient---setting up camp when we have light, but we don't want to overdo it and squander part of the day. We have a long way to go. Bad habits can become routine."

"So, about an hour?"

"At least an hour." A moment later, Centaur added, "Why are you smiling?"

"I'm going to bathe in an hour."

"We're 60 kays from Marsh Bay."

"We can heat water, can't we? I prefer a good soak, but a sponge bath will do if there's hot water and soap."

"In two more days we'll be in Marsh Bay. Why don't you just wait?"

"You may not have noticed, but I'm a woman. Women prefer to bathe often enough that dirt will wash off, instead of having to be peeled."

"Women."

I haven't had much success with women. Don't get me wrong, I like women, really like women, but I haven't formed a significant relationship with any. My direct approach---fueled by my physicality---has provided many interactions, but the kind of women receptive to such an approach don't stick around long enough to form an intellectual or emotional bond. I wasn't equipped to court women desiring a sustained relationship. My friends were envious of how easy it was for me to establish these casual connections. Some of them who never dated as adolescents were already married. I didn't want to get married, but it would be nice to have someone there for you when you needed her---and not just physically. There are things I think about that I'm not willing to discuss with another man. It would be wonderful to communicate with someone you have a common history you didn't have to compete with. References wouldn't have to be explained. Memories could be enjoyed. A confidant---that was warm and soft---that could console.

If Dinga wasn't taken, would I be interested in her? Possibly. She was extremely beautiful, in an exotic way. She was fit, but still sexy. You definitely knew she was a woman, but one you didn't have to look after. She could take care of herself. When her size betrayed her, she had the intellectual/social means of directing others to assist her. Her complexity would have restrained me in a past life, but now, after being incarcerated, and re-created, and becoming an Octagonal Knight, I was willing to wade through the mercurial unknown to discover the perpetual pearl. Exotic women fascinated me. I had become fixated on arbols, until my battle with the Octagonal Knight. Dinga was a changeling---someone who

43

could change their shape: human, raven, and something in between. When I choose to leave the Order, and am again eligible for re-creation, I wouldn't mind transforming into something that flew. Something larger than a raven. I wouldn't want to be that vulnerable. It takes awhile to become so mutated you no longer resemble a human. Dinga was one of those people who were death prone. She accomplished in a few weeks---how long she's been on Limbo---what it took others years, or ever, to do.

"We're close to Neutrality," stated Pulp. He was one of those gents whose height---he was four meters tall---wasn't the only thing that mutated. He looked like a tree. His skin was weathered cedar, from his bare ankles above his bark sandals, to his bare scalp above his one-piece moss jerkin. His head was out of proportion to his body. It was not only over-sized, but misshapen. His jaws were twice as large as a human's. Between them were two rows of flat equine molars. Pulp was a herbivore, in the most animalistic way. Whenever we stopped for a moment to rest, or to adjust a pack, or to free a pebble from a boot, he began chewing on the closest vegetation. Due to the high roughage content in his diet he had to eliminate waste more often than a human. He did so discretely. His ears, long and pointed, were higher on his head than a human's, stretching upward like antennae. Whenever an unusual sound was heard his ears rotated towards it. It was unnerving at first, but like a pulled tooth or haircut I eventually got used to it.

"I think it best we camp before we cross the boundary," continued Pulp. "It's safer on this side. We should take advantage of one more good night's sleep without a night watch."

"This clump of tender new sea sprouts didn't influence you, now, did it?" Centaur teased.

"Time for that bath," stated Dinga.

"The only water around here is sea water," Hornet countered. "You sure brine will enhance that beautiful black hair?"

"Better than dirt and grease."

"There's a creek up ahead," Pulp announced.

"Can you actually see that far away?" I questioned. "Since

becoming an Octagonal Knight my senses are enhanced, but incrementally."

"I can smell it."

"How, with these strong sea odors bombarding us?"

"That is the key. Freshwater smells different. The subtlety of it is what makes it stand out. If you listen closely you can hear the delicate trickle through the grass."

Focusing, I was able to filter-out the background noise, the sounds of the sea, the waves breaking, the wind, the seagulls. Like a buoy behind the mist I heard the gentle, distinct sound of organized liquid, flowing clear in purity, precise in movement.

About time I did something to balance the world. With our two cooking pans in hand I headed for that sound. "I'll be back in a couple of minutes with your water, Dinga." Not exactly fighting ogres, but it will make at least one person happy. The narrow stream was just a hundred meters up the coast. The water was completely hidden in the sea grass. I didn't see its channel until I was directly above it. It meandered to the edge of the bluff, where it dribbled onto the sand, forming a delta.

The pans were the same size as the stream. They dammed the flow briefly as water was forced into them. Something felt wrong. I shuddered as I returned the pans to my companions, who were setting up camp about halfway between the trail and the edge of the bluff.

Hornet had built a fire. I placed both pans of water on the platform of stones he had built for them in the middle of it. The uneasiness intensified. Bubbles began to appear on the bottom of the metal pans. "I better take them off before they get too hot," said Hornet. "I don't want to burn Dinga."

Dinga smiled. "I don't think it's possible to make the water too hot for me."

Hornet gently poured the water over Dinga's bent head. She emitted a pleasurable sigh, then her expression distorted, being replaced with shock. She screamed in a manner only a woman can. The hairs on my head and body stood up. As suddenly and as unexpected as the scream began, it stopped. Dinga wasn't making any sound at all. Something gelatinous was attached to her head. It slid down, into her mouth, disappearing

"She's not breathing," said Centaur.

Hornet held her with one arm as he probed her mouth with his hand. "I DON'T FEEL ANYTHING!"

"It's probably in her throat," said Pulp.

"HOW DO WE GET IT OUT?!"

"A tracheotomy," suggested Centaur, tentatively.

Hornet found a knife. He placed it where Dinga's chest met her throat. He paused. His hand was shaking. "I can't do it."

"I can," said Pulp. "After mutating---too many times to remember---nothing bothers me anymore."

"WAIT!" I said. The dread and uneasiness I felt had turned into sympathy. A gelatinous blob squeezed out of Dinga's mouth. It landed with a thud onto a patch of sand. We watched, transfixed, as the gel solidified. I felt horror, followed by resignation, then peace.

Dinga coughed as Hornet continued to hold her.

"Are you okay?" asked Centaur.

It took Dinga a couple of minutes to recover. She hugged Hornet, relishing the familiarity. "I thought I died again. I was more upset than sad. Why was I so death prone? Why was I such a klutz? I thought that part of my life was over. Was I going to mutate into something hideous again? Would I be re-created too far away for you to find me? What happened? I couldn't breathe--- then I could again."

"The gel was captured mistakenly by one of my pans," I explained. "It became distressed when it became trapped, and more so when it became heated. Like a tamed animal it sought someone---a human---for safety. It didn't realize it was killing you until it was almost too late. It fled to save you, but in doing so killed itself." It was remarkable what I was able to perceive since becoming an Octagonal Knight. And it was getting stronger---my ability to perceive. No, that was always there, but jumbled. The processing of the stimuli was improving.

Dinga became distraught, the shock of nearly dying a distant memory. "So I killed it?"

"It wasn't your decision," said Pulp. "If we were presented with the same dilemma what choice would we have made?"

"Help me," said Centaur in a quickened, agitated tone. The commotion had disturbed the fire, spreading it into the sea grass.

Hornet dumped the second pan onto the flames. It put out the fire in the immediate area, but the inferno continued to expand.

"This wind is our undoing," said Pulp as he stomped on the grass beside him.

"The entire prairie will be ablaze in another couple of minutes," said Centaur. "The only safe place is in the water."

We fled down the bluff and dunes to stand at the edge of the water, watching the chaos we created. Being oblivious to what was behind us, we were dragged to the ground by our ankles into the water. Our legs and arms were tied together like steers at a rodeo. As we were pulled underwater I caught a glimpse of our captors: seals.

Chapter 10

PEARL

Our trip was brief. We were dragged through a hole in the hull of a sunken ship. There was an air pocket in the cargo hold, two meters above the lowest part of the ship. We spit out water as we were pushed onto a platform sims above the water. The seals climbed onto another platform, where they transformed into black-skinned humans, some distinctly male, others distinctly female. There were six of them, but there were at least that many more in the wooden catacombs above us.

They stared at us, with a combination of loathing, despair, disgust, and pity. Two more seals entered from the water. After transforming, one of them said, "The fire put itself out when the wind changed direction. Two-hundred hectares have burned."

The seal men and women shook their heads. "Are we going to feed them to the sharks?" asked another.

"We have all made mistakes," spoke a third.

"An arsonist once, an arsonist forever."

"It will be years before the prairie is regenerated."

"They could replant."

"That will take weeks," Centaur blurted.

"At least you won't die, human."

"We don't have the wisdom to decide. The sea shall."

"The sea shall. A pearl for toil, empty for freedom."

A shell was retrieved from the ocean, and opened. Only moist flesh.

"The sea has decided."

"The humans are to be returned to shore."

Without fanfare we were dragged back into the water and deposited on the beach. Our limbs were untied. Before our circulation returned enough for us to stand, the seals were gone.

"Well, that was interesting," said Hornet.

"Not nearly as interesting as it would have been as slaves," Centaur stated.

"I thought only good people lived in the Positive Frontier," said Dinga.

"Good intentions are in the eye of the beholder," Pulp explained. "Selk are environmental caretakers. Because we weren't, we were considered to be evil."

"What gives them the right to decide?" asked Dinga.

"Be thankful the sea was on our side."

"Be thankful a pearl wasn't required to gain our freedom," Hornet declared.

"So, we have reverted to pagan mysticism?" I commented.

"Many on Limbo believe in a worldly god: Gaea."

"Organized religions, and their rituals, what a hypocritical waste. When I was in seminary the people there didn't behave any better than the heathens. True spirituality is in action, not dogma. Either you help or you harm. It's that simple."

"Wars are often started to determine which side is strong enough to impose their brand of virtue," stated Pulp.

"Shouldn't people just try to get along?" suggested Dinga. "What greater common good?"

"If a person believes in something passionately enough they will do whatever it takes to make it happen, for the common good."

"Isn't that egotistic?"

"GOOD people commonly have close-minded egos."

We crossed into Neutrality: Limbo's enormous belly was populated by those neither sanctimonious or retched. Moral extremes enveloped Neutrality in a misshapen circle. Chaos versus Order. Positive versus Negative. I felt more comfortable---more at home---in Neutrality than I did in the Positive Frontier. Octagonal Knights assisted the needy, but only as long as it balanced morality---a difficult task: sacrificing an individual to sustain a collective, allowing an infestation to diminish an overburdened population.

We camped a couple of kays into Neutrality. The fire had put itself out at the boundary, but we wanted to be far enough away from it that we couldn't smell the charred landscape. We chose not to build another fire that evening. We could wait until Marsh Bay for hot food and clean bodies.

As we slept under the stars, the night became still. Smoke drifted to my nostrils. Had the sea breeze shifted again or was it a memory? On tranquil nights, many kays and weeks from there, I still smell the scorched grass and earth.

Chapter 11

ODD TILT

My Octagonal awareness provided an ability to track---animals and people. And to a lesser extent, nature: weather, hydro and thermo dynamics, floral and geological strata. My skills weren't perfect, the gel and selk being examples of dangers I wasn't able to detour. But I was the most gifted in our small group, so I led, being given the position of SCOUT. Pulp was next in our queue, our ART, short for artillery. Now that Pebble had abandoned us Pulp was our best archer. Then came Hornet, ART2. Necessity required him to become more skilled in ranged weaponry. He didn't always hit his target, but his aim wasn't off enough to mistakenly strike us. Dinga followed him. Finally there was Centaur, our PROC, the most important position in a protective queue: the protector of our rears. The strongest was given that position, because it was the most vulnerable. One might think that being the leader of our group Centaur should be in front, but by being able to see us he was able to persistently confirm our safety.

We entered the Pewter Swamp early the following day. If we pushed we may have reached it before dark the day before, but certainly not Marsh Bay. There are few areas in Limbo safe enough to travel at night. Definitely not some place camouflaged in vegetation. The swamp began as a marsh, but after a kay a canopy formed. It was not only damp, but also gloomy. A dull grayness permeated our surroundings. The only thing mildly pleasant about the place was the raised road we walked upon. Water clustered in pools on both sides of us. Mosquitoes billowed in eddies of fetid air.

"How much further?" asked Dinga. "I've been nauseous since we entered this place. The rancid odors, you think, or being bit by mosquitoes?"

"Both probably," Pulp answered. "It's wonderful, isn't it? How one area smells so much different than another. Pine dominated in the Copper Forrest. And the sea after we left it. And now this pungent, earthy barrage."

"It smells like death," Centaur stated.

"How many more healing stones do we have?" Hornet asked.

"They won't help with nausea. And even if they did, we shouldn't waste them. I'm confident we'll need them for something more serious before we leave this place." Centaur stopped to thumb through his wallet. "Just three left."

"We have 30 more kays to go," I commented dryly. FYI, not pep talk. Harbingers of doom were never well received.

"Speculation or....?"

"A sixth sense? Octagonal awareness is able to perceive clusters of sentients: the interplay of moralities provides a beacon. The closest large cluster is 30 kays away. Will we have to walk farther than that? Certainly. As the foliage becomes denser the road will begin to wander."

"So, we're not going to reach Marsh Bay by sundim," Hornet commented.

"Unlikely. If our stamina holds out, we might arrive an hour after it gets dark---if we don't have too many delays."

"How many is too many?" spoke a chorus of shrilled voices. They were neither female nor male, neither child nor adult.

The trail suddenly ended. We were on the tip of a peninsula, murky water surrounding us on three sides. Small creatures, a third my height, more human than not, scurried over cypress and leaped from vines. They wore brightly colored clothing loosely over their lanky frames. Their features were somehow both rectilinear and rounded, perfectly, like being created from a straight edge and a French curve. Their skin was gray, blending in perfectly in the dim, indirect light. They laughed profusely: chirping guffaws.

They kept their distance, but not too far away where they couldn't see us.

"I believe the road, the lack of one, is an illusion," I said.

"What is real?" asked Hornet. "Should we travel forward where we think the road should be? Or has our last few steps also been an illusion and the true road behind us?"

"What do these creatures want with us?" asked Dinga.

"Our bewilderment, I believe," Centaur replied. "We are their entertainment."

"What's our plan? Chose a direction and sustain it until we---hopefully---reach Marsh Bay?"

"We could head to the coast," I suggested. "Then follow it until we reach Marsh Bay."

"Isn't Marsh Bay supposed to be inland?" asked Hornet.

"And the coastline isn't too straight," Centaur added. "It could take twice as long as traveling by road."

"More," I interjected.

"And that's without considering delays caused by brush and...." Centaur stepped off the road---inadvertently---losing a leg up to his knee, momentarily. "...gunk."

"You Neutrals just don't think outside the core, do you?" Pulp remarked. "Dinga can fly above the trees and locate the road's true route."

Dinga shivered.

Hornet hugged her, then backed away so he could see her. "What's wrong?"

"I'm not sure I can do it."

"Sure you can. We saw you transform, in the Copper Forest."

"I'm able to...transform. I'm not sure I want to." Before someone was able to respond, she explained. "When I changed a few days ago I didn't know anyone. I was also in shock. Dying, and coming back to life, repeatedly, does that to a person. In order for me to change I need to disrobe."

"We'll certainly turn around," said Centaur. "And you can

hide behind a tree."

"But you'll know that I'm naked. And I'll continue to be naked after I transform. Feathers will conceal, but that's not the same thing as wearing clothes."

"But...." Hornet began, before he was cut off by a look reserved for married women to use on their husbands.

"One of the joys in life is to share," Pulp stated. "Stories, personalities...sensuality of flesh and spirit."

Weakness bothered me. Why did some people not strive to do their best, for themselves and for those around them? "A few minutes in the sky might save us a couple of days of wandering aimlessly."

Apprehension and malaise transitioned to frustration---and fear. "I'M ALSO AFRAID I MIGHT NOT BE ABLE TO CHANGE BACK!"

Hornet attempted to console her again, but she wouldn't allow him. Wounded, and scared, animals needed their distance. "You don't have to do it," he insisted. "We'll eventually find our way out."

"EVENTUALLY?! I've had enough of this swamp. I'll do it. I'll undress, and transform. And if Gaea is willing, I'll transform back." She distanced herself from us, then closed her eyes. She concentrated, to the extent that sweat beaded her forehead. Black hairs grew on her body. They spread out and formed feathers. Her nose elongated. It became a beak. She kicked off her boots. Her feet widened and transformed into talons. With what remained of her hands she stripped off her clothes, revealing just a hint of the fine woman she was just minutes ago. When Dinga became determined, she went all out. No more delays---like taking the time to walk behind a tree to undress. Her arms became wings, her fingers, talons. Her transformation delayed as she momentarily retained a hybrid state, then the transformation resumed. Where a woman once stood was now a large jet-black raven. It looked at us with an odd tilt of its head. It looked first with its right eye, then its left. It looked down at the ground where an insect moved. Puzzlement from its feathered countenance. It looked up into the sky that was nearly blocked off by the swamp's canopy. It pushed off with its legs and flapped its wings. It spiraled upward through the interlocking branches until it became a large spec against the barely visible blue sky. It continued to rise higher, until it disappeared.

Hornet looked worried. Awkwardly, I clutched his shoulder, to convey sympathetically. I had never been chummy, self-reliance superseding companionship. An epiphany of solidarity overwhelmed me. I really was part of a group. These companions I had surrounded myself with---or they with me---had become my family. I wasn't saddened by my loss of independence.

Many minutes later Dinga was seen again, first as a black spec against the blue, then as a distinct shape that circled down to us.

The pixies didn't know how to react, first to Dinga's transformation, then to her flight. They finally decided on a course of action. They fired arrows at her. They were smaller than darts. They appeared to be more annoying to her than dangerous. Only one dart could be seen puncturing her. She detached it with a talon. It dropped to the murky water below. Before landing she dove at the pixies, scattering them. With an enemy no longer visible to take revenge upon she finally landed, directly in front of us. Cocking her head first this way, and then that way, she slowly transformed back, into a human. Hornet rushed up to her with her clothes. She looked shocked that Hornet was helping her. She backed away. "Who are you?"

Chapter 12

ADOLESCENCE

The pixies laughed. Hornet placed an arrow in his bow and let it fly. It hit its intended target in the chest, skewering it against a tree. The pixies no longer sounded so playful. Fury consumed them. Large swamp monsters erupted from the waters around us: hydras and crocodiles, and carnivorous plants. Hornet shot another arrow, it too met it mark. A second pixie hung by its ribcage. Horror replaced anger. The pixies fled. The swamp monsters dissipated as a road again appeared before us.

"You shouldn't have killed them," I chastised. Becoming an Octagonal Knight I felt it was now my duty to out the injustices of the world. Sometimes just an acknowledgement was enough to make a difference.

"They didn't intend to harm us," Pulp elucidated. "They just wanted to play."

"Do you call what they did to Dinga, PLAYING?"

"Why am I here?" asked Dinga, more upset then inquisitive. "Where is my apartment? Why was I taken to this place? Have you kidnapped me?" Frantically scanning her surroundings, she spotted Pulp for the first time. She fainted.

"All those monsters snapping at her heels, and she faints at the sight of me."

Centaur smiled. "She hasn't completely lost her senses, then."

Dinga woke. Her head was on Hornet's lap. She instantly stood up and moved away from him.

"I'm your...." Before Hornet could spit out the most accurate term for their relationship Dinga backed up again.

55

"Don't you remember me, Dinga?"

"Don't...EVER...call me a dog. When my benefactors find out...." Before she was able to complete her thought, her mind jumped to another. "I dreamt I was flying."

"Marsh Bay may have a cure for her," Centaur suggested. "If not, there should be someone there who can suggest where we can find one."

Hornet became fixated, a perpetual shocked expression staring at Dinga.

"I don't blame you for wanting me to be your girlfriend," she said to him. "You can't help yourself, not with the way I look." She frisked herself to examine her figure. "But don't touch, unless you have the means to pay, and looking at you, I would say it's extremely unlikely. Sometimes I give freebies to the guys I really like, but you're not my type. Now, this other guy..." She looked at Centaur. "I might be willing to give a free sample, written off as a marketing expense." She strutted over to Centaur and put her arm around his waist. Centaur looked mortified. Dinga was a fine woman, but also the companion of one of his best friends. I felt awful for Centaur---and Hornet---but even more thankful that is wasn't me she flirted with. There was a time when that might not have mattered, but not since I became an Octagonal Knight.

"So we'll arrive at Marsh Bay an hour or so after dark?" Hornet inquired.

Centaur separated himself from Dinga as gently as he could. "Maybe longer with this delay."

To say it was an uncomfortable afternoon and early evening was an understatement. A forced march through a hot, humid marsh accompanied by overt, undesired romantic invitations. Hornet's sadness at the loss of Dinga's memories began to transition into hurt feelings, then into jealousy. Centaur attempted to reassure him---on many occasions---but what could one say in such a situation.

The sun dimmed two hours before we reached Marsh Bay.

When Dinga was younger she apparently didn't have any sense of haste. The seductive manner she moved didn't help.

The fishing village smelled nearly as bad as the marsh. We shared two rooms at the village's lone inn, the LEECHES LAP. Dinga had a room to herself, the four of us sharing the other. It may have been safer to have one of the men stay with her, but with her state of mind, perhaps it wouldn't.

After dropping off our packs in our rooms we slipped down to the first floor to eat, drink, and---most importantly---find a cure for Dinga. The healer in Marsh Bay could do run-of-the-mill stuff, but couldn't restore memory. Berry, in the foothills of the Raspberry Mountains, was the best bet. In addition to having a gifted healer, it had an emporium. If Dinga couldn't be helped by traditional means, there were elemental alternatives. The greatest difficulty was getting there. It was 600 kays away, a week of travel under the best of circumstances.

"I say we go," I said. "We need to cure Dinga as quickly as we can."

"I second that," said Centaur as he gently detached Dinga's hand from his chest. Why did women think it was okay to do something like that in public? If men did that they would be arrested. "A delay, but not a drastic one. We'll be heading in the general direction. It will add an extra four or five days, but do we have any other options?"

"Don't I have a say in this?" Dinga whined. "Hiking 600 kays to lose my personality. Why not 1000 and cut off one of my mounds."

"Don't you want your memory back?"

"If this DINGA is as boring as you make her sound, leave me here. I'm quite gifted at making certain exchanges to obtain necessities." Dinga wasn't exaggerating. Before being sentenced she was a prostitute, one of those high-class girls that lived more luxuriously than many of her clients. Like most of us, Limbo changed her. Her prior profession didn't embarrass her, it was just something she was no longer willing to do.

"Did Dinga lose her memory all the way back to

adolescence?" asked Hornet.

What would that be like, waking up to find yourself in the body of someone twice your perceived age? We don't just change physically as we age, we grow intellectually and emotionally, perhaps even morally. Are children born innocent? Do they learn bad behavior? Or are they more neutral, their deviation from the center connected to stimuli?

Centaur was the most effective in convincing Dinga she should retain our stewardship. "Doesn't this place smell too bad to live in? Wouldn't you rather breathe fresh mountain air in a cosmopolitan city? Think of the interesting people you'll meet."

Dinga pouted. "All right, but if I'm not happy there I won't talk to any of you---ever." It was agreed.

Dinga wanted to stay up all night at the pub. After the second time sneaking downstairs she had to be tied to the bed. She enjoyed that until she learned she was going to be alone. She screamed a bit, but when she realized no one was listening she stopped, then begged to be released.

Hornet was concerned. "What if she doesn't revert back to her lovable, peaceful self after her memory returns?"

"I imagine we were all a bit immature at that age," I said. "I used to be anti-social. The only time I spoke to someone was when I complained about events that didn't benefit me."

"When Dinga's memory returns she'll be more mature," Pulp assured Hornet.

"What if she remembers disliking me?" asked Hornet.

"Girls marry different men than they date," Centaur insisted. "They become wiser. They learn there are negative consequences to the excitement they crave."

Chapter 13

HOW CUTE!

Dinga was grumpy. She apparently slept in longer during her youth. It took her half-an-hour to wake-up. Her petulance was replaced by exuberance. Its primary manifestation: flirtation. Coming to her senses, she no longer pined for Centaur. I was now her conquest. "How silly I have been," she said to me. "A man in uniform is much more distinguished than a barbarian. We'll travel the world together. Exploring exotic locations. Meeting exotic people. And at night---something just as memorable." The flirtation continued for most of that first day out of Marsh Bay, until Dinga got tired, then she began to complain. What a relief. Grumbling was easier to drown out.

Centaur frowned. "I overlooked something. Going around the Northern Sea instead of across it bypasses a sea voyage, but doesn't completely prevent us from having to board a boat. Few rivers have bridges. We'll have to take a few ferries, including one this morning."

"We can't," Hornet insisted. "Dinga can't."

"It will take us four days to reach Forks. That'll be our earliest opportunity to find a bridge. Those four days might take eight bushwhacking."

"Dinga could fly over the river," I suggested.

Hornet shushed him. "Don't let her hear you. She doesn't remember she can transform, into a bird. Do you want her to fly away?"

"Why don't we just ask her?" Pulp suggested. Before anyone could reply, the gent said loudly, "WOULD YOU LIKE TO GO ON A BOAT TODAY, DINGA?!"

Adolescents were complex. Sometimes they acted more like adults. Other times, more like children. Dinga had definitely acted more like a woman than a girl since she lost her memory, playfully, but in a worldly manner. She gained a couple of years of innocence instantaneously. She smiled widely, and had trouble staying in one place. She attempted to say something, but was too excited to get it out. She had finally worn herself out enough to say, "Can we go now? How long will we be on the boat? Should I pee first? Will there be food? Can I steer?"

Centaur turned towards Pulp. "You thought this would happen, didn't you?"

"Dinga did lose her memory. She can't be afraid of the water if she doesn't remember those two ships sinking. And...kids like boats."

"You like boats too, don't you?"

Pulp smiled.

The crossing wasn't entirely uneventful. Dinga became so spastic we thought she might accidentally fling herself into the water. She had to be pulled back from the brink more than once, one time a meter above the jaws of a crocodile. You would think the near death experience would have kept her to the interior of the craft. Instead it became a catalyst for her curiosity. "Where did the crocodile go? You think it's below us? Below our feet? Can I have one---a smaller one---for a pet?" She looked for another crocodile, but none appeared. "Can we go back across?"

"Later," Centaur replied. Which was true---there was another crossing---but days away, instead of minutes.

We immediately began our journey to Berry upon disembarking. We needed to be at least out of the Pewter Swamp before we camped for the night. We achieved our goal by noon. Seeing the sun again brightened our moods considerably. Dinga began to skip.

The prairie shrubs became sparser as we put more distance between us and the swamp. Late afternoon we came to a fork. It was obvious which road to take. The one on the left was packed earth, and wide. The right was barely a trail. It led to an unidentified community consisting of burrows in a hillside.

"Can we sleep there tonight?" suggested Dinga, enthusiastically.

"Sleeping is the easy part. I'm more concerned about waking up," Centaur responded dourly.

"It can't be that expensive," I added. I don't know why I was helping Dinga. Her advances and Hornet's reaction to them were painful. I do know. She looked so cute. Not an attractive cute. More like a kitten. She was enthusiastic and playful. To sway Centaur you had to appeal to his pragmatism. The utility must be obvious.

"Inexpensive or cheap, healing stones won't eradicate an infestation," he responded. Dinga looked at him sweetly. "Okay. It won't harm us to examine the accommodations---initially from a distance."

And a distance was the closest we could get. The denizens of the shantytown were about as enthusiastic meeting us as we were them. They blocked the trail equal distance from the fork and their settlement. Their dirty hides were partially concealed in rags. Dark, coarse hair covered what the rags didn't, on both the men and the women. The tops of their heads were laden with the same filaments, but more densely. Pinkish-gray faces, flat noses, and pointed ears confirmed their swine heritage. The town square was a wallow. It was apparent from the stench the people emitted that it was decorative. Tensions escalated, fueled by the inflexible standoff and careless comments, the latter an involuntary reflex to their shocking appearance. What had appeared to be mustaches on the men were actually tusks. They didn't appear to be carrying weapons, but were they necessary with those piercing protrusions defending them.

They were on the cusp of charging when Dinga blurted out, "HOW CUTE!"

The boars were so unhinged by this declaration they stumbled into one another as they stopped mid-stride. The ugliest of the boars strutted over to us. "You think we're cute?"

"Like a teddy bear," Dinga replied as she scratched him behind the ears. The creature grunted deeply, a powerful reverberation pulsating from his chest.

He gazed at the rest of us sternly. "Are we more attractive than your companions?"

"You're adorable, especially you." Dinga scratched the creature again. "When I was younger my best friend looked like you, but he was smaller. Full grown is cuddlier."

"The Unchanged lie. They are jealous of us. Their shun us to mask their insecurities. We are too cute and cuddly for them. THEIR ugliness embarrasses them."

"We must return to our kind," spoke Centaur. "It is uncomfortable being in the prescience of such beauty."

"True, true," spoke the gallery behind the lead boar.

"One more rub please before you go." Dinga enthusiastically stroked his head and back. Another loud, pleasurable growl, this time so powerful it nearly knocked us off our feet.

When we merged with the main road I said to Centaur, "You never asked about accommodations."

"Good job," Hornet told Dinga. "How did you ever come up with that?"

"Come up with what?"

Centaur sighed. "To be a naive child again."

"Maybe adolescents aren't that bad after all," I commented.

We pushed ourselves. We didn't stop again until the sun dimmed. A few more kays between us and the boars, then a few kays more. With rampant idle comments competing with unstable demeanors it was best to leave the neighborhood---and the next one. Being in open prairie it wasn't difficult setting up camp in the dark. It never got completely dark on Limbo, not with the sun transitioning into a full moon. Dinga looked younger---not physically: she still looked like a woman. It was her expressions and demeanor that made her look like a child. She was a joy to be around. Children are supposed to make one's life more interesting, more meaningful, more complex. If Dinga could stay this age forever....

Chapter 14

MISSTEP

The next three days were uneventful. We followed a river upstream, intermittently. The water lacked the focus of the wide groove the road had become. It meandered to the right, then to the left, and on occasion almost backwards before correcting itself. The days were dusty and warm, so lacking in stress it became tempting to take a nap. We fought it. Berry was still many days away. We couldn't afford any delays. Dinga's memories hadn't returned. We feared the longer she was an adolescent the more difficult it would be to transform her back into an adult. Her new personality was becoming engrained.

Dinga had a tendency to wander. Not too far, but far enough to get herself into trouble. Initially, it was boys. Since we had left the Pewter Swamp it had become nature. Everything fascinated her: mounds of earth, grass, shadows, but especially the water. It was like a rattle to her, or a mobile that spun in random patterns above her. There was movement in the river, and myriad textures and colors. Sometimes a child too curious got burned. She fell into the river once. The second time she got too close it was just a foot that got wet, but the timing was poorer. Her desire to experience the world around her persuaded her to take off her boots. Blisters developed initially....

"FEEK!" Dinga abruptly brought her foot back out of the water---what remained of it. An exaggeration. Most of the foot appeared to be intact, but it bled profusely, making it look worse. She climbed into Centaur's arms, which---understandably---bothered Hornet. The act was more loving than amorous, but it still stung. As Centaur comforted her, Pulp and I attended to her injury. Hornet looked on mortified. Pulp examined the foot visually while I rummaged for a---clean---sword cloth. I wrapped the foot with the cloth, then applied pressure.

"It appears to just be a surface wound," said Pulp. "Some flesh may have also been damaged, but no bone. Having been re-created a few times, and a changeling, she ought to heal quickly."

"But not quick enough to walk on her own today, or even tomorrow," I commented.

"We still have a healing stone," stated Hornet.

"I don't want to swallow no medicine," spoke Dinga defiantly through whimpers and grimaces.

Centaur looked down at her kindly, but sternly. "It will make you feel better. It will make all of us feel better. You need to take your medicine. Stick."

Centaur lowered himself to the ground, still holding Dinga. I placed a translucent stone in his---now free---hand. "Time to take your pill."

"I don't want to."

"Please." No reaction from Dinga. "Do it for me." Still, nothing. "It will make you feel better. Until your foot heals you won't be able to explore. You'll have to spend the next couple of days here, on the ground."

Dinga frowned, then snatched the pill from Centaur's hand. She immediately put it her mouth and swallowed it---tried to swallow it---nothing happened. She tried to swallow again. And again. She panicked on the last attempt, spitting out the capsule. I carefully picked it up with a cloth and cleaned and dried it. It was too expensive to accidentally activate.

"Water," said Centaur. Pulp handed him a leather bladder. "Drink this." Dinga did what she was told. She began to cough. "Not too much, just enough to wet your throat." I handed him the pill. "Try again, please." He held up his palm as she delicately picked it up with her forefinger and thumb. She frowned as she examined it, then closed her eyes. She made a sour face as she opened her mouth. She stuck out her tongue. She delicately set the pill at the base of her tongue. She placed her tongue back in her mouth and swallowed in a single motion.

Color began to return to her face. Calmness replaced panic and pain. She closed her eyes.

"That's one side-effect I could live with," I said.

"She's been through a lot," said Pulp. "It's probably the first peace-of-mind she's had since she lost her memory."

"Since she was arrested and sentenced," Hornet added. "So you think she's going to be alright? She won't permanently lose part of her foot?"

Pulp delicately pulled the sword cloth away from her foot. He poured some water on it, then used it to clean her foot. "It's not going to be perfect, but that might be due to her being re-created. It will leave a scar. That happens sometimes when the wound is too severe or too much of the body becomes displaced."

"Displaced?" Hornet questioned.

"Is lost. Like a limb. Or when something takes a bite out of you."

"What could have taken a bite out of Dinga?"

"Time to investigate." I walked down to the river, taking the stained sword cloth with me. "They really need to start making these in red." Pulp and Hornet followed me, the latter after looking at Centaur, his arms wrapped around Dinga in his lap. Sadness and exasperation.

Before rubbing the cloth on a rock I placed it in the water, saturating it. Ochre bled into the water, profusely initially, then a trickle, then intermittently. I fell backwards as I released the cloth. If I hadn't done so I would have been pulled forward, into the river. If my reactions weren't enhanced by my new profession I wouldn't have had time to make that decision.

"WHAT THE BORE WAS THAT!" Hornet spoke the words, but it could have been any one of us. We bent down to look at the

65

water, closely, but not too close. "Fish?"

I ran up the bank to my pack, then back down to the water. I dropped a piece of dried meat into the river. Three fish leapt out of the water, one of them successfully snagging it before it hit the surface.

"FEEK!" It was my turn to speak for all of us. "And I was thinking about washing in it tonight?"

"Piranha?" asked Hornet.

"Intriguing, isn't it?" Pulp replied. "This is why I left the Copper Forest."

"To have your foot amputated?" I questioned. "Your feet hurting you that much? You're not used to travelling so many kays in a day?"

"It's just so fascinating finding piranha here. Shouldn't they be in a jungle somewhere, instead of in a meandering river in a temperate prairie?"

"So it would make your day if you're attacked by a shark tonight, or a scorpion in the morning?"

"A shark perhaps. It wouldn't be that surprising to see a scorpion. It's warm and dry here, and we're not that far from the Alloy Desert."

Dinga's adolescence returned. Was Dinga's physiology that unstable or did the healing stone have something to do with it? Fortunately, her advances shifted to Pulp. She must have passed into that strange, experimental stage. Pulp found the situation amusing, and actually encouraged her, which Dinga eventually found frightening.

Dinga's hormone's found a new target---no not Hornet, he couldn't be that lucky. Hyenas heckled from across the river. They didn't look human, but not entirely like animals either. We ignored them. What other option did we have? We didn't want to get wet---or eaten by piranha. Adolescents being more sensitive to ridicule, Dinga launched an arrow at them. She must have been really upset, because she applied enough force behind it for it to reach the other side. The hyenas scattered, then returned, but at a safer distance.

Eventually they got bored and walked off on their hind legs, in a rude imitation of us.

"Do you think it's possible for animals to be re-created?" Hornet asked.

"Animals don't have souls," I replied.

"Maybe not the same souls we have, but they form personalities, implying the creation of distinct individuals," Pulp stated.

"If they had a soul wouldn't they be re-created?" Hornet questioned. "Animals aren't sterile. They reproduce."

"Implying they must die, truly die, instead of being re-created?" asked Pulp. "Maybe there isn't a correlation between being re-created and reproducing. Humans are sterile, but that doesn't mean animals must be to be re-created."

"It seems inconsistent to me," said Centaur. "But I guess lots of things are. Humans mutating when they're re-created. Animals when they're born."

"Who do you think Gaea punished more?" I asked. No one answered.

Chapter 15

THINGS THAT BURN YOU IN THE NIGHT

It was beginning to become monotonous: our routine, the terrain. The Aluminum Prairie was vast. Three-and-a-half days wandering through it already and at least seven more to go, more if you considered it extending past the Apple Woods. "Just a few kays more," Centaur assured us. Our destination today was Forks, a small village near the convergence of the Yellow and Blue rivers.

And yes, the river they formed was called the Green. Centaur continued to assure us, even after the sun dimmed. Dinga began to drag her feet. Initially it resulted in her being just a few meters behind us, but the distance was increasing. By the time it got dark it grew to ten strides. We waited for her to catch up. Her pace must have been contingent on the amount of separation, because she slowed considerably. By the time we got back up to full speed she had dropped back five meters. Centaur sighed. "I guess we're not going to reach Forks tonight. Let's set up camp." We were tired enough by then that we chose to not build a fire, resulting in us circumventing a hot meal.

"Travelling would be less difficult on a horse," I commented.

"And sleeping on a pillow-top mattress would be more comfortable," said Centaur. "Our jailors didn't supply either. We're in prison, not at a spa."

"Doesn't it seem odd to you that your namesake was created, but not what they derived from?" Hornet asked.

"Gaea created centaurs," Pulp stated.

"From what genes? Centaurs look like horses, not elk, or moose, or deer."

"So it proves that Gaea exists?" I questioned. "That centaurs aren't the result of a random mutation, but of a divine design?"

"How else would you explain it?" asked Pulp.

"I would like to ride a centaur," Dinga commented.

"No you wouldn't," Centaur assured her.

"It would be creepy if he turned around and looked at me, but if he promised not to it might be kind of fun."

Forks was across the river, between the Blue and Yellow rivers as they converged. There was a ferry, but it was on the other side. Signaling it was required, when someone was there to receive it---which there wasn't.

"How long do we wait?" asked Hornet.

"Until we lose our patience," Centaur grumbled. "Which for

me is just minutes away."

"Does the road continue on the other side?" I asked.

Centaur looked at his map. "It doesn't look like it."

Hornet became exasperated. "Then why not man the ferry? Or build the village on this side of the river?"

"Some people prefer privacy," Pulp stated.

"In place of trade? How does the village survive?"

"I personally hate privacy. Privacy is boring. But for some people it gives them peace of mind. Premeditated poverty is easier to cope with than arbitrary prosperity."

So we camped, again, this time along the banks of the Blue. The water definitely had a cleaner look to it than the Green. What we saw of the Yellow, beyond the convergence, looked murky, sediment, apparently, from the Platinum Mountains. We had only been away from an inn for four days, but when there is an expectation, and it is taken away, depression finds a foothold. There was not even a guarantee lodging would be better in an inn. And it could be expensive. But there was that expectation.

I had the first watch. Was a watch required this close to the Positive Frontier? Maybe not, but we weren't willing to risk a mishap. Painful potentially, but more importantly, inconvenient. Who would die? When would we be reunited with them? What shape would they be in, physically and morally? What subspecies?

I was as tired as the others, but one of the skills I acquired as an Octagonal Knight was the ability to delay sleep while retaining productivity and proficiency. With ease I monitored the flat, sparse terrain. It was too easy. With much concentration I forced myself to stay awake. I preferred to have a nerve-wracking watch within a dense forest, every leaf falling, branch swaying, or squirrel scurrying bringing potential, imagined danger.

We had built a fire for cooking, but had extinguished it prior to sundim. We didn't want to create a beacon. I mention this bit of seemingly trivial information, because the fire suddenly re-ignited, or so I thought.

A flame billowed in the still blackness of the overcast night. Did a sudden breeze whip it up? How could it without embers?

The tent erected for Dinga was ablaze. Changes in an adolescent's body created an enhanced desire for privacy. The rest of us slept outside. As I reached for my canteen, and any others I might find, I shouted to wake the others. We emptied the canteens. The tent continued to blaze. As the others ran to the river to refill their canteens, I did the only thing I could think of that would have an immediate impact. I flopped against the tent to smother the flames.

My companions extinguished what remained of the fire as another ignited, this time as an arc against our backs. Taking the first watch I retained my armor. It deflected the brunt of the heat. My companions weren't as fortunate. They screamed, as much from the shock of the sudden injury as from the pain.

As they extinguished one another's flames I sought the flame's catalyst. A florescent red toad the size of a dog opened its mouth and blew out a swirling mass of super-heated air. I sheltered my face with my arm. The flames parted as they streamed past me, my appendage an obstacle to the thermodynamic flow. I charged the toad before it could build up another burst of fire and release it. I unsheathed my sword. As a continuation of the motion it struck the creature with such fury it sliced it in two. The two halves burst into flames, disintegrating into ashes.

After permitting myself the briefest of moments to mentally recover from the death I caused, and the potential, supplemental destruction I prevented, I rushed back to my companions. The flames were now completely out. The men ripped apart what remained of the tent fabric with their blackened hands. There was nothing inside, not even a charred clump. DINGA!

We heard a shocked gasp. Dinga covered her mouth from the edge of camp. She wanted to cry, but she was too traumatized. Hornet rushed to her side, putting his arms around her. She shuddered, then broke down, weeping in his arms.

Centaur and Hornet were critically injured. It was agreed---demanded even---that they ingest the last two healing stones. My armor had protected me and Pulp's hide was as thick and fire-resistant as a redwood. The healing stones did their job---for ten gold each they had better. The third degree burns on Centaur and Hornet's backs and hands completely healed, not even leaving a scar. Pulp considered his burns to be superficial. Our doubts were reconciled after the dark, bubbly patches fell off a couple of days later.

"Where were you?" Hornet asked a still whimpering Dinga.

After taking a moment to compose herself, she replied, "A girl doesn't discuss such things."

"You could have been killed going off alone like that."

"I definitely wasn't going with someone."

"Couldn't you have at least waited until it got light?"

"Some things can't wait."

"You could have been hurt."

"I would have been more hurt if I was in my tent."

"She has you there," said Pulp.

"What was that thing?" asked Centaur.

"A toad," I answered. "But unlike any toad I have ever seen."

"It was zard," Pulp illuminated. "A Wizard's construct."

"Zards really exist then?" Centaur questioned.

"The Brotherhood was created to counter the Wizards. I can assure you, zards are very real."

"So this toad was just a soulless animatron?" I questioned. "A robot given a simple task."

"If only that was true. Many of the Wizard's constructs are just animated sticks and bones---or less often, lifeless flesh---but zards are created from black elem, souls of the deceased before they are re-created."

"Was the thing that attacked me my first day on Limbo a zard, then?" I asked.

"A stick golem attacked Stick," Centaur explained.

"It could have been," Pulp responded. "It depends on how intelligent it was and the number of tasks it preformed."

"Its main task, apparently, was to kill me," I said.

"Wizards like others to do their dirty work. It probably

71

wasn't created to attack you personally, just anyone who wandered by. Guard constructs generally don't require souls."

We attempted to return to sleep, however unlikely that was going to be. I know I wouldn't be able to.

Once my mind got working it was hard to shut it off. What was a soul? If it didn't consist of matter how could it exist? Was it just a figment of our imagination? Our collective thoughts? A grain of sand in the divine sea? Did it always exist---lying dormant until we took our first breath or the first synapses of our brain fired---or was it instantaneously created, a personalized, micro big bang? I liked to think of it as always existing, then it was likely it would always exist. A sudden existence meant a just as sudden non-existence, a permanent secession of being. Now that was something to keep one up at night.

Was the alternative any better? On the surface, living forever sounded great, but if a person wasn't designed for that---there were even safeguards built into the system to prevent it---how might he react to entering the true unknown? Space may appear to be the final frontier, but perpetual life, that was going to be the adventure. How would our minds react to it? Would we be able to cope? Would we go insane? We slept more for our minds to recuperate than for our bodies. Were they capable of staying awake for hundreds, even thousands of years? Why did our bodies have to age, our cells have to mutate? What was God preventing us from learning, if given enough time to do the research?

No, I definitely didn't get much sleep. I woke up more tired than when I went to bed. No zards today, please, no Wizard constructs, no harvested souls.

Chapter 16

IT BIT BACK

Camp was broken down quickly---what remained of it. Five more days until we reach Grove, in the Apple Woods, revised from six. We were now travelling 50 kays a day. That might sound like a lot, but most of that was through level, unobstructed terrain. Also, that's what a person was accustomed to on Limbo. Most people travel by foot. Could the centaurs fill that void? Not voluntarily. Other four-legged beasts? Oxen? Deer? Oxen were used to transport goods in some parts of the world, but rarely people. It was considered immoral---by many---to enslave any animal for any purpose. Do we know---for certain---it wasn't once a person?

It was finally Hornet's turn to become Dinga's designated suitor. Was it because she ran out of men? Or had something deep within remembered a relationship with him? It was easier to endure a tragedy in the embrace of familiar companionship.

Hornet confided in me. "This recycled relationship feels platonic, more like friends seeing one another after spending many years apart than spouses or lovers. Even if Dinga's memory returns I'm not sure our relationship will. The days apart feel like years."

Centaur should have been the one to talk to Hornet. He was married. A long relationship to me was seeing the girl in the morning. It was unlikely I would ever have a relationship, now---a real one. Like priests and nuns, I was married to the divine. I didn't regret or covet. The sacrificial benefits far exceeded the selfish detriments. But if I wasn't going to enjoy matrimonial bliss I was determined those I was most close to did. "If what the two of you had was real, not some romantic fantasy, it's likely to return."

"What if the time apart was too long?"

"It has just been a few days."

"You know what I mean. People do drift apart. Dinga might not progress emotionally in the same manner that she did originally."

"A pebble dropped in a creek may change its course. The water still has to go downstream, eventually reaching the sea."

"Unless it's trapped in a basin: a depression."

"You're certainly glum today."

Hornet looked sorrowfully back at me.

"I guess if I had what you had I would be too. Sometimes things that are meant to be just happen. If the two of you are suppose to be together it will happen. A little memory loss---and re-maturing---won't prevent that from happening. Fate. Luck. Destiny. Call it what you will."

The next four days passed expeditiously. We were in a routine now---beyond tedious---we had transitioned to rote. Our legs instinctively propelled us forward. We were tired at the end of the day, but not exhausted. The dimming of the sun was a better indicator to mark the termination of our travel than our fatigue.

Midway through our fifth day we entered the Apple Woods. A majority of the trees weren't fruit bearing, just the ones that interested us. After a week of trail rations we were susceptible to supplementing our diet. In addition to apples, there were pears, and plums, and cherries. Eating too much fruit was supposed to give one a belly ache. We didn't care. A little discomfort was a fair trade for something fresh with flavor. Some of the fruit was too fresh, which Hornet was first to discover.

After he bit into an apple, it bit back. The worm was carnivorous. It not only bit a chunk out of his tongue, it made an escape route through his cheek. We deadened the pain and cleaned both injures with the last of our wine. We bandaged his cheek the best we could then hoped for a good healer in the village. We were out of healing stones. How strange, that a magical, alchemical derivative had become a staple.

Grove was across the river. Unlike Forks, there was

someone manning the ferry. Not just manning it, but eager to take us across. "I apologize, but there is a one copper fee---per person."

Centaur opened his wallet and frowned. "And the protection?"

"Grove doesn't have a militia, or an expensive wall. There's a hedge, but it doesn't even keep insects away---which we encourage. Without bees our orchards wouldn't be as bountiful."

"Do you have of a market for your fruit? This isn't the most populated part of Limbo."

"Some of it goes to Berry. Occasionally, a freight-hauler delivers a dried bundle to Marsh Bay, which is then shipped to the Central Peninsula or Cape Town. Most of it heads north to Kenwood."

"You must wish you lived in a more modern society. With better transportation and refrigeration you could make a bundle."

"At the cost of our serenity?"

"Fruit harvesting can't be that boisterous?"

"True, but an increase in production would require an increase in population, and possibly tourism. We enjoy company, but a handful of guests a week, not hundreds. If we required stress we would have moved to a city. I would rather take a peaceful solitary stroll through the woods than become a tour guide."

This far upstream the river was narrow. A ford was possible, but probably not practical. The water looked too deep to be crossed haphazardly. Decades ago travel must have been unbearable. If it wasn't for mining in the Platinum Mountains and agriculture on the Berry Peninsula this part of Limbo would have remained unpopulated---by the non-mutated.

The crossing took just a minute, not long enough for Dinga to get too worked up. "Maybe we can take a longer trip some time," she suggested. "Will we follow the river to Berry? Wouldn't it be faster if we took a boat?"

Centaur answered. "The river does go all the way to Berry, but we'd be going upstream. Even if we could afford to buy a couple of canoes---which we can't---it would take more effort--- rowing, than walking."

75

Dinga got quiet, which she sustained the remainder of the day.

I whispered to Centaur, "If we were closer to the sea we might be able to save a couple of weeks."

"We're going to Berry to cure Dinga."

"There are other cities, with other healers."

"I'm surprised you would even consider delaying Dinga's recovery."

"Because I'm an Octagonal Knight? Knights are proponents of Neutrality. We correct imbalance. We right wrongs, but for the benefit of all. Sometimes helping an individual harms the group."

"Do you believe that dogma?"

"Dogma? Doing something to benefit all is extremely moral. Being as physically oriented as I am I require focus. Ambiguity gets me into trouble. Details may be gray, but not objectives. Dinga's fear of boats will return, but west or east of the Northern Sea?"

Grove was extremely hospitable. Its citizens fawned over us like family reuniting. Hornet was treated like he was a small child that had skinned his knee or been stung by a bee. His hand was held and he was hugged. He blushed. His benefactors weren't exclusively female, but enough of them were. It was a good sign whenever the female population rivaled the male. Eighty percent of Limbo's inmates were male. For so many females to cluster together they had to feel comfortable. Respect and lack of violence were virtually guaranteed.

Grove was as beautiful as it was friendly. It wasn't just the people who were aesthetically pleasing---their demeanor making wholesomely attractive people even more so. Every residence had flower beds, adjacent to the structures and on both sides of the sidewalks leading up to them. The town's lone, meandering street was paved with beautiful stones, colorful and polished, like pebbles in an alpine lake.

Hornet was escorted to the village's healer. She was the most remarkable woman I had ever seen: extraordinarily attractive, but professional. She was one of those women who wasn't aware how beautiful she was. Every movement of her face, every contortion of her body caressed my soul. The attraction was of too high an order to be sensual. Watching her was like examining a work of art---in motion---two dimensions expressed in three, or three in four. I had never been attracted to intelligent women. Intellect can get in the way, a supplemental personality to compete with. I had trouble enough communicating with one woman. Three of us was a crowd. But this woman changed how I viewed women. Her intelligence, instead of distracting from her personality, enhanced it. She was a piece cake, but with a fruit filling, topped with ice cream. Being an Octagonal Knight I could never have a relationship with this woman, not to the degree she deserved. Our relationship lasted just a moment: a series of glances representing introduction, courting, companionship, and separation.

Like a moth to a flame, the healer was drawn to Hornet. She examined his cheek, then the rest of his body. If she hadn't acted so professionally the contact would have been viewed as inappropriate. She was very thorough in her examination. "An injury to one can become an injury to all," she explained. "The health of a body can affect the health of its components. The wound will heal more efficiently if it is the focus. What you wish to cultivate will not achieve its potential if it must fight weeds for nutrients. A moment, please."

The healer walked to a table cluttered with glass vials. Using tongs she extracted four dried leaves from one of the vessels, and, what looked like, a small, dehydrated carrot from another. She placed all into a stone bowl. Using a stone mortar, she ground them. She added water, slowly, just enough to congeal the powder. Using a spatula, she gently transferred the contents of the bowl onto a cloth, which she covered with a second cloth. From a third vial, much smaller than the other two, she extracted its contents, using tongs: what looked to be a solitary spherical confection.

She faced Hornet. "Eat this." She dropped it into his outstretched hand.

He examined it. Then examined it some more. Then waited. Contemplating the consequences of swallowing it? Possibly. Or just trying to get up the nerve.

Dinga walked up to him. "Men are such babies when it comes to going to the doctor or taking medicine." She snatched it from his hand and put it in his mouth. It happened so suddenly, and so unexpectedly, Hornet didn't have time to think. Instinctively, he chewed and swallowed.

"You shouldn't have done that," the healer said mechanically. It couldn't have been the first time one of her patients---or a member of the patient's entourage---did something stupid. "Your touch may have activated the penta."

"Penta?" It apparently wasn't just people Dinga forgot.

"The active ingredients."

"What could have happened to me?"

"Your energy may have been restored."

"And that's bad?"

"When one has a limited supply of herbs."

"I don't feel any different."

But Hornet did. "It feels like hundreds of ants are crawling over me, but in a good way, like they're massaging me." Hornet felt his cheek. "It doesn't appear to be healing it."

"That's because it's an energy penta, not a healing one. When intensive healing occurs, matter is transferred to the injury from other parts of the body. A boost to the system lessens the shock. Now, pick up that compress---those two pieces of cloth. Place it on your cheek. Apply some pressure. The ointment needs to be able to seep."

Whatever it was---in the ointment---it was working. Hornet was beginning to look uncomfortable.

"You may wish to sit down."

"I'll be okay."

Hornet began to pale. Before he fainted, Dinga forcibly directed him into a chair. Color returned to his face.

"Five minutes more, and we'll see how well that cheek healed," spoke the healer.

"Do you think it's possible to teach me how to do that,

mixing dried leaves and stuff together to make medicine?" asked Dinga.

"If you're receptive. You may wish to consult your friends. It could take months to learn how to…."

"MONTHS?!"

"Alchemy is as much an art as a science. It takes practice to properly grind and mix the ingredients. That's after finding and collecting the elem-infused herbs."

"Months?"

"Off world it takes three years to become a doctor. Time to examine that cheek."

The healer removed the compress---with her hands. But the healing should have run its course, by now. And it wasn't like healing was going to burn or electrocute her. The hole had filled in. There was still evidence of an injury, but not substantial enough to notice across a room.

Softly with hesitation, Centaur asked the healer, "How much do we owe you?"

"Healing is a calling, not a vocation. Donations are accepted, but not required."

"How do you stay in business?" I asked her.

"People find ways to sustain necessities."

Centaur begrudgingly gave her two gold coins. The materials alone were worth considerably more than that, but it was the best we could do if we wished to reach our destination.

The healer dropped the coins into a wooden box on a small table beside the door. It would take seconds for someone to snag it and run off. But apparently not in Grove.

"Do you have a place to stay?" she asked.

"Not yet," Centaur replied. "We're comfortable camping, but Dinga would like a bath."

"I would?"

"You used to, before…."

"Now that you mention it, I would like to take a bath…with soap…and a lot of bubbles. I guess a bath was one of those things I liked before AND after."

"If you don't mind sleeping on the floor you can stay here," the healer suggested. "There's a tub in back---a donation."

Hornet looked puzzled. "This building didn't look large enough from the outside to accommodate a bathhouse."

"It doesn't. The tub's out back."

It was Dinga's turn to look puzzled. "Then how do you...?"

"Bathe discretely? Grovellians will provide privacy, when it's requested. It's disrespectful to give unwanted attention. Being a healer I'm required to give professional attention to potentially embarrassing displays. I'm adept at distinguishing platonic from non-platonic. An accidental glimpse won't debilitate me."

"We wouldn't want to impose," said Centaur.

"Of course we can," Dinga countered. She whispered to us loudly, "Some people consider it rude to decline an offer. You'll embarrass her---badly---if you refuse. You'll imply she and her house aren't worthy."

"Well, if that's the case," said Pulp. "We generously accept your offer, madam." He bowed deeply. For a gent that was quite impressive, like a tree bending in a windstorm.

Pulp caused a commotion. For every person who thought of him as a monster, another two treated him like a celebrity. It wasn't every day that someone met a mighty gent. It was even rarer for them to frequent their business or home. Those in smaller settlements tended to be more curious than fearful. Without a mob mob-mentality rarely occurred. Hate, distrust, was usually a group activity.

Chapter 17

SISTER

In the morning the healer treated us to a light breakfast. As we left the hamlet we were goodbyed as warmly as we were welcomed.

Five more days until Berry. Three more days of prairie, then foothills. I was looking forward to different scenery. My physical heritage made me susceptible to boredom. The one day reprieve into a deciduous forest was pleasant, but it felt temporary. The novelty wore off after the last tree was passed, creating its non-existence. Before we abandoned the forest we filled our packs with fruit and nuts. Our trail rations were sufficient sustenance---physically, but not emotionally.

The first day, and evening, passed without incident. During our second I paused to examine an odd trench that intersected our route. A sticky, acidic residue covered its walls. "It might be best we compressed and kept our wits about us." A kay later we passed a small grove of trees. Most were dead. The remainder were on the precipice of joining them. Vertical trenches were cut into their trunks, covered with the sticky substance.

A kay after that we found a porcupine---what was left of it. It looked like it was made of wax and had melted in the sun. Only bones and a portion of its barbed hide remained. The sticky substance spread out from the carcass like a corona.

Dinga wore a stunned expression. "What could have done that?"

"It looks like slug slime," I commented.

"But more acidic," said Pulp.

Centaur smiled. "Anyone have a large salt shaker?"

"You could use my skin," said Dinga. "I need a bath."

"You just had one," Hornet countered.

"That was yesterday. Clean girls are more susceptible to romantic overtures. Store that away for future reference."

Hornet and Dinga's renewed relationship was definitely blossoming. No more than flirtations so far, but she was directing them at the right person.

We never saw the giant slug, if that's what created the trenches, and killed the porcupine. If we hadn't been on the road so long our curiosity might have exceeded our weariness. Investigations tended to be more fruitful in the morning: physical activity being more vigorous; acuity and spirit, more crisp.

We spotted the Raspberry Mountains the end of our second day. They were still almost 100 kays away, but having them this close---close enough to stretch out an arm and touch---cheered us up immensely, supplying us with the energy we needed to make that final push.

"Let's not stop at all," Hornet suggested. "If we walk through the night we'll arrive a day early."

"It would be a challenge," I added enthusiastically.

"An adventure," Pulp amended.

Dinga was noncommittal. It may be fun, but it would bring her closer to losing herself, the self that supplanted that boring, older woman.

"Someone is more likely to trip in the middle of the night," stated Centaur. "And monsters are more likely to attack. We don't have any healing stones, and every step takes us farther away from that healer. We're in an open, Neutral prairie, but how well will we be able to defend ourselves after our energy is exhausted?"

We didn't always agree to Centaur's suggestions, but they were usually the most prudent. Before it got too dark to diminish our navigation and safety, we camped.

The following day, en route, cheetahs surrounded us. One of them charged. Something didn't feel right. It---they---didn't emit any animosity. Competitiveness, but playful, not violent. On the precipice of a counterattack I called out, "WAIT!" It still surprised me how disciplined we were as a group. Everyone held back. Putting your life in someone else's hand earns trust. After touching Hornet with one of its paws, the cheetah darted off. Our reaction: a mixture of amused and perplexed expressions. Additional cheetahs played this game, it continuing until all participated.

"Well, that was interesting," stated Centaur. "Not the wisest thing to do. If Stick hadn't warned us…. How did you know?"

"Since I became an Octagonal Knight my…awareness…has improved."

"Something in the armor?" Hornet conjectured.

"Perhaps? I've heard of armor and weapons being enchanted. The thought of me being surrounded by infused elem is exhilarating, but also unsettling."

"Those cheetahs must have been male," said Dinga. "Guys will make a game out of anything. The more dangerous the better."

"It reminds me of a game I played with the arbols," Pulp shared, "but they were female. There was also I lot of touching."

I sighed. "Tell me again why we left the Copper Forest so suddenly?"

Centaur answered. "Let's see. You were beat up from defeating that Octagonal Knight. I was bent over from carrying a herd of equines. Hornet was almost pummeled to death, and drowned."

"So you agree, we should have stayed there a couple of weeks to recover?"

"We were concerned if we stayed there much longer the arbols might take back the pearl."

"They wouldn't have," stated Pulp.

"Why couldn't you have said that then?" I asked.

"Because you hadn't met me."

"Technicalities."

"You have a pearl?" asked Dinga. "Can I see it?"

"Two pearls," Hornet declared.

We looked at one another. What harm was there, in Dinga seeing them?

Hornet removed two small bags from his pack. He extracted a small metallic green sphere from one of them. He placed it in Dinga's hand. It began to glow. "Did I do that?" she asked.

"It's powered by the sun," Centaur responded.

Dinga held it between her thumb and forefinger. "It's so beautiful. Can I see the other one?"

Hornet set a metallic blue sphere in her other hand. When she brought the two together to compare, the one on her palm---the blue one---bolted, like it had been struck. Instead of falling to the ground after it left her hand it stopped midway. Her other hand, the one holding the blue sphere, jerked towards it, like the two were attached, by a string. Hornet came to her rescue. He snagged the blue sphere, then lifted it, until it was level with the other. Dinga took it from him with her unencumbered hand. She brought the two spheres together, then separated them, repeatedly. It looked like she was exercising. She smiled unabashedly. The display initially made me happy, then depressed me. In a few more days she may no longer have the capacity. She twisted and turned. "I can't control it, not entirely. It wants me to turn...that way." She motioned with her head towards the Raspberry Mountains.

"Could the next sphere be there?" Hornet asked.

"Let's check," said Centaur. "Can we borrow those for a minute, Dinga? We need to start moving, but you'll have time to hold them one more time." Dinga faced Centaur with her arms extended. "Hornet, you ought to be the one to test them."

"They frighten you?"

"They make me uneasy. If you don't mind."

Hornet held each of her hands briefly as the spheres were transferred. An electromagnetic mist began to form at the point of contact, evaporating quickly after it was broken.

"Oh," Dinga whimpered softly.

It was the first time they had such a contact since she lost her memory.

Hornet permitted the spheres to direct him. He turned slowly around, stopping in the direction Dinga had been facing. "The force is about the same. Which means the next sphere is still hundreds of kays away, doesn't it?"

Centaur nodded. "It also confirms it hasn't moved. It's in the same direction."

"What are you talking about?" asked Dinga.

"The spheres form a transport portal," I declared. "If we find all six we'll be able to escape."

"One of us," added Centaur. "Most of the portable ones were constructed for a single use."

That's the first time that was mentioned. If only one of us was going to escape who should it be? I no longer wished to leave this planet---maybe I never did. Pulp certainly was content here. That left Centaur, Hornet, and Dinga. Would Hornet and Dinga be willing to separate once her memories return? Centaur would be the logical choice, but would he ever be happy on the outside? Would the real world remind him of his wife? Would his freedom compensate for the lack of adventure?

We must have been thinking similar thoughts---all of us--- because the next few kays we kept to ourselves---emotionally, not physically. There was safety in numbers, closely clustered. We were reminded of potential dangers when the cheetahs pseudo-attacked.

We saw an additional cheetah later in the day. A praying mantis the size of a cow had skewered it with one of its razor-sharp legs. It tore bits of flesh before shoveling it into its mouth.

"How awful," said Dinga before she buried her head in Hornet's shoulder.

"It's surprising we haven't seen more giant insects," said Pulp. "The grasslands of the Berry Peninsula used to be called the Pestilence Prairie."

"The Aluminum Prairie does sound safer," Centaur stated.

"Marketing, you think?" I questioned.

"It's still pretty desolate here except for Berry and Kenwood.

Where are they going?" Centaur was referring to Dinga and Hornet walking rapidly towards the river. My lack of response was as effective as any retort. "It's been more than a week. Does that mean it will be over quicker because they can't wait any longer, or longer, because they want to make up for lost time?"

"Can't it be both," suggested Pulp.

"I'll get the cards."

When Dinga and Hornet returned the radiance that surrounded them was almost blinding. They were flush and drenched, and unable to communicate. They didn't completely recover until we camped. Maintaining our policy of what we didn't know wouldn't hurt us, the event wasn't discussed.

Everything was back to normal the following day, until the evening. Just one day remained before we reached Berry. Things were about to change. For the better, or for the worse, they were going to change.

"I should be happy, but I'm dreading having my memory returned," Dinga shared. "If I become this other person, I'll lose who I am."

"But this isn't really you," Hornet pleaded.

"If feels like it is. Sometimes criminal's minds are modified to cure them of their corruption. Is it just to alter them? Or are we killing them to allow another to possess their body? If my memories return will someone else possess MY body?"

"Does your body truly belong to you? Or are you just borrowing it until the other returns?"

"I don't think you will lose your current memories when your prior self returns," said Pulp.

"So I will share my memories, like having a sister in my head?" Dinga stood up and walked to the edge of camp. She was smiling.

Chapter 18

BERRY

In the morning Dinga kept to herself. She was very observant of her surroundings, as if she was experiencing everything for the first---or possibly the last---time.

Midday we came to a crossroads. To the west was Filbert, in the Huckleberry Forest. To the south was Violet, along the Northern Strait. And finally, to the north, was Berry---our destination---in the upper foothills of the Raspberry Mountains. We also intercepted a creek, the Purple, a meandering stream--- horizontally and vertically---that would accompany our climb.

The climb wasn't always steep, but it was incessant: a 1500 meter ascent extending seven kays. The cascading water provided enough moisture to the canyon we ascended to modify the scenery considerably. Damp earth, even mud, replaced the dust that billowed after every step since we left the Apple Woods. Replacing the brittle grass were verdant shrubs and ferns, and a mixture of cottonwoods and oaks that transitioned to pines. The temperature was noticeably cooler. Initially from the creek spray, but as the day progressed, instead of it getting warmer, the temperature sustained. It actually dropped a couple of degrees when we entered Vineyard Valley, the shelf Berry occupied.

Berry was aptly named. We passed through blackberry briars and strawberry patches, raspberry hedges and cherry orchards. We slowed as we came closer to our destination, our full bellies slowing us down.

The dirt road became a stone boulevard. Blossoming cherry trees shaded tiled benches, each mosaic unique, the majority depicting nature.

"Time to take a break," Dinga declared as she removed her pack and dropped heavily onto one of the benches.

"With us being so close?" Centaur questioned.

"Haven't you ever paused a moment before walking into a dentist's office?" Pulp commented.

Hornet considered joining her, but didn't. She looked so pensive. Abruptly, she stood up, and replaced her pack. "You ready?" he asked her.

"As ready as I'll ever be."

Dinga wasn't the only person who occupied a bench. Most were individuals, but there were a few couples, in various states of platonic and amorous intercourse.

Berry was walled, but in an inviting manner. Berry vines draped over them, most flowering, with white, pink, red, and blue blossoms. Fifteen towers rose above the city walls: three within the city, four guarding the southern and western gates, four more book-ending the creek's entry into and egress out of the city, the final four protecting elongated spans. The towers were also covered with flowering vines. An armored guard was stationed upon each perimeter tower. Their lower levels were leased out to local businesses.

Two guards in purple uniforms greeted us at the southern gate. Silver and gold berries drooped from silver and gold chains attached to their heavily armored hearts. "Welcome to Berry," greeted the older, more adorned man. "Admission is a silver per person the first day, three coppers after that."

"Do we need to pay in advance?" asked Centaur.

"Just for the first day, but no one chooses to spend just one day in Berry."

Centaur gave him five silver coins, leaving us with just enough money to pay for a healer and a night or two of lodging.

"Maybe we can wash dishes or something," I suggested.

"What is your business here?" asked the other guard. He wasn't as jovial as his partner. Having a three-meter tall gent accompanying us didn't help.

"We wish to find a healer," said Centaur. "Dinga is ill."

"She looks fine to me."

"Exceptionally fine," added the first guard.

Dinga blushed as she smiled at the man. Women were definitely fond of compliments, especially when it came from men in uniform.

Noticing my armor for the first time, the younger guard said in an embarrassed tone, "Octagonal Knights are always welcome here, sir---free of charge. Allow me to give you a refund." He handed me a silver coin.

Centaur chuckled. "Think of the money we could make if we taught you to sing and dance."

"The Healing Tower is the first one you come to," spoke the older guard. "Lodging is in the Western District. Many of the inns have great views of the peaks."

Beyond the gate the boulevard persisted, but with houses similar to the ones in Grove replacing the cherry trees. They clustered closely to the road and to each other. The hodgepodge of stone and vegetation reminded me of summer in the mountains. My family owned a rustic cabin, mandatory for a physical family with means. The tower the guard spoke of was a kay away. It was draped in a mural of grapes and the myriad varieties of berries that grew in the region.

The people we passed were friendly, blatantly content with their lives. It was impossible for us not to be infected by the pleasantness, the peaceful exuberance permeating our pores.

The lobby of the tower was occupied by a woman in a white pantsuit, adorned with a single silver berry. She sat behind a desk. Rolled scrolls filled the grid organizer behind her. She sat on the only chair in the room. She ignored us as she went about her business, which involved looking at everything around her but us.

Centaur became impatient. "We need to see a healer."

"Of course," she replied. "Why else would you be here."

"Can we see one now?"

"You'll have to take a number."

"What number?"

"Take one from the top of my desk."

We looked on top of her desk. There was a basin carved into the top of it, with numbered balls in it.

"Any ball?"

"The numbers I call are in the order they shall be chosen."

"How many other people are waiting?"

"You are the only ones who have come in after closing hours."

"So we have to wait until tomorrow?"

"If you pick the proper number and are here when we open tomorrow, you'll be the first served."

"If you're closed, why are you still here?"

"Sometimes people like to reserve a number for the following day. We take pride in our renewed effort to create efficiency."

"When do you open tomorrow?"

"At four, but I recommend arriving at least ten minutes earlier. If you can't be here when your number is called we appreciate you informing us ahead of time. We reserve the right to bill no shows. Good day. The advanced reservation period is over."

"Do you think there's another healer in the city," I asked, dryly.

"If there was how could this one stay in business?" Hornet responded.

Leaving the Healing Tower we entered a spectacular sight. The town was aglow. Lights replaced the sun that had dimmed while we were inside. The mica in the stone streets glittered. A fire had been lit at the top of each tower, creating---simultaneously---exhilaration and warmth.

We walked to the center of town, to the base of the Civic Tower. Stained glass in the shape of berries glowed from the flickering illumination. An avenue as broad, and as well constructed as the one we were on, began at the base of the tower. We turned onto it, heading west. It terminated at the western gate, now closed.

COBBER CASTLE was chiseled on the left tower.

"That sounds like a place to sleep---and eat," said Pulp. "I'm in the mood for a good home-cooked meal."

"I thought you didn't like cooked food?" Centaur commented.

"Sometimes I get a hot tooth. I just have to be careful I don't eat anything with meat in it."

"On moral grounds?" I asked.

"Dietary. I acquired more than large molars during my transformation. I'll become seriously ill if I mistakenly eat meat."

"Even a small piece?" asked Hornet.

"It depends on how small, but yes, the pain might be less intense, but still something I wouldn't want to experience."

"Do you miss the taste of meat?" asked Centaur.

"Sometimes. Other times the thought of meat makes me nauseous. Worst is when someone is cooking it, permeating the air."

"So, overall, you don't miss eating meat---that much," said Dinga.

"Except on those rare occasions I crave it. That fleshy chewiness, that warmth as it's squeezed down my throat. Sometimes I contemplate if that one bite might be worth the hours of agony that follow."

"Do you ever give into temptation?"

"I haven't so far, but living in the Copper Forrest there are plenty of things to distract me---soft, pretty, very willing to distract, things." Pulp looked very dreamy-eyed when he finished speaking.

What would it be like to live without conscience, the moment surpassing future consequences? In the Positive Frontier it was balanced with good intention. What would such a lack of restraint be like without a check? The Negative Frontier would be a living hell, but to those who live there would it be paradise? Million of hectares of the worst of the worst, mutating into more extreme versions of themselves. And we were travelling there, voluntarily?

We reserved three rooms high in the tower before eating--- my position reducing the rent by a third. Did I deserve the perk? I righted wrongs, but so did others, just not in an official capacity. Should I be rewarded for doing my job? Others weren't, for following their conscience.

The meal in the pub below consisted of berry products: jellies and jams, pies and sorbets, breads and cakes, wines and schnapps. It was good, but more variety would have been better, with protein in it. Buying locally was admirable, but it didn't have to be exclusive. And where were the nuts? They also grew on trees. Were they out of season? Nuts weren't as savory as meat, but they had at least a similar nutritional value.

Chapter 19

CURE

The next morning we had blueberry pancakes with freshly squeezed juice---and bacon. From what animal, we weren't certain. It didn't exactly taste like pork, or beef, or chicken or fish. Our curiosity didn't exceed the potential trauma of confirming some of the more disturbing possibilities.

There were already five people in front of the Healing Tower when we arrived. Fortunately our number was called first. The clinic was at the top of the tower, eight flights up. We climbed a spiral staircase past six recovery rooms and a lab. The healer was a gray-haired man. It was rare for a Limboan to show signs of aging. He looked overworked, which likely was the origin of the obstacles: receptionist and stairs. Perseverance, apparently, equated to severity of illness or injury. The healer wore a simple white robe. He didn't wear any ornamentation, which worried me, until I saw

20 metallic berries hanging on the wall, twice as many as I've seen anyone wear so far.

"Do you wish me to disrobe?" Dinga asked the healer as she began undressing.

"If you wish," he responded. "But I don't think it will be necessary for what ails you." Dinga instantly re-buttoned her shirt. "You're healthy, physically, both of you, so your ailment must be mental."

"I've lost my memory." Dinga did a double-take. "What do you mean BOTH OF US?"

"You're pregnant. Our jailors prefer women not to bear children---bad publicity. But sometimes mistakes are made, early in a pregnancy."

"But I wasn't pregnant when I was sentenced."

"You're mistaken. Sometimes women aren't aware until late in their pregnancy."

"I think a woman knows if she is capable of becoming pregnant. It's been months since I've...."

"Not exactly," Hornet interrupted.

"I never took the birth-control antidote. That would have been fatal in my line of work.... Enough of what they put in the water supply should have still been in my system.... I didn't think we could become pregnant on Limbo."

"I didn't either," the healer replied. "Once we enter Limbo our bodies change, including becoming sterile."

"There are other ways?"

"I think you'll have to disrobe after all, and you too, young man. The rest of you can wait downstairs. Within the lobby, if you don't mind. If it's crowded some people will give up, even before taking a number. Just once I would like to get off work before sundim. Now, if this young woman is really pregnant.... Common illnesses, and fractures, have become too routine.... Miss, I'll examine you first."

"Dinga. My name is Dinga."

"Dinga, I'll examine you first, then...."

"Hornet."

"Then Hornet in about 20 minutes. I'll page you when it's your turn."

Centaur, Pulp, Hornet and I climbed back down to the lobby. It was full. That explained why there weren't any chairs in it: there was no room. Our entry dislocated a similar number of people. Those nearest the exit either had to push back---or leave. They chose the less confrontational route.

Hornet was eventually called back up, then the rest of us. "Dinga is definitely pregnant," stated the healer. "And Hornet IS the father."

"I don't understand," Hornet responded dispassionately.

"Neither do I. Neither of you is sterile. Why have our jailors become suddenly lax after a hundred years of following strict procedures? I hope I still remember how to deliver a baby. I haven't delivered one since I lost my license."

"It didn't involve a delivery?"

"Not exactly. It was for performing abortions during a brief period it was illegal. I was sentenced to Dartmoor for being a mass murderer."

"How about Dinga's memory?" asked Centaur. "Can you restore it? If she is going to have a baby it's important she remember its father."

"You see those vials over there?" The healer pointed to the red, black, and purple bottles on a counter. "The medicines I have developed are from select berries. Elem sometimes collect in pockets, like metal in veins. Certain berries are good receptacles for these pockets. The red potion is for strength, the purple for physical restoration, and the black, to cure diseases."

"There isn't anything for memory restoration, then?" Hornet asked.

"There is, but it is much rarer. I'm not even permitted to store it in my tower. You see, the civics consider it too valuable for a single individual to possess."

"So you can't help us?"

"The civics may be willing to come to some kind of

arrangement."

"What do we have that they want?" I asked.

"You. You're reputation precedes you---your order's."

"Am I to become a sentry? A gate guard?"

"I don't believe they would choose to waste your skills on something so tedious. You'll need to speak to them, in the Civic Tower, for the particulars."

"We can go to the emporium," Centaur suggested.

"If we still had one. I apologize."

"It's not your fault," Dinga assured him. She had been silent since we rejoined her. Who wouldn't be shocked upon learning they had become pregnant on an inhospitable---supposedly infertile---world.

"But it is. The stones most commonly sold are for healing, and I can supply the same for a fraction of what the Wizards charge. They don't supply their services for the benefit of mankind. Profit is their motivation, and peripherally for the gossip they overhear. The Berry Peninsula is peaceful and quiet. The potential reconnaissance didn't warrant retaining their business operation. Their departure benefited me doubly. This tower used to belong to the Wizards."

Hornet hesitantly hugged Dinga. She had finally broken out of her shell, but was it safe to make contact with her? I didn't envy him. Dinga was a beautiful woman, but she was messed up: hot, cold, kind, mean, a memorable past, an inconsistent present, a questionable future. But they were now in it together---forever---a bond created that could never be completely broken. She hugged him back, initially reflexively with the same intensity, then more vigorously. He responded in kind. The embrace was more loving than passionate. We felt grateful to be in their prescience, not trapped.

"Before you leave I have something for you." The healer climbed down the stairs.

"I guess congratulations are in order," said Centaur. He hugged Dinga and shook Hornet's hand. "I didn't know you had it in you---in any of us."

Pulp leaned down and hugged both of them.

95

"Does that mean we now have to be careful who we….?"

"Or what we," Centaur added. "Your fascination with the exotic will, one day, be your undoing."

"I don't believe so," stated Pulp. "The loss of our infertility, not Stick's dalliances with mutants. Dinga and Hornet are special. You have seen how imperative their need to bond becomes. And that glow that surrounds them afterwards." Dinga and Hornet blushed. "This pregnancy didn't happen by accident."

"Our jailors?"

"Or Gaea."

"Superstition," I interjected. "Fables created to explain the unexplainable. Ancient religions were established to cope and to consolidate power."

"One day people may feel the same about modern religions," said Pulp.

"There is no dogma in the Aspects---principles to live by and to explain---not random criteria to confirm and enforce mandates to retain power."

The concept of Gaea scared me. I didn't believe in the supernatural, but there was part of me, a very small part that was open to the possibility. Few people were completely atheist. Many prayed to God when they were desperate. God didn't exist, but if He or She or It did, there was still hope. If a supreme being had some ability to control our lives that meant we weren't entirely in control. I needed to be in control. Not in control of others, but of myself. That's why I didn't have friends, serious friends I could share my thoughts with. If someone knew too much about you they could control you.

The healer returned with a leather pouch. He handed it to Dinga. She opened it. Inside were at least a dozen stones.

Centaur said, "I thought you couldn't…."

"Prenatal medication. Take just one a week. They may not help, but they won't hurt."

She hugged the healer. "Thank you."

"I'm not entirely doing it for you. My obligation as a healer,

96

and the continuation of my livelihood, demands it. How many patients would I have if I become known as the doctor that wasn't able to save Limbo's first child?"

The civics were expecting us. The mayor wore a purple tunic so cluttered with medals they tangled, becoming one large mass on his chest. The eleven story Civic Tower had a magnificent view of the entire city, and the mountains, hills, and prairie that surrounded it.

"We need your help," began the mayor, without preamble. He looked like he was six or seven. With the ample supply of medications available it wasn't surprising. Then why did the healer allow himself to appear so old? "The Road-At-The-Top-Of-The-World has become too dangerous. Not only is the route to Sweet Falls closed, we no longer have access to Alpine Meadows, where many of our most valuable berries grow."

"And in return, you will give us the memory serum?" asked Hornet.

"In addition to a few other rare elixirs. For an Octagonal Knight to provide such a valuable service, the reward must be great."

"An Octagonal Knight does not trade his services for a reward," I stated.

"Maybe not, but your companions may wish to. You'll certainly wish to protect them as they perform their task."

"What must we do?" asked Centaur.

"A hydra has nested in the high country. Instead of spewing fire, it discharges frost, strong enough to not only knock over trees, but to freeze someone in place. Three companies of town militia have been sent. None have returned. We dare not send any more. Our defense has been decimated. Larger cities have an unlimited supply of citizens willing to train as militia---we don't. A draft wouldn't go over well on a planet populated by people relocated against their will."

"Can you keep Dinga safe while we're gone?" asked Hornet.

"I don't want to be left behind," whined Dinga.

"It's no longer just you you must consider," stated Centaur.

Dinga sighed, then she smiled. And finally, enlightenment. "I'll stay, but on the condition I spend most of that time with the healer. If I'm going to have this...baby...I need to learn...everything. What I should and shouldn't eat and drink. What kind of activity I should and shouldn't participate in. What symptoms I might have. What the pregnancy will do to my body. What it will be like to give birth. What happens after the baby is born. I'll wish to feed the baby naturally. What I should eat to maximize its nutrition. It's going to be heartrending raising it. When should I tell it its mommy and daddy are criminals? All the people around it are criminals. It's living in a prison without the possibility of parole. There are things out there that will wish to kill it for sport. And when it dies---Gaea forbid before it's an adult---it will become mutated, possibly grotesquely."

Hornet put his arm around her. "I'll also be there."

Dinga closed her eyes as she floated in his warm embrace. She turned to kiss him on the lips tenderly. "Return safely---and quickly. I need those memories back."

We waited until the following day to begin our excursion, not wishing to camp after a partial day of travel. We spent the remainder of the day sightseeing. The stream the city borrowed flowed through a greenway designed for it. Numerous bridges spanned it, its relatively flat course through town permitting paddleboats to traverse it.

The seven story Art Tower was on an island in the middle of the stream. Every level housed a different medium: painting, sculpture, writing, even a primitive form of photography using stone plates covered with chemicals that when exposed to light dissolved channels in the rock. Fumes from the process was toxic, forcing the stonographers to create their art outside. Our stonograph was taken as a tribute. But as heroes that killed the hydra, or the most recent group to be killed by it?

Chapter 20

BURIED

Dinga wished us well---sadly.

"We'll return in a couple of days," Hornet assured her.

She smiled. "I'm looking forward to my baby's mother and father getting to know each other again."

The western gate opened stiffly. It had been weeks since someone had left the city in that direction. "Someone needs to lubricate it before we return," Centaur demanded. "It will be extremely inconvenient---for all of us---if we can't reenter the city after killing the hydra."

I prepared myself mentally for battle. I knew that as an Octagonal Knight I was going to survive, but that journey to the brink would still be painful. And my companions? Death to them would be more dire, with them possibly muting into something like the thing we were going to fight. Would I ever see them again?

Moments after losing sight of Berry, a mountain lion leapt from a cliff towards us. My companions and I instinctively went into a defensive stance, with shields up and weapons out. It wasn't necessary. "You wouldn't happen to have some extra food on you, friends?" spoke the large, tawny cat as it rubbed its body against us. "I'm helpless." It flopped on its side. It definitely looked less-frightening now, but maybe that's what it wanted us to believe. A trap perhaps? I remained cautious. "I haven't eaten in days. If I don't eat something soon I'm going to expire, evaporate into the ether." Receiving no response, it stood back up, and rubbed its body against us again. "Please. Can you spare a morsel? I'm fond of chicken. I prefer drumsticks, but I'll settle for a wing. Ground beef? Any minced meat will do. These choppers aren't as strong as

99

they used to be. It's easier for me to eat if the meat's chopped up a bit first."

"If Dinga was here she would have already emptied our packs," Hornet commented.

We continued on, ignoring the beggar. The cat wasn't swayed. The rubbing and darting in front of us was beginning to get annoying. Centaur had enough of it. "ALL RIGHT! We have some place to be, and you're going to delay us long enough that we'll have to return in the dark, won't you?" He gave it a sandwich.

"Thank you, thank you," it mumbled as it ate. After gumming the bread, it had trouble breaking apart the slice of ham. It pummeled the piece of meat against a rock, eventually shredding it into small enough pieces to be swallowed. "With passersby no longer passing by I'm on the brink of starving to death." After consuming the last of the meat it began to lick its chops. "You wouldn't happen to have a bit more?" It looked up. We were many strides from it already, almost out of sight. It climbed onto the ledge it had leapt from.   It stretched out its paws, together in front of it. "They'll be back," it spoke dreamily as its eyes slowly shut. With a start its eyes popped back open. "Unless...."

The road climbed gradually at first, then more extremely, as switchbacks. I was beginning to get winded. After walking 600 kays in 15 days one would expect to be in better shape, but most of those kays were flat. The higher the elevation the thinner the air, which made climbing even more strenuous.

We hit snow half-an-hour after escaping the perilous belly of that mountain cat. It began as scattered, slushy patches that dribbled down the muddy road that had become as narrow as a trail. Our feet had become wet, refreshing at first, but ultimately uncomfortable, more unsettling than painful. The anguish kicked in after the snow completely covered the road. The cold penetrated our feet through our footwear. When I say our, I meant their. An Octagonal Knight's protective armor included his feet. Through the sturdy, but lightweight boots I NOTICED the cold.

Centaur was the first to slip. "FEEK!"

Hornet reached out a hand to pull him up, but instead of helping him, he was pulled down.

Centaur attempted to stand up on his own. The best he could do was get into a crouch before falling back down, this time on the other side of his body---the side that had been dry. "Aren't you going to at least make an attempt to help us?" he asked Pulp.

"You disappoint me, believing all gents lack common sense."

Centaur also looked up at me.

"I don't think this armor rusts, but why risk it," I responded.

In small, stepped movements Centaur and Hornet finally rose to their feet. They brushed off the snow that hadn't melted on them---yet. We resumed our climb to what the Berrillians called the POLAR PLATEAU.

"It must be spring," I commented. "The snow would be more solid if it was still winter, and it would be warmer if it was summer."

"The road is sometimes cleared, isn't it?" spoke Centaur. "I think I saw a stonograph of this area without snow."

"I didn't think there were seasons on Limbo," Hornet commented.

"There are definitely seasons," Pulp replied. "But they are inconsistent in length. You can thank the Wizards for that. The seasons must occur in order: fall after summer, spring after winter. But sometimes winter lasts just a week. I remember that happening to summer 15 years ago. Someone must have been in a bad mood."

"So, in those years summers are short this snow pack may not completely melt?" Hornet hypothesized.

"Or if the Wizards are particularly cantankerous, they could prevent an area from receiving rain for a couple of years, transforming a forest into a desert."

"Don't they have any morals?"

"They're TRUE NEUTRALS. That's why the Wizards Keep is in the center of Limbo. They do what they wish, not intentionally doing harm, or helping others."

Octagonal Knights were also considered to be True Neutrals,

but they approached their morality differently. Instead of doing what they wish as they abandoned the world around them, they actively integrated, modifying their environment to achieve Neutrality---modifying the subtleties that created imbalance. Wizards may be the epitome of selfishness. In contrast, Knights were selfless---doing only for others, even if it was contrary to their sensibilities. Was I proud of what I had become? What I was becoming? It was a necessary evil. Loved, loathed, unappreciated---I was still needed. The inhabitants of Limbo were too imbalanced to subsist on their own.

Two-hundred meters above the tree-line we crested. We entered a broad expanse of snow and ice. The plain was relatively flat, the extensive white-wash marred by only boulders---sporadically---and the snowmelt their sun-absorbing warmth created. The road was non-existent. Wooden poles began at the top of the pass and continued in a straight line as far as the eye could see. Mountains, jagged and pock-marked by snow, enveloped the plateau. Their elevation varied from one to two thousand meters above the 3000 meter plain. Water fell from the mountain nearest to us, its peripheral spray forming an icy helix.

The sun finally fought its way through the clouds, but it wasn't welcomed---not now. The warmth it created was countered twice fold by the glare off the snow and ice. My visor provided limited protection. Sunglasses were needed. In a society where survival was a daily struggle some things weren't contemplated---not enough to develop the complex process of manufacturing them.

"What's that, over there?" asked Hornet. That perked us up. We didn't know where the hydra might be, or what it might look like. It had multiple heads that blew out frost, but how many, and how powerful was the frost? How large was it? Would we be able to see it from a distance, or would it suddenly appear, bursting through the snow?

Whatever it was, it wasn't the hydra. It was stationary, and glittery---and large---many times the size of a person.

"Let's investigate," suggested Pulp.

"Is that wise?" asked Hornet.

"We have to start somewhere, looking for that hydra," said Centaur. "It could give us a clue."

I headed for the object. Two steps from the poles I dropped chest-deep into the snow.

"Should we stay near the poles?" asked Hornet.

"I didn't get wet and cold for nothing," I declared. My mission resumed. Enduring the brunt of breaking trail my energy became depleted much sooner than my companions. I slowed considerably. Hornet passed me, as did Pulp, and finally Centaur. It took Hornet a couple of minutes to become exhausted. Pulp replaced him. Centaur also took a turn leading, but wasn't able to sustain as long as the long-legged gent.

We believed the iridescent object to be about half a kay away, but just a few meters more became a few meters more. Its size was what made it appear closer than it was. It was over 20 meters long---the part of it that was visible. Being partially buried it could have been significantly longer.

"Is it a fallen tree?" asked Hornet. "Are those ice crystals on it?"

"If it is, that's the oddest bark I've ever seen," spoke Centaur. "It overlaps."

Whatever it was, most of it was buried in the snow. Just the top of the middle portion was exposed. Its two ends were completely hidden. I was first to touch it. The trunk was as smooth and hard as cedar, but the coloring was wrong. It was iridescent, like fish scales.

My companions began to examine the object, spreading out along its length. Pulp and Hornet backed away. Centaur and I didn't know what provoked their reaction, but we followed their lead. We stopped after 40 meters, then backed up another 20.

"Is it hibernating?" asked Hornet.

"Possibly," said Pulp. "A month long coma to us is a nap to them."

Now that its identity was revealed, it became apparent. Nothing quite looked like a drak, even half-buried.

103

"Do you think it's playing with us?" asked Hornet. "Like how a cat plays with a mouse?" We backed up again.

Centaur shouted something unintelligible. The sound carried across the plain, echoing back to us after the waves bounced off the mountains. Another back up. We kept at least one eye on the monster at all times. Still no movement.

"WHY THE BORE DID YOU DO THAT?!" I shouted at him nearly as loud.

Centaur smirked. "Just a little experiment."

"Could it have frozen to death?" suggested Hornet.

"I've never heard of one doing that before," said Pulp. "It's more likely hibernating. If we leave it alone it may stay that way."

"Would it hibernate in the middle of the snow like that?" asked Centaur.

"I think it's dead," I said. "Even draks die---eventually."

"Are you willing to test that theory?" asked Centaur.

Hibernation meant it was still alive, but in a low-energy state. I should have sensed something. I began walking back towards it. My companions shoed me back to them, trying to be as quiet about it as possible. Aware now what it was, I pictured that clump of snow at one end as its buried head, and the flat end, its tail. Its wings must be buried beneath it.

I cleared snow off its back, being gentle at first, mindful that at any moment it might snap its head around and either bite or blow fire or frost or something just as deadly at me. Still not sensing any movement---not even a breath or a heartbeat---I cleared snow off it in a more forceful manner, working my way to its head. It must have been partially twisted, because I felt a sharp ridge on the far side of it, which would make it its back. I didn't find any arms, so they must be buried beneath it like its wings. Viewing it now as an object instead of an antagonist, I was drawn to its beauty. The colors of its scales---reds, yellows, and blues---flowed from one to another like a rainbow. The scales sparkled in the sunlight, like diamonds. If draks weren't so dangerous, the market for their hides would be tremendously lucrative.

104

As I got closer to its head, its body became narrower. It widened again as its head appeared. I paused, becoming frightened, again. I listened for breathing and a heartbeat. I could hear nothing over my own, which had calmed for a couple minutes, but now was deafening. I hastily cleared snow off its head: a bandage hurting less if it is removed in one yank. Its mouth was partly opened, revealing two rows of sharp dagger-sized teeth. It appeared to be grinning at me. Its eyes were open.

Something hit me from behind. I fell face down into the snow. I was poked in the back of my neck as my body was rocked back and forth. I could hear my companions rushing to my defense: a desperate compacting of snow. My situation was becoming hopeless. My, now exposed, lower arm and hand became mangled. I saw legs beside me. Two swords and an axe sliced through the air. My wet, sticky neck became suddenly cool when what was pressing against it was knocked away. It became quiet, except for the panting of my companions. I attempted to stand, but fainted when I got to my knees.

I awoke to the smell and sound of meat roasting over a fire. They weren't cooking the drak, were they? Revenge is sweet, but was the drak edible? After being dead for weeks? I felt my arms, hands, and the back of my neck. My skin was smooth, without any trace of injury. I sat up, slamming into the drak.

"Works well as a wind break," Centaur commented. Large rodents on skewers roasted over a fire.

"We thought you could use a hot meal after healing," said Hornet. "That healing elixir the healer gave us works better than a healing stone. The hard part was getting it down your throat. Being in liquid form, we even put some on your wounds."

"So it wasn't the drak?"

"Those things." Centaur pointed at the savory varmints skewered over the fire that had melted its way to exposed earth. "I think they were originally attracted to the drak, but you were easier to get their teeth into. Their white fur camouflaged them so well we didn't see them coming. They knew what they were doing.

They went for major arteries. You lost a lot of blood. Another minute or two and you would have found yourself in the Octagonal Prism."

"When I do, I'll put a request in to augment this armor with a neck guard," I said as I felt my bare, surprising smooth, neck.

After devouring the delicious strips of meat---everything tastes better after a travesty---we returned to the buried road. The sun hid again, giving our eyes relief, but making it suddenly much colder. The wind picked-up too. We warmed up after we began moving, but once one is chilled to the bone it was difficult to fully recover.

Chapter 21

GOLEM

Three kays after rejoining the road we spotted tracks. They appeared to wander aimlessly, going a bit this way, then a bit that way. They intersected the route before us intermittently, indicating a high probability of it being coincidental. They were obviously made by something bipedal, and from their spacing, it was either very small or traveled very slowly. The tracks, slightly smaller than a man's, were without definition. They didn't have any distinguishing characteristics, their length being about the same as their width, not square, but not circular either. The tracks were as deep as ours, indicating the thing that made them either weighed as much as a full-grown man or had been particularly forceful in its steps.

The mystery was revealed, sooner than anticipated, our

conjectures not yet expired. Something the size of a child veered in front of us. It appeared to be completely oblivious to the near collision, its non-linear trod persisting without interruption. So shocked were we of its peculiar---and sudden---appearance, we held fast in our tracks, examining the thing mentally. And a thing it was: a jumble of sticks and stones. Its limbs were wooden, as was its neck. Its hands, feet, torso, and head were made of stone. The irregular, wooden dowels connecting the stones looked like a child's toy. Its feet were flat, like stepping stones. Its hands curved to a point, like a shovel. Its head was crudely human. Its mouth, a hole drilled completely through. Its eyes, nose, and ears, mere indentations.

It stopped in front of us. It put its hands on its hips, chipping away a sliver of its midsection. Something sounding very much like a sigh blew through the hole in its head. "I might as well come with you." The voice sounded like a person whispering on a desolate mountain---alone---into a cold wind that scraped scree across exposed stone.

"What if we don't want you to join us?" asked Centaur.

"I think it's my decision where I go," it spoke, hollow and echoing. "You could run away from me, but I'll eventually catch up to you."

"Why would you even want to travel with us?" I asked.

"Looking around...." Its head swiveled, making a full revolution. "...isn't it apparent my options are limited. My decision-making is imperfect at the moment, so I thought you might do it for me."

"But you don't know where we're going."

"It won't be run of the mill, or you wouldn't be up here. I don't even mind if you all are crazy. I find crazy interesting. Never a boring day when you're crazy, no sir."

"Don't you fear for your safety? With little effort we could pick you up and throw you against one of these boulders," stated Pulp.

The sticks-and-stones-man laughed in that melancholy way one who is sad does, to attempt to cheer himself up, or to pacify those around him who think he should be happy. "Giant, if I might so sarcastically call you that. I haven't been frightened of anything in 40 years. Angry, annoyed, yes, but hardly frightened."

"Gent."

"Gent, giant, what's the difference? Names change, but people don't."

"Come along, if you wish," Centaur finally relented, "but do as we say or we will discard you the first opportunity that arises. Our quest will terminate when a hydra---or we---die. Don't make any sounds or movements that will announce our approach, or distract us once we're in battle."

"I can guarantee, when I wish to be, I can be exceptionally quiet and immobile."

Five kays into the Polar Plateau there still wasn't any sign of the hydra. We paused to scan our surroundings. There were no tracks except our own behind us.

"Did you lose something?" asked the sticks-and-stones-man.

"Doesn't that stone head of yours have enough room to store even a half-hour's worth of memory?" Centaur berated. "We seek the hydra."

"Why do you assume it's here?"

"That's what the mayor of Berry said. Isn't this where travelers and militia have been attacked?"

"When was the last time someone was attacked?"

"Two...three weeks ago, I think."

"And you expect the hydra to starve to death waiting around two or three weeks for the likes of you?"

"So we need to find the hydra's new food source?" I conjectured.

"Very good, and where might this food source be located?"

"We haven't seen much of anything since we climbed up to this plateau," said Hornet. "Except for a dead, frozen drak, and...."

"Sleeks," the sticks-and-stones-man assisted.

"And they are back in the direction we came from?" Pulp conjectured.

"But where?" asked Centaur. "Shouldn't we have seen the hydra by now?"

The sticks-and-stones-man sighed.

"Where did the sleeks come from?" I asked. I turned to face my companions. "You said they snuck up on me, but from which direction? Did you notice any tracks?"

"They came from the north," said Hornet.

We could have chosen a more direct route, but that meant traveling many kays up to our armpits in frozen precipitation. Instead of making the diagonal we backtracked along the snow poles, back to where we broke trail to the drak. Travel was effortless in the trough we had previously created. We paused at the enormous carcass. How could one not be transfixed by the sight of such a creature? The sticks-and-stones-man let out another sigh.

Past the creature we had to break trail again. Ten minutes later a large awkwardly shaped beast was seen in the distance. Approaching it, details began to form. Six bluish-brown serpents dug into the ground at six distinct locations and angles. They merged as apertures of a common body. The creature's four legs were massive, as was the tail that counterbalanced the awkward movements it made.

"A bit of advice," offered the sticks-and-stones-man. We all listened. It may have been lacking size and social grace, but it was more knowledgeable of the local environment. "Hydras don't move very fast with their stubby legs and oscillating heads. This particular hydra may breathe out potentially deadly frost from all of its six heads, but its range is poor, rarely exceeding 10 meters. After a head attacks in this manner, the frost must be built up again before it can be discharged. This takes a minute or more. Thirdly, concentrate on one head at a time. Every head destroyed reduces its number of attacks."

We made our approach. One of the heads noticed us as it joyfully chewed on a sleek. The creature may not have had great intelligence, but it did have the capacity to communicate internally. Within seconds the other heads turned towards us.

"Aren't you going to help us?" Centaur asked the sticks-and-stones-man, who stopped suddenly, creating a distance between himself and us.

"I can watch better from here."

The hydra ran towards us awkwardly, its heads bounding randomly like a female athlete wearing a poorly supporting sports bra. "THE FAR LEFT HEAD!" shouted Centaur. Four bows released four arrows, two of them striking the same head. So closely together was their penetration the combined impact was enough to severe it.

"THE FAR RIGHT!" Three arrows struck this time, with a similar outcome. Too close now for another aerial barrage, we threw down our bows and reached for swords, axes, and hammers. The hydra's four remaining heads blew their frosty breath at us--- simultaneously. To counter the back thrust required the hydra to plant its feet, delaying its approach.

"BACK AWAY!" Pulp cautioned. "WE CAN CHARGE IT ONCE ITS BREATH EXPIRES!"

It was quite easy actually. The hydra's stationary stability prevented it from chasing us. A few extra meters this way or that way brought us outside its range. As soon as the discharge expired we charged the beast, one man per head. Centaur and I easily dispatched our opponents. Hornet and Pulp had some trouble. Hornet's opponent kept missing him. The awkward thrusts made it difficult to retaliate. Perseverance prevailed, three spaced swings severing the head. Pulp appeared hesitant. The likely culprit: positivity fused into him causing him psychological stress. Ultimately KILL OR BE KILLED overwhelmed the moral dilemma, permitting him to eliminate his opponent. Without intellect to direct the hydra, its body collapsed.

"Exhilarating," spoke the sticks-and-stones-man, who had walked up to us after the hydra lost its last head. "I might even join you in your next battle. My heart hasn't raced like this since...." It became void of speech and movement as it tried to remember, almost, on the verge of retrieving the strand, but losing it at the last moment---a fish breaking free a couple of meters from the pole.

We headed back to the road after the briefest of celebrations. We could celebrate more exuberantly after we returned to Berry, preferably before dark.

We passed the drak carcass a final time. "Do you know what happened here?" Hornet asked the sticks-and-stones-man. "Isn't it rare for a drak to die? I don't even see signs of a struggle."

"It happened two months ago. Nimbus Weedwood was hunting for hydras when he spotted something unusual on the snow-dusted tundra. You see, the reason for the hydra being so bold in this area was the absence of its only predator, the aforementioned Nimbus Weedwood. A man wearing a flowing gray robe stood alone and helpless. Nimbus, being cursed with a curious nature, landed beside him. The man's reaction was an exaggerated smile. Nimbus was perplexed. The man raised an arm, the five rings he wore prominently displayed. Nimbus floated. He saw his body beside him, then the world went dark. When he recovered his vision he saw two stick legs beneath him, attached to two stone feet. The Wizard---who else could the man be---commanded the former drak to attack his former body. Astonishment was the last expression the Wizard's face would ever reveal. Nimbus pummeled him with his two stone fists. The Wizard, unprepared for this attack, was unable to defend himself. His body was consumed days later by the hydra you killed."

"So you are the drak? Or were."

"Alas, I was. I am Nimbus Weedwood. Once a mighty drak. Now, a simple mixed-medium golem."

"A freewill golem created from black elem: elem essence?" I inquired.

"Wizards call it gray elem, but you are essentially correct. I believe I was an experiment. If the Wizards could steal a drak's soul, they could steal anyone's. The one thing he overlooked was the might of a drak's freewill. He could transform me, but he couldn't control me."

"Have any other Wizards been here?" asked Centaur. "To investigate, or enact revenge?"

"Not that I'm aware of, but my senses aren't as finely tuned as they were when I was a drak."

"Is there any way for you to return to your original body?" asked Hornet.

"If you mean my drak body, it's extremely unlikely. It looks to be in better shape than it actually is. The cold and snow and its natural defenses have preserved it, but not entirely. It is beginning to decay."

"What are your plans, in addition to following us?" asked Centaur.

"To eventually die, and be re-created into a drak. But I fear what I have been through has affected me so severely that I'll be re-created into another form."

"I thought a person can only be re-created as a drak once," said Hornet.

"Who told you that?"

"A drak I met in the Bluewoods."

"Mist has his philosophies, doesn't he? Actually we don't know, not really. Too few of us have died to formulate a hypothesis."

"So no draks have actually been re-created as draks?"

"Not so far, but that doesn't mean we can't."

"You could kill yourself to accelerate the process," I suggested.

"I don't think I could. Draks have a strong sense of self-preservation. I will follow you instead, as likely an activity to guarantee my inevitable demise."

Our discussion made time pass quickly. Before we realized it, we were already halfway down the switchbacks we had climbed in the morning. We had to hike the flat portion in the dark, but with Berry's lights in the distance guiding us we did so without hardship.

Chapter 22

TRIANGULATION

At the closed western gate Centaur spoke to Nimbus Weedwood. "Golems are rare, but not unheard of. Self-willed golems, just rumors. I recommend you keep silent in public. The fewer questions that are asked, the better."

"I'll have to compensate for my silence when we leave Berry."

"I'm sure you will."

Before spewing the vocal barrage we feared necessary to make our prescience known, the gate opened before us. The guards not being derelict reassured me. It was said the quality of an establishment could be ascertained by the cleanliness of its restrooms. The same could be said for the readiness of a watch post. Even if the threats were few, diligence confirmed an attention to detail and relayed that even minor incursions were taken seriously.

Before reuniting with Dinga we had an audience with the mayor. He was pleased to see us. Either we had destroyed the hydra, or at least escaped it unharmed, giving him hope that is wasn't invincible. We told our tale, cautiously circumventing the events surrounding Nimbus.

"And what might this be?" The mayor looked down at the golem. How could someone not notice the animated jumble of sticks and stones?

"We found it near the hydra," Centaur answered. "Spoils of one of its many victories, perhaps. It was one of the few artifacts near its lair that was salvageable."

The mayor's eyes lit up. "So there are others?"

113

ERIC CARLTON NEPERUD

"Just a figure of speech. There were other things, but nothing of great value, not valuable enough to return with. After the snow thaws---if it ever does---more trinkets will likely become unearthed."

"Intriguing," the mayor spoke softly to himself. "The salvage may pay for the replacement of the guards and reparations to their families. I still might win this election." In a much louder voice he said, "This construct, of course, must be surrendered to the city. It's unlikely its previous owner will return to claim it. Unfortunate for him, fortuitous for Berry. The transfer of non-claimed possessions to the settlement of residence is standard procedure."

"How do you know this OWNER ever lived in Berry?" I asked.

"We don't. But since we were first to claim the artifact another settlement must prove, without doubt, that the said artifact belonged to one of its citizens."

I was becoming concerned. Nimbus was a valuable asset. He was annoying at times, but not enough to supersede his vast knowledge. We couldn't afford to lose our encyclopedia.

A politician is no better than the advisors that surround him. One such man whispered to him, "Possessing such a thing will reek of impropriety. As citizens of Berry toil to pay their taxes the mayor's personal servant performs his every whim."

"It will be put into the general service of the city."

"It won't be perceived that way. Allow these HEROES to retain their toy. Prancing around with it will promote the militia: JOIN TODAY TO RECEIVE EXOTIC REWARDS."

The mayor handed Centaur the memory serum. "With Berry's compliments. Our militia is short-handed. We have positions for you all if you're interested. Not only is a food and housing allowance provided, there's a death benefit, the money going to either the re-created---if he finds his way back to Berry within a month---or a designated beneficiary."

The advisor whispered, "We have discontinued the death benefit due to too many payouts. The coffers are empty."

"After a year of service, of course," the mayor added. "We

114

can't have someone dying on us the first week, can we? Taxes should not be wasted on the death prone."

The advisor looked at the mayor, then Pulp, then back at the mayor, relaying to him more in those glances than a five-minute briefing. Gents were rumored to be unstable: cordial one minute, rampaging a village the next.

"Well, thank you again for exterminating the hydra." The mayor shook our hands and showed us the door.

Centaur smiled, the amusing nature of bureaucrats superseding their insolence. "Time for us to be going. There's a woman waiting for us, and you know how much they like that."

Dinga was so preoccupied with her discussion of pregnancy she didn't notice us entering the Healing Tower. I've been in many battles, seeing things too gruesome to describe, but listening to a couple of minutes of that intimate conversation between the healer and Dinga debilitated me to a degree that required me---and Pulp and Centaur---to leave the room. I don't think Hornet was doing any better, but he was determined that Dinga ingest the truth serum.

The healer, Hornet, and Dinga joined us downstairs a quarter later. She was draped around him. "I'm so sorry about the way I acted," she whispered to him.

"It's okay," he reassured. "It wasn't really you. Not yet. Not the you you grew into."

"But it was still me. Even if I didn't remember you, I still should have acted better."

"You became an adolescent. Sometimes they do foolish things."

"Foolish?" Dinga's eyes momentarily flashed, then they softened again. "That younger version of me also apologizes. Seeing you through my eyes she now realizes she nearly sabotaged one of the best things that ever happened to her. I don't think either of us will take you for granted again."

Hornet and Dinga embraced, then kissed. "I believe the reunited couple needs some time alone...to become reacquainted," suggested the healer. "We'll talk in the morning. Certain potions will be prepared and made available to you."

The next morning the healer handed each of us two vials of a red STRENGTH elixir, two vials of a purple RESTORATION elixir, and one vial of a black CURE elixir. "These are more efficient than the healing stones the Wizards sell. For minor healing a partial dose will suffice."

"Thank you," said Centaur.

"I wouldn't mind going on an adventure myself, but as you see from the line of people outside, I'm needed here. I don't even have time for my research. If I should ever have some free time I believe I could conclude it. I'm very close."

A heated discussion erupted between Hornet and Dinga. "I'M NOT STAYING BEHIND!" Dinga demanded. "Not only would I miss you all, I wouldn't be able to learn that much about elemental energy manipulation. I need to be in the field."

"What about the baby?"

"The healer says I can be quite active, and even should be the first two months."

"What if you get hurt, or killed and re-created? What would that do to the baby?"

"I'm not THAT death prone. A baby needs a father as much as a mother in a place like this. I don't want to raise a child alone because its father got killed and mutated into a monster…. Okay, I'll make a compromise. I'll return here in ONE month, so I can be safely taken care of, and our baby born healthy."

"Five weeks."

Dinga glared at him.

"Dinga will be fine, except for the mood swings and the healthier than normal appetite after she gets over the morning sickness," the healer assured him.

"Will any of the potions help with that?" I asked.

"The mood swings or the nausea? Not really, but if pregnancy becomes commonplace on Limbo either I or the Wizards, or both, will eventually come up with something."

Before leaving Berry we connected the two pieces of the transport portal we already had together. The two spheres retained a meter's separation---where the forces of attraction and repulsion were balanced. Hornet held the green sphere tightly before him in two hands. The blue sphere floated freely to his left, an eighth of a turn counter-clockwise from due east.

"Do you think the next sphere could have moved that much since the last time we checked it?" he asked.

"Unlikely," said Centaur.

"But we have," said Dinga.

"But not enough to change the angle that much. Unless...."

"What?" asked Hornet

"Unless there's another sphere"

"Aren't there four more spheres?" asked Dinga.

"Are you saying the spheres are now reacting to a different piece of the portal?" I concluded. "Than the one they reacted to in Gnotting Hill?"

"So we're now closer to the fourth sphere than the third," Dinga conjectured.

"We're much closer," said Hornet. "The pressure is at least twice as much as it was in the Copper Forest."

"So we're almost there. The next sphere isn't in the Negative Frontier." Relief flooded Pulp's features. The gent joined our group to share our adventures, but that didn't make it any less disturbing for him pass through regions inhabited by contrary moral extremes.

Centaur unrolled his map. We were in the center of the western peninsula, formed by the convergence of the Northern and Western Straits at the Crosshairs. "How strong a pull do you estimate it be, relative to what it was in the Copper Forest? More than twice?"

"Almost three times," Hornet answered.

Centaur placed his finger on the far coast of the Northern Strait.

"So it might be on an island," said Pulp.

117

"Or underwater," I added.

Dinga squirmed. Now that her memories of the two ships sinking returned the only water she cared to get into was in a bathtub.

The sticks-and-stones-man jumped up and down, clinking his stones together.

"Is there some room we may borrow to have a private conversation?" asked Centaur.

"You may use my office," the healer responded. "It's past the time I normally make my rounds."

After the healer left, Centaur looked at Nimbus. "Okay, talk, but make it quiet and brief. We don't know who might be listening."

"The force of attraction between two bodies is inversely proportional to the square of the distance between them." Silence. "It means the forces between them increase at a greater rate than the distance between them."

Dinga frowned. "So we're not as close as we thought?"

Centaur recalculated, placing his finger on a new location. "Beyond the Northern Spine, but still in Neutrality?"

Pulp moved Centaur's finger further east. "I guess I had to return to the Negative Frontier eventually."

"I didn't think Positives ventured that far from home," Hornet commented.

"Let's just say I didn't always live in the Copper Forest. Let's leave it at that."

"How many weeks do you think it will take?"

"Three weeks," I conjectured.

Centaur scrutinized me.

"We've come almost halfway and it's only taken us two weeks."

"As the crow flies. There's a significant body of water between us and the Northern Spine. Then there's the crossing of the mountains."

Hornet looked at Dinga hesitantly. "How much of that

younger version of yourself is still in you? Can she convince you to take one more sea voyage?" He traced the route a ship might make with a finger. "We could completely bypass the Northern Spine if we traveled by boat."

"NO BOAT!" Dinga barked. Her emotions got the best of her. She broke down, concealing her sobs in Hornet's shoulder.

"So a dry journey it is," stated Centaur matter-of-factly.

It was my turn to study the map. Since becoming an Octagonal Knight I have become more attuned to moral nuances. Positive versus Negative. Chaos versus Order. It bothered me---sometimes---that I had to be Neutral. Why couldn't I be a DEFENDER OF THE PEOPLE instead of a PROPONENT OF NEUTRALITY? Did championing Neutrality mean I was antagonistic to the moral extremes---all of them---even those regarded as being beneficial? "The people, monsters, what have you, living in the ordered part of the Negative Frontier act badly, but in an organized manner?"

"Just consistent," Pulp answered. "They may torture you before they eat you, but they'll do it the same way every time. If we have an idea how they are going to react, we have a better opportunity to defeat them. The Chaotic beasties are the ones we have to worry about."

"Aren't you one of those Chaotic beasties?"

"Positive Chaotics are playful. The Negative ones will laugh, but as you cry. They'll pull your arm off one day. The next, they'll allow you to escape, giving you hope, before they track you down and slaughter you, followed by either consuming you raw or cooking you on a skewer, depending on personal preference."

"There is a way you can pinpoint the location of the next sphere more accurately," spoke Nimbus Weedwood, who already ascertained our ultimate goal, by piecing together the conversations we've had. Silence. "You can triangulate. Add the current force line to your map. In a week or so draw a new force line. Where they cross should mark the sphere's location."

We were stunned. A man---thing, actually---constructed of sticks and stones had more intelligence and common sense than the lot of us combined.

Dinga looked at the map. She felt guilty adding to our travel time, but not that guilty. "It's not that far around the Northern Sea. And after that it's a straight shot to the Northern Spine."

Centaur grunted. "It looks like we have a plan. Let's estimate Gnotting Hill's force line, to get a head start on finding the fourth sphere---the original third."

"The portal will practically reconstruct itself," stated Hornet. He looked at Dinga. Seriousness replaced frivolity. "Do you still want to travel with us, knowing that our next destination is in Negative Frontier?"

"If it becomes too dangerous, I'll leave---for our baby's sake," Dinga promised him. "I don't want to be left out."

Chapter 23

CONSTELLATION

"The most direct route is through the Polar Plains," I stated.

"But is it the quickest?" Centaur questioned.

"The mountains are going to be prettier than the plains," said Pulp.

"You'll be able to see them from the Foothills."

"You can see a woman from a distance too, but is that the same as being next to her?"

Centaur let out a loud breath.

"Dinga never saw the snow," said Hornet.

"You have never seen snow?"

"Hornet means since I've been to Limbo. I would like to see what you saw yesterday, but I understand if we need to go around to save time."

"It's more important to her than that," Hornet added. "Her memory has returned, but supplementary to the person she had become. It didn't displace her."

"So you're saying that adolescent is still inside Dinga, sharing her body?" I conjectured.

"It's more comforting than invasive," Dinga clarified. "Like a best friend. I've become her mentor."

"You've become your own mentor?"

"Yes....no. Are you the same person you were five years ago?"

"I don't think I would like someone sharing my thoughts. I would never have any peace. I could never wander off somewhere by myself."

"It's one of the major differences between men and women. Women seek companionship. Men are sometimes smothered by it."

Hornet look offended. "I could never be smothered by you?"

"We are newlyweds---the Limbo equivalent. In five years you might think differently. There is a reason lone wolves are always male."

"So you consider us married?"

"Does that make you nervous? Do you already feel smothered?"

"I never really thought about it. I believed we would one day get married, especially with you being pregnant. But to already be...."

"People do get married on Limbo," stated Pulp. "I don't think I'll ever feel the need---casual, temporary relationships are more my style---I have lived in the Chaotic Frontier for more than a decade. We haven't regressed into cavemen. There are still ceremonies."

Dinga began to glow. No, not like after she and Hornet returned from the woods. It was an emotional radiance.

"I know that look," said Centaur. "My wife had it every time she left me to be with her lover. I thought it was her enthusiasm for the gym."

We all looked at him.

"She came home sweaty with a content look on her face."

"So, across the mountains or around?" I asked him.

Centaur studied his map. "I guess across. We probably won't be saving any time anyway. It will be slower, but half the distance. I don't think I have the heart to dampen Dinga's enthusiasm."

"Do you ever wish you had kids?" asked Pulp.

Centaur smiled.

Dinga's enthusiasm for the snow didn't disappoint. There was a lot of stomping, and falling, and throwing snowballs, not all of them happily received. There was a brief dampening of our collective mood when Nimbus's body was passed. "It's magnificent," she informed him.

"It WAS magnificent." Nimbus glanced one final time to the right, then became steadfast in not looking back. That part of his life was now over. He sighed loudly.

Before leaving the Polar Plain we broke for lunch, primarily BONCH, a travel food the Berrillians created, consisting of dried berries, nuts, and chocolate.

"This is really good," I stated.

"It better be considering Dinga gave most of the rest of our food to that freeloading cat," Centaur declared.

"It was so needy, and so cute," Dinga explained. "OUCH!" Dinga leapt up from where she was sitting in the snow. The rest of us remained standing, our mental scars from that cold, wet day not yet healed. The seat of her pants was missing. What should have been a lovely sight was a constellation of blistering boils. Hornet found something to cover her with, then applied all three varieties of ointments. He didn't wish to experiment on such a delicate region. It must have stung, indicative of her reaction, but anxiety transitioned to relief a moment later. As Hornet held a towel in front of her for privacy Dinga changed into her extra breeches.

Pulp smiled mischievously. "What does the adolescent part of you think about her first snow?"

"Both of us would prefer a hot bath? How much longer?"

"Two days," said Centaur.

"Feek."

"That's the Dinga we've missed," I commented. "Our charming sister has returned."

"Bore you."

"What do think attacked her?" Hornet asked the golem. "A sleek?"

"Possibly. They never bothered me."

"How many people---or things---are foolish enough to attack a drak?" I asked.

"They haven't attacked me since I became a golem, either."

"How many things eat sticks and stones?"

"You would be surprised."

"Are we safe?" asked Centaur.

"If you keep moving. Sleeks won't attack a group...unless it's unaware."

"So you wouldn't recommend us camping here?"

"Unless you maintained an extremely diligent watch."

We didn't camp until the snow began to recede, in a sheltered valley a few meters above the tree line. That evening was without incident, as was the following. We didn't begin a permanent descent until midway through the third day. We passed through the seasons, winter becoming spring, spring becoming summer.

"I've developed a disturbing theory," Centaur shared. "The extended winter up here isn't normal, is it?"

"Winters are long up here, but not this long," Nimbus confirmed.

"Has there ever been a winter that lasted this long?"

"Not since I've been living in the Raspberry Mountains."

"I believe the Wizards have modified the weather up here to conceal their experiment."

"But the winter will eventually recede," stated Dinga. "As I understand the mechanics behind it, the longer the weather is displaced the more difficult it is to retain it."

"Do they believe your body will eventually become too decayed to incriminate them?" asked Hornet.

"Or they are just hoping for a delay?" asked Pulp. "But for what?"

Sweet Falls was a hamlet. Its only industry was a chocolate factory---but considered to be the best in Limbo. It's where the chocolate in bonch came from. Chocolate not being as bulky as fruit, was easier to haul. Being a novelty item, the product provided the potential for substantial profit---if safely delivered. Chocolate was heat sensitive, so spoilage was an issue, making it even more lucrative for the vigilant freight-hauler. Wishing to be more than a one-company town, rooms where rented at a discount, as a marketing tool to encourage tourism.

"If you're not going to eat those chocolates...." Dinga commented as she swooped in to snatch the truffles from the room Centaur, Pulp, and I shared.

"We just walked in," I said.

"Are you eating for just two, or for three...or ten?" Centaur teased.

Dinga's eyes got big. "You don't think that's possible, do you? Nothing's the same here as it is in the real world." Dinga looked like she was going to be sick.

"Morning sickness?" Hornet asked her.

"It's not morning," I stated.

"It's more likely to occur in the morning, but not exclusively," Centaur clarified. "It's too early in her pregnancy, though, to be morning sickness."

"How do you know so much about it? You never had kids."

"My wife miscarried. Our relationship wasn't the same after that. I believe I reminded her too much of the tragedy, so she took her comfort elsewhere."

"I'm sorry, Centaur."

"She was pregnant when I killed her. I didn't know it at the time."

"Are we sent to Limbo to be punished or to be redeemed?"

"A little of both," Nimbus commented.

"Time will tell," added Pulp.

"I'm not physically sick," said Dinga after a moment of silence. "But that got me thinking. What if this pregnancy doesn't progress normally? My baby could be born in 13 weeks instead of 27, or in 54. I was thinking about what I had become, what I mutated into. What guarantee do we have that this baby will be born? Is it possible that I might instead lay an egg? I wish the healer was here."

"Second regrets on accompanying us?" asked Hornet.

"No, I don't want to be back in Berry. I wish he was here, with us."

"Whatever happens, it will be wonderful," said Pulp, enthusiastically. "One child or ten. Live birth or egg. This will be the most remarkable thing that has happened on Limbo since the first mutation."

"It's much easier to be enthusiastic from a distance."

Too much of a good thing---even chocolate---was detrimental to your health---reminding me of the flaws of moral extremes. We ate other things in Sweet Falls, like berries, and fruit, and nuts, but the chocolate was what made us sick. Not enough to vomit, but uncomfortable enough that we weren't able to sleep--- much. We promised ourselves we would never do that again.

We were given chocolate when we left. It was inadvertently left behind. Not the wisest move, considering its value as barter. But if it was out of reach we couldn't be tempted.

Nimbus wasn't affected by overconsumption. He apparently didn't eat at all. He had to receive energy from the sun. From elem? Through the gradual consumption of his being? Now that would be disturbing. You're sustained as long as enough of your body remained to be consumed.

Chapter 24

FEATHERED

It took another three days to reach Owlwood. With Nimbus's stray thoughts perpetually bombarding us, the hours passed rapidly.

"So, draks are Gaea's greatest achievement?" Dinga often prompted Nimbus. Because she actually enjoyed his orations? Possibly. To mock him? Most definitely. Likely a combination of both.

"We are. Irrefutably. Nothing is more powerful." At times Nimbus considered himself to still be a drak. Others, a martyred has-been.

"The Brotherhood...." Pulp began.

"As a group the Brotherhood is more powerful than a single drak, but alone is a gent a match for even a juvenile drak? Remember the hydra? I didn't even consider it a pest. It was simply a snack."

"Will draks ever group together?" asked Dinga.

"Unlikely. The only thing larger than our bodies is our egos. We don't want to share glory. No one is our equal, even other draks. If we ever collaborated everyone would want to be in charge."

"You don't seem to mind not being in charge," said Centaur.

"Because I choose not to be."

"Because you're no longer a drak?" asked Hornet.

"How can I be coerced when living in this body is my greatest sorrow?"

"Why are some demons large and others small?" asked

Dinga. "Why is Pulp shaped like a human and you're shaped---used to be shaped---like a drak?"

"I don't know."

"That's a first," said Centaur.

"I'm not omnipotent. Gaea knows. I ascertain. I believe there is more than one layer of re-creation polarization. Positive versus Negative cross-indexed with Chaos versus Order is the first. Does size and shape comprise the next?"

"Maybe everyone---everything---on Limbo is composed of something like elem," Dinga suggested. "Its morality, its size, its shape, its personality is a cluster of sub-molecular particles. If the Wizards can discover what makes lightening or a golem, why can't they, or we, discover the combination of particles that comprise a drak?"

"You discussed this with the healer, didn't you?" Hornet interrogated. "You couldn't have spent all that time deliberating your pregnancy."

"The healer analyzes penta by contrasting their differences. Most elem manipulators study their common components. His calculations from subtractions are essentially my calculations from additions, from a different perspective. Healing is fluid based. Logical considering a majority of the body is water. It takes five elem to form a penta. For healing, four of them must be liquid based---elem aqus. The fifth is dependent on the type of healing. Being air-based, elem aero has an electrical component. It isn't a stretch to predict energy being restored to a person who consumes it. For tissue to be healed, elem terra is required. It consists of matter, and the body requires matter to rebuild itself. For a body to be cleansed of toxins, elem fiero is required. Diseases are literally burned out of the body."

"Do you have any hypotheses about penta that don't involve healing?" I asked.

"I'm developing them. That's why I feel it's dire to immerse myself in diverse environments. I require dynamic encounters with penta in order to study it."

"Can you help Dinga?" Hornet asked the sticks-and-stones-man. "Being elementally enhanced you must have some knowledge of pental mechanics."

"When my drak body was stolen from me I lost my elemental abilities, but that's beside the point. Mutants use elemental energy innately. We don't think about using it any more than you think about walking or breathing. The terra-forming residues that mutated me also gave me my elemental powers."

The road to Owlwood straddled Gold Creek until its termination, where it merged with Silver Creek to form the Pearl River. At the confluence a toll was demanded to cross the wooden bridge connecting Owlwood to the Berry and Grove Highways. Owlwood was the peninsula's crossroads, bestowing it a status and population it didn't warrant otherwise. It was just days from Kenwood and Berry, the Raspberry and Platinum Mountains, the Alloy Desert and the Northern Sea. The silhouette of an owl carved into the trunk of a pine tree was attached to the toll collector's green jerkin. I became upset when I wasn't offered free admission, but checked myself before I made a commotion. Boasting was acceptable if your actions could back it up, but a person shouldn't expect exclusive privileges due to his status or reputation. I was ashamed I permitted my circumstance to inflict me with arrogance. The benefits of being an Octagonal Knight are to remedy imbalance, not to collect freebies. I was given this power less than a month ago and I was already letting it to go to my head. Maybe I wasn't worthy. I was determined to work even harder---mentally, physically, and emotionally---to live up to the standards of the Octagonal Order.

I briefly reneged on that promise when the cost of room and board nearly bankrupted us. It wasn't that the rooms and the food were expensive---our wallets were nearly empty. Why hadn't we asked for a monetary reward in addition to the memory serum? Our dinner consisted of an unnamed fowl. We felt it was for the best to retain our ignorance.

We visited the City Hall in the morning, hoping there was some exterminating work to be done. There was just one bounty: the removal of a flock of feathered-ursine valued at 140 G. 140 goblin units, not 140 gold.

"What's today's rate for a goblin unit?" Centaur asked the mayor.

"Eighteen-hundredths."

"THAT WILL BARELY COVER OUR EXPENSES!" Assuming the consumption of a penta or two was required to complete the job.

"There is a herd of samtaurs already on their trail," the mayor informed us. "They do so for the common good. They're going to donate their reward to the poor."

"What do these feathered-ursine look like?" I asked.

"You'll know them when you see them. They're three meters tall, brown fur mingled with feathers. Their bodies look like a bear's. Their heads, like a fowl's. Be wary of their beaks. And try not to get too close to them. If they squeeze you, it'll be your last embrace. We'll need their beaks---as proof of their demise. The Bear Buffet will pay you five silvers per carcass---if the meat is fresh. The furrier, four per coat, damages deducted. This flock of feathered-ursine is in a bad mood. While venting they've destroyed three deep-wood cabins---and the people within them. We don't care too much what happens to those loners---living in isolation like that they deserve what they get---but if the feathered-ursine are acting this aggressive it won't be long before they attack the town. Good day...and good hunting."

Owlwood didn't have the tax base to build walls. The oaks and maples the forest primarily consisted of began where the town ended. It was understandable why the mayor was so concerned. If the feathered-ursine entered the town they would do so with little or no warning. If I was in charge I would have had the forest cut back a hundred meters.

After we pieced together the portal I intended to return to Owlwood to do something about that. Not just Owlwood, but all the small villages and hamlets without adequate defenses. If I wasn't leaving Limbo. I still hadn't decided if I would leave if given the opportunity. If more than one person could pass through the portal, would I be foolish not to go? It could be my only opportunity to leave this place.

I perused the forest, ascertaining the work the clearing would entail. There was something homey about having the woods next to the town. No transition. A natural flow: nature into civilization. Maybe there was more to Owlwood not clearing vegetation from its perimeter. Sometimes aesthetics were as important as safety. Existence might consist of circumventing complications. But to live, we sometimes had to throw caution to the wind. For every speck of dust billowing back at us was a stumble into the magnificent unknown.

We headed northwest, into the heart of the forest. The only roads in the Owlwoods were the highways that maintained an aesthetic and psychosomatically sheltered proximity to Silver Creek and the Pearl River. A jumble of narrow trails invaded the forest--- tendrils seeking the isolated bastions of modest existence. My companions were hesitant of wandering too far from town. I reassured them, my innate Octagonal senses guaranteeing we not become lost.

A kay into our excursion the forest became denser. Not just the canopy. The undergrowth was becoming tangled, knots of vegetation congregating so tightly nothing short of a machete would have permitted us to penetrate those areas not already breached. Even those, we occasionally had to hack at, the forest determined to retake its own.

We walked single file, resulting in me doing most of the hacking. I didn't mind, I having the best weapon for the job. Nimbus kept to the rear, in anticipation of the events that were expected to unfold before him. Centaur was still officially the proc, the sticks-and-stones-man a mere spectator.

"What exactly is a samtaur?" Hornet asked.

"It's equine, like a centaur, but larger," Pulp replied. "They believe they exist to assist. Their self-worth is attached to their deeds---symbolized by precious metals and gems affixed to their

130

headbands. The more valuable the medallion or jewel the more valuable they are to society."

"They may have had an earlier start, but we have the decisive advantage," spoke Dinga. "Being bigger than us, they're going to have a more difficult time moving through the brambles."

"I hope you're right," said Hornet. "I would hate for us to get scratched up for nothing."

We found one of the destroyed cabins. The ceiling hadn't just collapsed, or the walls knocked over. The small structure was torn to shreds.

"It won't take long for this place to go back to nature," I commented.

"Which may have been the feathered-ursines' goal," Pulp hypothesized. "There has to be a reason for their rampage--- encroachment into their territory, perhaps, or hunted for their meat and hides."

"Sometimes people react a certain way because that is who they are," said Nimbus. "It might just be their nature. Remember, we are in Neutrality. Unless someone of Frontier stock has wandered into Neutrality, those who act bad here aren't trying to. It's our perception that has attached meanness or violence to their actions. A predator hunting for food isn't evil. No more than its prey is suicidal for allowing itself to become prey."

A second destroyed cabin was found. If possible, the forest was becoming even more dense. We could see just 10 meters in front of us, the trails nearly reclaimed. The feathered-ursine could be a dozen paces away and we wouldn't know it.

Frustration permeated Centaur's features. "How are we ever going to find them in here?"

"Go to where the feathered-ursine are most likely to appear," suggested Nimbus.

"Of course. Why didn't I think of that? Could you be a little more specific?"

If a person broke it down in the simplest of terms the solution was quite obvious. I shared my epiphany. "We know the feathered-ursine are attacking the cabins, so if we find a cabin that's still standing they'll eventually come to us."

The plan would have worked better is we knew exactly where the cabins were. "Visibility might be better above the forest," Dinga suggested. "The only way something as large as a cabin could be built in this forest is for a chunk of it to be cleared away."

"Are you sure you want to do this?" Hornet questioned her. "Aren't you concerned about what happened to you the last time you flew?"

"Of course. There hasn't been a minute I haven't thought about it since it happened---since my memory returned. And the fear is growing. I don't know if it's the transformation into an animal, or not being able to change back. Or getting stuck in that intermediate stage. You don't know what it was like after that final transformation. I fear if I don't transform soon I might lose the nerve entirely."

"And you couldn't have chosen another time to experiment? A safer time?"

"Without the prodding, the necessity behind it, I don't think I would have ever got up the nerve. I begged to tag along, so I need to pull my weight. It would be foolish not to take advantage of the opportunities presented. Please support me in this. It's difficult enough without you begging me not to. Oh, and have my clothes ready when I change back. I've never been the most modest person, but I will soon be a mother. Gentlemen, turn around please."

When Dinga was determined to do something, she didn't hesitate. Waves of air rushed past us as a black bird spiraled through a narrow gap in the canopy. The dense vegetation concealed her seconds later. Maneuvering through the tangled, interconnected forest must have been like putting together a jigsaw puzzle.

We waited. If we couldn't see the sky it was unlikely she could see us. It might take her hours to find us if we began wandering aimlessly again.

She returned ten minutes later. Hornet had her clothes ready as she transformed back. She did so, so quickly, we barely had time to turn away, catching a glimpse of her distinctive feminine features.

At times it bothered me that I no longer was attracted to women. I still appreciated their free-flowing forms, but there was a lack of sexual desire. Did helping others compensate for not helping myself? All priests had to eventually determine that for themselves. Many sects permitted relationships. The Octagonal Order wasn't one of them. Was I psychologically changed or did the armor exude a pheromone that diminished certain urges? I wasn't completely emotionless when it came to the other gender, but the subtle bursts were brief, like the sun shining through on a cloudy day---for just a minute---then being blocked again. Sexual desires were definitely distractions. If I was to focus on maintaining Neutrality, I couldn't be distracted, not if I wanted to operate at optimal proficiency.

"We need to head due west. There's a clearing a kay away. There looks to be a cabin within it, but from my perspective I couldn't tell if it was still standing or rubble."

I led us westward using my internal compass. As we entered the clearing from the east, seven samtaurs entered it from the south. They looked more torn up from the tangles than we did. "Salvation Troup #8, currently ranked third in the Samtaur League, claim this cabin," spoke an equine wearing a ruby in his headband. His voice was somehow both deep and nasally. His bearded upper torso looked very human. His lower torso was quadrupedal. It was less muscular than a horse's---more like a deer. Only one of his companions had a gem in his headband: a sapphire. The other five wore either silver or gold medallions.

"Good day," Centaur greeted them. "We too seek the feathered-ursine. Have you seen any signs of them?"

"Only a cabin the heathens destroyed. May Gaea preserve their souls in a worthy shell." He rolled a foreleg in a circular motion. "Being here first, we demand salvation rights."

"I believe everyone is eligible for the reward," stated

133

Hornet.

"The honor of defeating the dishonorable is what WE seek."

"We could form a coalition?" suggested Dinga. "You collect the honor and we collect the reward."

"If would be dishonorable to concede a reward that wasn't earned. If we share the kill we must share the honor. We are just three honor points away from second place. If we defeat the feathered-ursine alone we receive five points. If we share the honor with you we receive only two. Partial honor is no honor."

A man with hair and beard below his waist angrily opened the door to his cabin and yelled, "YOU OGRE BORERS! Can't you take a hint that a man wants to be left alone. You have an entire planet to bother and you choose to hassle me." He looked like he hadn't bathed in a year, maybe five. His frothy beard and hair concealed the rags he wore. Without anyone else around was a person obligated to wear clothing? He must have been so used to the filth and stench he no longer noticed it.

"We were just leaving," said Centaur. "Sorry to bother you." We followed Centaur, away from the cabin.

"Whoa," spoke the ruby samtaur. "That's the way we're heading. TO GLORY!" He kicked his way through the brambles, heading north. His companions followed him.

"I guess that leaves west for us," said Hornet.

"We need to stay here," I stated. "The feathered-ursine will come here next. I don't actually see or hear or smell them. It's more of a feeling. Intuition, you might call it. I don't know if it's like one of Lynn's premonitions." Lynn was a lynx-once-human who traveled with us prior to finding the first sphere.

"She considered it a convoluted predictive science," said Hornet.

"Or it might just be some sixth sense Octagonal Knights have. I wish there was some manual to study. I really ought to travel to the Octagonal Prism."

Centaur turned to Dinga. "Do you mind going on another reconnaissance mission?"

"Not with that hermit so close. He's creepy."

She wasn't the only person bothered by the recluse. We backed away from the cabin, a hundred meters or so. We listened closely, trying to distinguish feathered-ursine from the cacophony of the forest. Never hearing one before we used our imaginations on how one would sound. Being bird-like, squawking was likely, quite powerful, due to their size, intermittently laced with growls.

We weren't disappointed. The sound we finally heard was a cross between a hawk, an owl, and a goose---all at ultimate volume. We also heard banging, like hammers against wood, and a loud crash. We rushed back to the hermit's cabin. The return journey was much quicker than our departure. We had already cut our path thought the forest, facilitating a moderately straight jog.

I was the first to enter the clearing. The feathered-ursine were bent over the collapsed cabin, equally spaced along its perimeter. With their rear ends up in the air, they resembled bears searching for something on, or in, the ground. Getting closer, their beaks became more distinctive. They were pecking at the fallen structure, like chickens eating dried corn. They looked like they were just tearing apart the wood, but they must also be eating what lay beneath it, including the hermit.

"Well, I guess we should attack them while they're occupied," I suggested once my companions caught up with me.

"That's assuming the one we're attacking isn't rescued by his friends," said Centaur. "There's too many to fight simultaneously."

We had to decide something soon. The cabin was already half-destroyed. If the feathered-ursines' goal was to bring it the ground quickly they would have succeeded already. They relished the gradual demise: a banana slowly pealed, a candy bar slowly unwrapped.

"We could stick them with arrows," Hornet suggested. "By the time they realize what happened half might be dead."

"That's a big might there," said Pulp. "I'm not sure riling them up is what we want to do."

"We need to take them on one at a time," Centaur insisted.

135

"What if we fought them on one of these narrow trails?" Hornet suggested.

"They'll just go through the brambles," said Pulp.

"They'll follow the path of least resistance," Nimbus advised.

"They might be reduced to having to fight us one at a time, but won't that limit us too?" asked Centaur.

"I believe I'll be able to handle anything one on one," I declared.

"Then a second one, and a third, and a fourth? You're well-conditioned, but even you will eventually tire."

"You could draw them into one of those coves, two or three of you fighting them at the entrance," Nimbus recommended.

We followed his advice. The plan was implemented---perfectly. After finding a widening of the trail Hornet returned to the now flattened cabin. He shot an arrow at the closest beast and ran. The flock caught up with him, but not before they were met by Centaur, Pulp, and me. One by one the creatures were hacked and pummeled. The last two broke through together. A little too late. For the most part, mutations balanced. Something that gained strength typically lost intellect. The awkwardness of stumbling through the brambles was the delay we needed to position ourselves properly. We were worn out when it ended, but we were triumphant, with minimal bruises and scratches---nothing requiring a healing stone.

We were only able to carry three of the carcasses back to town. It was exhausting, taking as much out of us as looking for and fighting the creatures. They weighed 200 kilos each. Hornet and I shared one, with Pulp and Centaur somehow able to drag one by themselves. Dinga wished to help, but being pregnant we insisted she didn't. Nimbus, well, even if he volunteered---which he didn't---was much too small---and fragile---to assist us. One yank would have torn one of those stick arms out of its stone socket.

Chapter 25

SALVATION

After relieving ourselves of the beaks and carcasses---we remembered to cut out the beaks of the creatures we did not carry---we returned to the NIGHT OWL, the inn we stayed in the previous night. We were intercepted by the herd of samtaurs we saw in the forest. They had their own feathered-ursine. "We feel sorrow for your lack of honor," spoke the ruby-banded one. "While simultaneously feeling exalted for the increase of our own."

"We've already collected our reward," said Centaur.

The END OF DAYS may not have arrived, but it had called and was on its way. The samtaurs looked lost. Their mission not only became more problematic, but now unachievable. With an abrupt burst of enthusiasm their leader said, "Knowledge of a universal success is sometimes reward enough. We'll be on our way after delivering these carcasses to the Bear Buffet. The Redemption Revival awaits us. We must atone for our sins. Even in doing Gaea's work, perfection isn't achieved in the manner it is accomplished."

I felt a stirring. There was definitely a kinship between the samtaurs and me. Not necessarily a friendly one. Not even cordial. More like having the same hobby, or being in the same profession.

If I could cleanse myself of my impurities maybe I would feel more deserving being an Octagonal Knight. "We need to go with them. I do, anyway. This Redemption Revival can't replace the Octagonal Prism, but some is better than none. I must strengthen within before my full potential can be expressed as external deeds."

"How far out of our way is it?" Centaur questioned.

"Three days---each way," stated Pulp.

"We should stay together," Hornet insisted.

"We're not going to abandon Stick, are we?" asked Dinga.

"WAIT UP!" Centaur shouted after the samtaurs. They had just delivered their beaks and carcasses and were beginning to leave the village.

Nimbus sighed. "I guess this means I go back into mute mode."

Sometimes first impressions weren't the best indicator of a relationship. The samtaurs may have been stern with us the first couple of times we interacted, but they were now delighted upon learning our desire to go to the Redemption Revival. Their leader was called 4-Green. The samtaurs believed in divine intervention. When they became old enough to declare their intention to devote their lives to Gaea and the betterment of her children, a new name was randomly chosen for them. A plaque was placed on the ground. The first raindrop designated a number, their common name. The second, a color, their surname. Each color represented a classification of personality. The samtaur zodiac consisted of the three primary colors, the three secondaries, the three shades (white, gray, and black), plus three composites (aqua, brown, and pink).

The samtaurs were very considerate in traveling at a pace slow enough for us to keep up. In the time it took us to travel to our first camp, along the banks of Silver Creek, the samtaurs could have already arrived at the Redemption Revival.

Their diet consisted of grass, but they enthusiastically ate the dried berries and nuts we offered to them. They declined the chocolate, apologizing for not being able to metabolize the caffeine in it. They were polite when we spoke of our adventures, grimacing when we came to a particularly impure part. They enjoyed talking about themselves more, in particular, their great moral deeds. Another hot topic was the specifics of their moral peers, allies, and rivals in the battle for salvation.

Trogs were spoken of often. "They live in a mountain city," 19-Brown informed us. "Their tunnel boulevards stretch for kays.

Their population numbers 10,000, more than any human city west of Kenwood, but you wouldn't know it by the sounds of the city. They talk infrequently, and then just in whispers. Some of their kind don't speak at all. They believe that even the most direct statement can be laden with subconscious falsehoods, the less a person speaks the less they can lie. There is no greater glory than telling the truth."

"They believe even the movements of one's body can relay falsehoods," spoke 11-gray, "so they are very economical and precise when walking, or reaching for a glass of water. Even alone, because they are their own worst critics. Lying to oneself is as depraved---even worse---than lying to others."

"They spend too much time hidden in their caves," 4-Green criticized. "They should be aiding Gaea's children, bringing honor onto themselves. The trogs rarely do anything dishonorable, but in conjunction with their lack of honorable deeds they barely exceed Neutral."

The creek needed to be crossed. There was a ford, but it was at least a day out of our way.

"We can carry you across," suggested 12-Blue.

Dinga's eyes got wide and she began to bounce on the tips of her toes. "Please." Her adult memories may have returned, but supplemental to, not displacing, her adolescent mannerisms. Dinga was a hyperbole---a woman who alternated between serious and playful unpredictably. Hornet was either the bravest man I know, or the most foolish.

I caught Centaur's eye. He grimaced. His joyride upon an equine had been reconciled, but the emotional scars remained. "A generous offer," I stated. "The loss of dignity...."

"The humble never lose their dignity," 4-Green responded. "What act is more dignified than giving?"

"Are your backs as strong as your will?"

"It is true the body isn't always as strong as the soul. An overextension can affect future deeds."

Dinga not only dropped her ice cream. Someone stole it before it could be picked up and brushed off.

"Caution can be contemplated independently."

As Dinga was ferried across, the rest of us held onto a samtaur as it led us.

The most direct route to the Redemption Revival was off trail, a bushwhacking of parched prairie taking two days. It was held on the edge of the Allow Desert, 30 kays into the Frontier. A majority of the mutants living there were Positive and Ordered. At the far end of the desert rose the foothills of the Platinum Mountains. They were much dryer than the hills surrounding the Raspberry Mountains. Vegetation didn't grow on them until the 2000 meter level---an inverse tree-line. The peaks weren't as high as those in the Raspberry Mountains, but the chain was much longer. From north to south they stretched 250 kays, the foothills adding another 100.

The samtaurs called the desert, SALVATION SAND. The masu, the winged demons with a human head and feline torso, the PLAIN OF PEACE. The kocra, an avian hybrid, the WHITE LOWLANDS, the salt deposits being prominent from the sky. The trogs didn't call it anything, they rarely venturing that far from Trogdom.

A shrine marked the center of the Revival. Three arched entrances faced the three groups of revivalists. The triangular ziggurat rose 25 meters. It was stark, being the only pinnacle, manmade or natural, for kays.

Our samtaur companions joined their kindred. They exchanged greetings, sounding more like they were reciting resumes than giving cordial salutations. Honorable deeds were listed, those achieved since the last revival being mandatory. Past deeds deemed particularly honorable were also spoken of, but in a more condensed form.

Becoming unintentionally abandoned we visited the other two races. The masu were more humble than the samtaurs---and less ostentatious. They didn't wear ornamentation of any kind. I had trouble telling them apart. One seemed to speak for all, but that one kept changing. "Has your companionship been joyful?"

asked the current speaker.

"With the samtaurs?" asked Centaur.

The masu slowly shut his eyes and reopened them. "They are exceedingly honorable. Without their service many of Gaea's children wouldn't be able to live their lives properly. Gaea bless them."

"Does your kind perform such missions of self-sacrifice?" asked Dinga.

"Masu approach our service to Gaea differently," spoke the next speaker. "We assist others after we are asked. We do not wish to intrude if our service isn't earnestly desired. If we are needed badly enough someone will contact us. We are willing to do whatever is required to help others, including sacrificing ourselves, but we don't wish to become accomplices to those becoming complacent with their own Gaea given abilities. Creating lazy children doesn't honor Her."

The masu ate what looked---and smelled---like rotten fruit and decayed animals. They ate solemnly, the sole purpose of the activity the replenishing of nourishment. After speaking to them we learned that in believing in the sanctity of life they ate only dead matter: fruit fallen from a tree, berries dropped from a bush, or meat from an animal that died from natural causes or from a predator who left part of its prey behind.

The kocra ate enthusiastically, ripping flesh from freshly slaughtered mammals: sheep, goats, swine, even cattle. "Would you like to join us?" spoke a red-feathered kocra with a yellow ribbon around its neck. It used it as a napkin, its bloody mouth turning it orange. "Gaea has provided a vast bounty today. The farm we inspected had too many animals. It was surprising none of the animals had starved to death from the overpopulation. Gaea provided our hunting skills. We must praise Her by keeping the standard of living high. Too many of one species lowers the quality of life. It will be a joyous day when the trogs ascend. Why does Gaea allow their population to swell? Why hasn't disease destroyed them years ago? Gaea must have a plan. Whatever it is She chooses to keep it to herself."

After making our rounds, visiting the other species, we returned to the samtaurs. "Have you cleansed your sins yet?" asked 4-Green.

"Do we talk to someone or immerse ourselves in water?" I asked. "What's the procedure here?" Every culture had its method of atoning. Some repented. Others performed deeds. The self was sacrificed---physically---emotionally---sometimes financially. Rituals were performed. When parishioners of physicality wished to atone they ran laps.

"The shrine must be entered, individually."

"Is there something we must do in the shrine?" asked Centaur.

"To each his own."

4-Green gave us our space as we contemplated.

"That was a bit open-ended." Hornet examined the shrine, visually, from where he stood. "Does it matter what entrance we use? It's apparent from the location of their congregations each species has one designated for them."

"We could just randomly choose an entrance," Dinga suggested. "With at least one of us passing through each of them, and no more than two."

"We must proceed prudently," said Centaur. "We don't want to start a religious war with us in the middle of it. Does entering beneath the samtaur archway honor them or disgrace them? Do we honor them more than the masu and kocra, or disgrace them? Which group, or groups, will be less easily offended?"

"We are overthinking this," said Pulp. "Let's just enter the temple. No matter the outcome, it's guaranteed to be interesting

"Try the top of the pyramid." The sticks-and-stones-man spoke so softly that only I was able to hear. With those large ears of his Pulp may have also been able to hear---if he cared.

As my companions continued to contemplate I approached the shrine. The blocks were larger than they appeared from a distance, forcing me to climb instead of step. Twenty-three steps were climbed---yes, I counted them. I expected the shrine to be flat on top. Instead, it was sunken the height of one block. I dropped into the depression.

The name HENRY O'TOOLE was chiseled in stone. Was he the man the shrine was built for, or a vandal? Why was his pre-Limboan name used? It was no longer who he was. Was the name there because of its lack of meaning, as an attempt to be odd for odd's sake, like painting a canvas white? Or was there a deeper meaning?

I looked at the plains to the east, the mountains to the west, and the desert below me. I could understand now why the shrine was built in the desert. Its contrast to the barren landscape made it bolder, more pronounced. My thoughts also had become more pronounced. My sins were so insignificant compared to the world as a whole. Why must I waste so much effort condemning myself for them? They won't harm the world, not substantially, and not for long. Stepping into a creek and churning its bed may make the water murky, but minutes later the creek runs clear. Are doing good deeds also a waste of time? For that one person I help it isn't. And maybe helping that one person creates an opportunity for him or her or it to help someone else.

I climbed back down, fully revived. My companions were dispersed among the samtaurs, masu, and kocra. Had they entered the temple already, or were they still contemplating? Heated discussions were occurring, among the three races, and within my group. From the distance I was away from them it sounded like insects buzzing---or static.

The sun dimmed, the disparity of temperatures between the desert and the mountains creating complex, splashes of colors in the sky. For that brief moment all races were silent.

We erected camp under the moonlight, then formulated a strategy---after much debate. "I think we should head for the Northern Sea as soon as we break camp," spoke Hornet. "It's time we found another sphere."

"I would like to see more of the world before I have this baby," said Dinga.

"I wouldn't mind staying here one more day," said Pulp. "It's the last opportunity we have to converse with people of goodwill. It's amazing, isn't it, how three groups so alike in ideals could be so different."

Hornet smiled. "A last exaggerated breath before sinking."

"Something like that."

"I would like to travel to Trogdom," said Centaur. "Trogs are unmatched in their crafting of weapons and armor. Entering the Negative Frontier we need to utilize every advantage."

"I thought terrans made the best weapons?" asked Hornet.

"They do, but in a very limited variety. Being the ones to harvest the ore and smelt it into metals trogs are capable of custom-making nearly anything, be it a pan, a sword, or a chest plate."

"What do you think, Stick?" asked Dinga.

"I don't need to upgrade, but we are more likely to succeed if the rest of you are properly equipped. Taking a few extra days to find the next sphere shouldn't affect our acquisition. It's probably been in the Negative Frontier for years, decades even."

"Portals have been around that long?" asked Centaur.

"Since Dartmoor was created I believe. Improvements in technology tend to occur in clusters---one feeding another."

Hornet acquiesced. "I can wait a few more days."

"And I," said Dinga. "I need to get in as many experiences as possible. In a couple of months I'll be trapped in a city until the baby pops out of me."

"You do know child-birth is more involved than that," said Centaur.

Daggers were thrown his way, flaming and venomous. "I haven't been on Limbo that long. If I'm lucky I'll just lay an egg."

Hornet looked horrified.

"Isn't it the father's duty after that to take care of it? As Hornet sits on it for months I'll continue to explore the world."

"I guess I'm also willing to leave today," said Pulp. "The people here are already repeating themselves."

"Then it's decided," Centaur declared.

We asked for directions to the trogs before leaving. The masu and the kocra gave aerial directions. The samtaurs suggested we gallop 30 kays to the north, where we would intersect a road that would take us to that ford of Silver Creek. From there we would head west to Silverton, the largest human settlement in the Platinum Mountains, where we would procure directions for our final leg. We wished our travel companions well, in particular, 4-Green, who now wore a diamond in his headband.

Chapter 26

PARTIALS

We headed due north through barren salt flats. After you got over the concept of having a stationary sun, it became more beneficial than detrimental. If you knew where you were in the world you could determine your direction, day or night, assuming the sky was clear enough to perceive the orb. It was well past noon when we spotted the road. There were plenty of false alarms: heat waves producing images we permitted our imaginations to provide details. The road, a few kays from the base of the foothills, paralleled them the remainder of the day. The evening was spent peacefully without incident.

Midway through the next day we saw a string of cottonwoods in the direction we travelled.

"Silver Creek?" asked Hornet.

"Or another," Centaur answered. "It's welcomed whatever name we wish to call it."

It was Silver Creek. And there was no longer just a ford to cross. A plank bridge had been built, without railings, comfortably wide for single file, too narrow for two abreast. An easy task unencumbered can become onerous carrying a third of your weight carelessly on your back.

"Just because a bridge was built doesn't mean we must use it," I stated.

"It would be more fun, though," Pulp replied. "It's been weeks since I've been on something like this. I miss the aerial acrobatics almost as much as I miss the arbols."

"Please," said Dinga sweetly.

"We don't all have to cross the same way," said Hornet.

"Yes, we do," Centaur responded firmly. "Danger is proportional to the degree we scatter." Dinga looked at him with puppy dog eyes. "Okay. We can cross the bridge. Did I really have any choice in the matter?"

"You think it would be better for us to be tied together?" I asked him.

"If we had something to hold onto, maybe. If one of us goes, we might all go. Togetherness is great, but at the cost of none of us completing our mission? And who would protect our gear until we're re-created and return?"

We kept to our protective queue as we crossed. Fighting the elements wasn't the same as fighting a monster, but it provided us some comfort. I made it across first, then Hornet, and.... Dinga was looking this way, and that way, up and down, upstream, downstream, to the right, to the left. The end of the bridge was just a couple of steps away. She pounced. The planks weren't sodden, but they weren't completely dry either. Dinga skidded. Before she recovered she ran out of footing. She was so close to the water she barely made a splash. It was more a slide in than a kerplunk. She was initially scared to death, then ecstatic. She would have floated for kays if we didn't insist she come to shore. She shook like a dog when Hornet came up to her with a towel. Her clothes clung to her. She may have played like a girl, but she was definitely a woman.

Athletes didn't believe in luck, but...randomness was

definitely a factor in everything we did, and accomplished. If I never met Centaur or Hornet where would I be today? An Octagonal Knight? Someone attempting to reconstruct a transport portal? If Dinga died how long would we have waited for her? How long would have been our delay to find the next pearl? Would our group have disbanded? If God, or Gaea, exists does He or She dictate our actions---all of them? How much free will do we have?

After Hornet spent a couple of minutes drying---and embracing---her she smiled broadly. "I'm going to do that again."

"No...you're...not." Centaur was firm, but not loud. The competency of the prior determining the intensity of the latter.

Dinga frowned---briefly---abruptly breaking into a smile. She hugged Centaur, relaying her fondness for him, and her residual dampness.

We turned left at the crossroads. We climbed casually onto and around rolling, dusty hills. The MOGULS, as they were called, had more rocks than shrubs. Sage filled the air, in those periods it wasn't saturated with the dust our boots kicked up. It coated our breeches and jerkins, hair and armor, making mine look more pewter than platinum.

A sign at the base of the Moguls informed us Silverton was 107 kays away.

"We could travel through the night," I suggested. I was anxious for something to happen. The physically inclined were easily bored. A couple of more hours of exertion didn't bother me.

"Not safely," Centaur responded. "With hills surrounding us, and the angle of the moonlight---nearly horizontal this far from the center---we would be in almost complete darkness. The footing is bad enough already."

Near the end of the day we entered a settlement. One large mogul was on the left side of the road, two smaller ones on the right. Small doors and windows were carved out of them, the largest being half of what was standard for a human residence. A woman in a brightly colored blouse stuck her head out a window in the first mogul on the right.

"IT'S A HALFLING!" Dinga barked.

147

"I'm hardly that fat," she replied in an offended tone. "I'm a quarterling."

"Who are you calling fat?" spoke a woman from a window in the left mogul. She was wearing a brightly colored blouse like the first woman, but she was twice her size. "Halflings are not fat. You're an undernourished runt."

"Petite is the proper term."

"No bigger than one of my mounds."

"What's all this shouting?" spoke a third woman, this time poking her head out of a window in the second mogul on the right. She was of a size between the first two women. She wore the same style of blouse. "You should just agree. You're fat, and you're a runt."

"And you're Miss Perfect?" spoke the quarterling.

"They always say the in-betweens are the worst," said the halfling.

"Not cute."

"Or mature."

"A thirdling is just right: Not too big, not too small. Not too childish, not too frumpy. Not too hard, not too soft."

"If we may interrupt," said Centaur. "Would you happen to have a room or two for rent?"

"GAEA!" bellowed the quarterling. "Now that's a big one."

"And look at his bald friend," spoke the halfling. "You know what they say about bald men."

"And look at their toy," said the thirdling. "I don't think I'll ever be too old to play with something like that." I was closest to Nimbus, so I put a hand over his mouth. He squirmed, but he wasn't able to comment back, not intelligibly anyway.

"I guess we could put you up somewhere," said the quarterling.

"There's an auditorium that might be large enough," spoke the halfling.

"The men will be back before dark," spoke the thirdling. "They are more interested in adventurous tales than we are. With seven or eight husbands each there's a lot of work to do. They'll probably get all worked up from your stories and become amorous. Why couldn't I live on a world with more women than men? Not only could we split up the chores, we could split up the nightly duties. What I would do for one good night of sleep."

Being isolated on the fringes of civilization the partials, as they were collectively called, didn't have variety in their diet. What grew best in the Moguls were potatoes, carrots, and onions. An occasional lizard entered their diet, but they were few and far between. We gave the women half of our remaining berries, nuts, and chocolate. They were particularly pleased with the candy.

"I'll take eight pieces of chocolate over eight men any day," chirped the quarterling.

"They last longer too," chuckled the halfling.

"I haven't felt this good since the men left for three days to go on that hunting trip," said the thirdling.

The men returned a quarter before sundim. They came in all sizes, but other than that, they looked about the same. They wore gray jumpsuits, covered with dirt. Their hair was bushy, not long, or short. They smiled as they marched and sang off-color songs. Like being put through a multi-filtered sieve, the partials broke off from the pack one by one, entering the doorway properly sized for them.

After washing up, the now blue jean overall-wearing men left their homes and began prompting us to tell them of our adventures. They wanted to know every detail, every tree, every blow, every beautiful woman we saw. Being conservative they never left the Moguls, but they still craved knowledge of the rest of the world. They lived vicariously through the few travelers that passed through.

We were called to dinner at sundim. We followed the partial men to what the women had called the Auditorium. The entrance into the room was tall enough for me to enter without stooping, but just barely. Pulp wasn't as fortunate. The room must have consumed the entire mogul. There were enough chairs and tables for three dozen partials. A place was cleared for us in the center of the room. Being too large for chairs, we sat on straw mats. There was a bank of windows on both sides of the door, to illuminate the room during the day. From the five meter high ceiling hung three candle chandeliers, fully lit. They didn't put off as much light as the sun, but it was bright enough to see one another and the food we consumed.

The partial men spent most of their days farming, on terraces they cut out of moguls west of their village. Other times they went hunting. When the weather was poor they did home repairs---if they were needed---but they mainly bothered their wives. Seeing the sun in the morning always put the women in a good mood.

Our dinner consisted of carrots and onions wrapped in a potato tortilla. We washed it down with water that was especially refreshing: cold and sweet. It had come from a small snowmelt creek that flowed into the Silver. The minerals in the Platinum Mountains gave it its flavor. Platinum Mountain water was considered to be the best in Limbo. Dusties---a diminutive race resembling mice, named for their coloring and aversion to bathing---even bottled it, distributing it to human settlements. Sitting in bottles for weeks it didn't taste as good as from the source, but it was still better than most local water.

For dessert we had berry scones dipped in cream. We supplied the berries. The flour for the dough came from the small field of wheat the partials harvested recently. The cream, from the wild mountain goats. Believing, like most Positive and Neutral Limboans, that any animal could have once been human, they weren't caged. There was a difference in opinion whether milking a once-human was immoral. The partials philosophy: if they didn't want to be milked, then they shouldn't have behaved in the manner necessary to mutate them into a goat.

After telling more of our tales we were left in peace to sleep on our mats. The women left after they washed dishes. The extra hour or two of sleep they got was probably welcomed as much as the chocolate we shared with them.

We were wakened by the sound of two dozen men eating what remained of the previous night's meal. The women didn't mind cooking, but they were only going to do it once a day. The men wished us well, then asked if we needed their help. "On your next adventure, perhaps?" We politely declined.

We said our goodbyes to the women after packing our belongings.

"Please come back," said the quarterling.

"You wore the men out enough they didn't bother us in the night," spoke the halfling.

"And please bring back some chocolate," spoke the thirdling.

"Let's push," suggested Centaur. "There's less than a hundred kays to go. Even with the climb ahead of us I think we can still make it to Silverton in two days."

The opportunities for camping became more promising. The shrubs became more frequent and fuller. We even began seeing pines. Grass began to grow beside, and even on, the dusty road. The dust departed. It became cooler as we continued to gain elevation.

Did it make is easier, or more difficult, to travel through beautiful scenery? There were many distractions: many opportunities to peruse the splendor, or take a nap. We climbed, but not excessively. The pace was consistent, but pleasant. There were some insects, but more ambiance than pest.

Centaur looked up at the sun. "It's time. Ten more minutes before it's too dim to see."

Centaur couldn't have picked a better spot: a relatively flat, grassy shelf beside the creek. The water was accessible for filling canteens and washing. There was enough wood to build a fire. And we were so far into the Positive Frontier that it was unlikely anything dangerous would be attracted to it. For once we drifted off to sleep without worries. For once---but there was always tomorrow, and the next day, week, and month.

Five kays from camp we left the moguls for some serious terrain. Granite peaks surrounded us. Between them were 75 meter tall firs. The air had become more moist, not necessarily muggy, but substantial in contrast to the desert and Moguls. The temperature didn't fluctuate noticeably, the warmth of the day being offset by the increase in elevation. It was cool, but not cold, comfortable in concert with the toil of our climb. Lakes began to appear, formed by long-departed glaciers---the terra-forming equivalent. Snow was seen, but not passed through. We finally crested, 15 kays past the final mogul. We didn't instantly drop on the other side of the pass, nor come to a plateau like the one in the Raspberry Mountains. The terrain was inconsistent. We ascended as much as we descended, repeatedly, as we traversed the shoulders between the numerous peaks. For every 100 meters we dropped, we gained it back the next kay.

Chapter 27

SILVERTON

Silverton was built at the base of three mountains. Its 700 citizens were concentrated in a single irregularly-shaped tower enveloped by a 20-meter wide wooden rind.

The tower's lower levels were granite, the flakes of mica in it causing it to intermittently sparkle like the frosty icing of a winter morn. The tower's echelon was constructed of silver, seven distinct pinnacles of varying height. The tower's many windows were paned, a rarity on Limbo.

Silver Creek passed beneath the city, flowing from the south canyon into the east.

Being so far from the stationary sun, its rays were nearly horizontal. The perpetual late afternoon light reflected off the tower in a spectacular fashion. It was like we had discovered Shangri-La, or Mt. Olympus.

Half the city must have been on the wooden planking. Hundreds of eyes watched us as we walked up a stone ramp. I felt conspicuous, like I had done something wrong. There are things that we know that others don't. Does that mean we are obligated to speak of them? If WE rebuilt the transport portal must we share it? Should we? Would it be wise to free thousands of criminals? Should we even free ourselves? Do we have the right to make that decision?

We walked past the rocking chairs, benches, and tables, some with umbrellas bent sharply outward to block the intense high-elevation rays. Many of the Silvertonians were reading, a rarity on Limbo, the number of books published each year limited by hand-written tedium. Most were scribed by monks living in the Southern Spine. Trogs also replicated manuscripts, but they had a tendency to edit. A large **T** stamped on the cover confirmed their approval of its contents, but to most people it was a warning, of it being excessively abridged. Sometimes the heart of a book was completely exorcised, voiding its plot. The advantage of reading a trog approved book was its precise lettering. If one was to find a copy of a book so deeming in character that it didn't need to be edited it was worth whatever price one might have to pay. Alas, trogs were notorious for their lack of approval. To a trog, having a bad day meant actually liking something.

Silvertonians liked to play games, the most popular involving tiles. Imaginary ogres battled imaginary arbols in the forest and on top of mountains.

There were also polite discussions. Intimate for the most part, encompassing just two or three individuals.

The most common activity, though, was WATCHING: people, the landscape, the sky. At the moment we were the focus of their attention. Not many people traveled the outskirts of Limbo,

153

not when it also meant a 2500 meter climb.

At the five-meter tall red iron gate at the tower's east entrance stood a single guard in silver armor. On the center of his breast plate was stenciled Silverton's tower with its seven pinnacles, each painted a different color of the rainbow. "That will be five silvers for the first day. Two-silvers-five each additional day."

"That's immoral," I blurted.

"Actually, it's as moral as it can be. The amount is recalculated each season, and it includes room and board. Everyone is treated equally here, with those being here longest receiving first choice of rooms. The rooms are exactly the same. Their location determines their desirability. Most of the fee you pay goes to maintaining the city---a majority of that going to food procurement. A small percent is assigned for administration and defense of the city. The books are open to the public. They are on display in the accounting office."

"It still seems a little high," said Centaur.

"Food grows poorly at this elevation. Much of it must be imported. Invoices of food purchases are also in the accounting office, as are the amounts of food our farmers produce."

We paid the initial fee, determined to stay at least one night. If we hadn't received that reward in Owlwood we would have been destitute.

We were escorted to our rooms by a hostess. Everyone worked in Silverton. The minimum wage barely covered the daily fee, but there were numerous jobs that paid more if one wished to pamper themselves. The rooms weren't technically all the same, just those within the same class: married, single, or double. The single rooms were much smaller than the other two classes, but they were completely private. The double rooms had two beds. The married rooms had one large bed. Hornet and Dinga chose the married arrangement, Centaur and I the double. Because Nimbus wasn't considered a living entity he could share a single with Pulp. It couldn't have been a pleasant arrangement. An ex-drak and a

154

gent cramped together in a space small enough for the gent to touch opposite walls simultaneously. Even laying diagonally Pulp's legs stuck out nearly a meter past the bed. There were advantages being as tall as he was, but few of them occurred in the civilized parts of humanity.

Every room had a window with a view.

Every room was constructed of wood: walls, ceilings, and floor, lightly stained, preserving but not concealing the wood's natural color and texture.

Restrooms were communal. The showers, toilets, and wash basins sparkled. The water must have come from the stream. Most cities in Limbo didn't have running water. The water was slightly cooler than room temperature. Refreshing was the best way to describe it, warmer than its source, but just barely. Vents were found in the floor of each room, but being late spring, no air passed through them.

The one glitch in our accommodations was when it was discovered that Hornet and Dinga weren't properly married. They either had to change their sleeping arrangement or formalize their union. All marriages in Silverton were civic---and public. Matrimony being rare---with the inequitable ratio of women to men, and multiple death-mutations---it was treated as a holiday. All expenses were paid, primarily consisting of a ring being tattooed around the couple's wrists and a special dessert being made.

"We're grown-ups," Dinga complained. "Why should it matter if we're married?"

"We were planning to get married anyway," Hornet reminded her. "This is as good a time as any."

"When I look back, fondly, at this proposal, I'm going to remember it differently."

"This is a very romantic setting."

"I didn't say I wasn't going to agree to being married here, I just wish the particulars were different."

Navigating Silverton would have been complicated if it wasn't for the numerous maps stenciled in corridor walls. Those who built Silverton apparently didn't believe in stairs. Rising from one level of the tower to another consisted of taking a ramp. Sometimes the walkways went up and down in the same stretch.

The center of the tower was hollow and open to the sky, facilitating illumination to interior rooms and corridors. The dining area and social halls consumed a majority of this space. The dining room may not have had a view of the exterior, but in compensation a mural covered the interior column, depicting scenes from the nine moralities of Limbo. Some of the places and creatures I recognized, many I didn't.

There wasn't a single dining room, but many, adjacent to one another, connected by archways. Areas above and below could be seen through the seemingly random openings in the ceiling and floor, covered with glass for safety.

Dinner consisted of potatoes, carrots, and mushrooms, each cooked separately in their own flavorful seasonings. Multi-grain bread was served in small loaves. Our main source of protein was a three-bean salad. One of the beans may have actually been an insect. I didn't ask. I ate the entire entrée, being thankful for the protein, in whatever form it took.

After our dishes were cleared it was time for the marriage ceremony. I felt guilty that someone had served and cleaned up after me. I understood that it was their job, what they did to sleep in a soft, warm bed, and to eat delicious food, but it still seemed wrong. They weren't my servants. But most people would consider the work more desirable than doing guard duty, or cleaning rooms, or farming, or maintaining the sewer. When I left a tip the server appeared perplexed. He chased after me to return the money.

"No, it's yours, for a job well done."

He became defensive. "Why wouldn't I do a good job?"

"Servers generally don't make a lot of money. It's customary to leave a tip."

He looked more confused. "So you tip everyone you think doesn't make a lot of money?"

"Just servers. Well, sometimes the person who caries my bags."

"You can't carry you own bags? Are you injured?"

"It's a service some hotels provide."

"And they charge you for this SERVICE?"

"Most don't. It's just customary for you tip them."

"So you pay extra money to people just doing their job? My friend Cricket does guard city. Did you tip him?"

"Guards usually aren't tipped. They are fully compensated, in their pay."

"But he makes less than me."

"Doing such an important job?"

"How likely is it for something to attack us, living this far into the Positive Frontier? Cricket is more of a lifeguard, providing first aid to people who get too much sun. He collects fees too, but only a few times each day. Guarding Silverton is a paid vacation. The fresh air. The scenic views."

"Here." I doubled the server's tip. "Give half to Cricket. Even someone living in paradise occasionally needs something. New clothes. A book, perhaps. A tropical vacation."

"We're living in the best place on Limbo, why would we want to go someplace else? And what purpose was there in buying our own books? Silverton's library has plenty. Why waste a month's wages on something you finish in half that time? Thank you nevertheless. Sometimes traveling salesmen come to Silverton. I wouldn't mind buying an orange or two."

I returned to the table my---single---friends shared.

"What was that all about?" asked Centaur.

"Some Octagonal Knight stuff. You wouldn't understand."

"You gave more of our money away, didn't you?"

"We got plenty now. He needed it more than we did."

"You sure about that? We have hundreds of kays to go before reaching the Negative Frontier. That means possibly subsisting on what we have for weeks."

"Oh, we'll come into more money by then. If Hornet's luck runs out, Gaea will provide." I did believe that. Manifest destiny. Whatever you wanted to call it. We were imprisoned on Limbo to reconstruct the transport portal. We being Centaur, Hornet, and I.

Any possibly Dinga and Pulp. Dinga becoming pregnant wasn't a coincidence. I wouldn't be surprised if Pebble showed up again. And then there was Nimbus, and who knows who else might join our group---temporarily or permanently---before our mission is complete. Some of the people helping us may not even be aware of it. Subtle pushes to nudge us back on the path.

   The sun had dimmed, but there was still light coming from the central column---now, more from below. Light was dispersed through the city using the same ductwork as heating, transmitted by a series of mirrors.

   Hornet and Dinga stood in the center of the dining/social hall. They each wore a robe. Hornet's was black on top and white on the bottom. Dinga's, the colors reversed. The woman conducting the ceremony was the mayor. She wore a loose fitting white dress with small green, brown, blue, and white flowers. Up close it looked like a bouquet. From a distance, mountains, forest, and a lake. Her long auburn hair was tied back in a pony tail. Following local custom, her feet were bare. The nails on one foot were painted green. On the other, blue. She looked to be eight--- as did most people on Limbo, its regenerative nature retaining our youth---but her wise, sad eyes revealed she was much older, her lifespan probably measured in decades instead of years. She smiled, externally. She was required to participate in this festive occasion inconsequential to her mood. I was drawn to the tattoo bracelet wrapped around her wrist. It was broken.

   "It is a welcomed occasion when a woman and a man agree to bond. With the chaos our imprisonment has created, and the unbalanced ratio of women to men, it is rare for such unions to occur. Since I was elected mayor 14 years ago I have joined only 39 couples. Each time I felt rejuvenated. Our society becomes more commonplace, albeit for just a moment. Do you both desire this union, until re-creation do you part?"

   "Yes," spoke Hornet and Dinga in unison.

   "Then as mayor of Silverton I sanction the union of Dinga Polygulch and Hornet Polygulch. Huckleberry?" The tattoo artist leapt from where he was sitting. The design he stenciled on each of their wrists was elaborate, much more detailed than one could distinguish from a distance. Within the interconnected gold rings was the name of their sanctioned mate---in silver---one letter per link. The artist had to be particularly careful when the bracelet was close to completion. It was a terrible omen for the links not to connect.

"May I present Dinga and Hornet," the mayor said as she held each of their hands and raised them. "The 40th couple married under the administration of Frond Sun Coast of the village of Silverton, located in the heart of the Platinum Mountains."

A robust cheer erupted. "Shouldn't you be giving us permission to kiss?" asked Dinga.

"If you haven't kissed yet, you shouldn't be getting married."

In the manner they did, it was far too polished for them to be unfamiliar with the concept.

The crowd dispersed, abruptly, being too honest to participate in well-wishing small talk. They didn't know Hornet and Dinga, and the couple probably wouldn't be staying in Silverton long enough for them to get to know them. Most of the diners returned to their rooms or to the deck to watch and listen to the nocturnal wonders nature had to offer. Those not leaving clustered together, talking and playing tiles. The wedding cake was chocolate with peanut butter frosting---great alone, but better together. Most people helped themselves to a slice or two before leaving the dining area. Rarely being offered such a treat, each member of our group had three, washed down by a crisp, clear, flavorful crystal decanter of snowmelt.

I caught the mayor as she was about to leave. "Please stay," I insisted. "We need some advice." Hornet and Dinga left a few minutes earlier to do what I assumed newlyweds were suppose to do on their wedding night. The rest of us didn't have such a pressing engagement.

The mayor smiled warmly---just a hint of sadness retained in her eyes---as she sat beside me. My heart leapt. Maybe an

159

Octagonal Knight didn't have to be completely emotionless. Why was I feeling this way, now? I had been on Limbo for many years, and had met many women. Never had I been attracted to anyone as strongly as I was to the mayor. Being in her prescience was more filling than the largest, most comprehensive buffet. Was it possible for an Octagonal Knight to have a romance? Was it wise to do so? Not only would it be a distraction, a loved one could be used as leverage against me.

I was too enamored to speak. Centaur picked up the slack. "We would like to meet with the trogs. They may be able to assist us in the completion of our journey."

"In the manner you speak of your journey, you seek more than a destination." Mayor Frond spoke in a voice both authoritative and beautiful. Few women possessed such duality. Most came off as too strong or too bossy, society branding them as unattractive, or too sweet, regulating their knowledge and abilities to social issues.

As I opened my mouth to speak---pleasing Frond had freed me from my stupor---Nimbus kicked me, reminding me of secrecy. I didn't want to lie to Frond---I couldn't disappoint her---but I wasn't permitted to share our mission with her either. I was dumbfounded. To Frond I must have just appeared dumb.

Pulp bailed me out. People assumed with his size that he was strong, but stupid, the typical giant stereotype. In most instances such stereotypes proved true. The MUTATIONAL BALANCE is what people call the leveling of post re-creation attributes and abilities. Increased strength is countered by decreased intelligence or agility. For Pulp to retain his intelligence, and in many ways improve upon it---he used his past experiences to make wise decisions---he had to be deficient in something else--- something hidden possibly, engrained, but sporadic. "We prefer to not go into details. The more people who know the greater the probability for danger---to all."

"Well spoken, but for me to assist you I must have some knowledge of your mission. Trogs don't like to be bothered. For me to be an accomplice in disturbing them I must believe it necessary."

"Our mission will take us to dangerous lands. The trogs' formidable metallurgical skills will assist our safety."

"So you seek only an improvement in your armor?"

"We wouldn't turn down a well-balanced blade," Centaur answered.

"Is your quest of noble intent, or for self-interest?"

It was my turn to speak. I couldn't have Frond think I was some simple hired henchman. "We must admit what we seek is primarily for personal gain. But if successful, the ramifications of our accomplishment will have global consequences."

"Positive or Negative? Do they bring more Order or more Chaos?"

"I guarantee you we'll be thinning out the East as we progress through the completion of our mission."

"Aren't Octagonal Knights supposed to be Neutral in such matters?"

"The immoral bulge warrants a balancing. To protect those traveling with me I sometimes must take swift action. I promise you, my judgments won't be enacted unjustly."

"The problem with instigating a decrease in a Limboan population is its temporary nature. It's unlikely a sound defeat will inspire a change in morality. Often the opposite occurs. Those in the Negative Frontier don't need additional motivation to become more ill-mannered.

"I commend your honesty. On the surface it might have appeared more personally beneficial to tell me what you perceived would influence a positive response. As we age our skin isn't the only thing that becomes thinner. Trogs also treasure honesty, above all else, even their treasure hordes. Personally, I believe a partial truth is adequate. Whole truths are often too cruel. The trogs may assist you. They hesitate in their own use of force, but they wouldn't be saddened by the elimination of those living in the East, even temporarily. In the morning I will direct you to them. Sleep well. If you don't in Silverton, who won't anywhere." Frond's eyes became particularly sad.

As I started to leave, the mayor held me back. "You appear troubled."

"There are ramifications of being an Octagonal Knight I wasn't aware when I first accepted the position."

"All professions have their benefits and liabilities."

"What liabilities could there be as mayor?"

"Many. The obvious one being responsible for making decisions for an entire city. I'm no dictator, but I do create policies, and must bring up issues for discussion, and solutions to problems to a vote. Personally, the greatest liability to my job is my inability to travel. Being mayor I must make myself available."

"I admire your dedication. If traveling is that important to you, couldn't you step down as mayor? You've been doing it for quite a while. Fourteen years?"

"If completing a term of office is all that was holding me back, I would have already departed. The problem is I am the best person available for the job. My duty is here, in this capacity."

"Wouldn't the people of Silverton understand if you wished to retire? There has to be someone else capable of running the city."

"Silverton would understand, but I wouldn't. If something went wrong with the city I would always question whether it could have been prevented if I was mayor."

"May I ask a personal question?" The mayor smiled tentatively and nodded. "Does your wrist chain being broken mean you are no longer married?"

"I was married once, shortly after I became mayor. My husband had as much wanderlust as I. That was one of the things---the main thing---that brought us together. Few in Silverton have such affliction. When you live in paradise, why would you wish to leave it? He wanted to see the world, as I did, but I felt I couldn't leave Silverton. He left, first for just a short excursion into the mountains, then into the Moguls, and finally into the desert and the plains beyond. The increased freedom of movement each time only made the desire to see new places expand within him. He eventually made his way into Neutrality. I told him about where I was born and he wanted to see it for himself. Before he reached the Sun Coast, abnormals attacked him. Abnormals are those men and women whose bodies mutated inconsistently. An elongated arm might be mismatched with a shrunken leg, a claw, or a hoof. Being shunned from society, due to their grotesque nature, they have become angry. They do not attack because they're cruel. It's more a defense mechanism. They just don't want everyone to go away, they need them to. My husband, living in the Positive Frontier most of his life, underestimated their ferocity. He was killed and re-created, breaking the marriage bond. We could have re-bonded, but the slight mutation he received only heightened his wanderlust. He abandoned me for good. What an odd expression: for good. Is there a morality attached to permanence?"

"And you haven't thought about remarrying in all those years since?"

"I am married---to my city. Bigamy is forbidden here. Try to sleep well tonight. I haven't slept well in over 13 years."

Chapter 28

BELOW

I didn't sleep well. After many tosses and turns I came to the conclusion it wouldn't have worked out. I didn't entirely give up on the concept of loving someone, but the person, place, and time would have to be perfect for it to happen. I couldn't force the issue, not with the responsibility I assumed when I defeated the Octagonal Knight and dressed myself in his armor.

We had two options when it came to traveling to Trogdom: above or below ground. It was 20 kays to Trogdom on the surface, none of them on a road. Or we could use an abandoned tunnel beneath Silverton that was used for commerce before the trogs became more reclusive. We had been down a hole or two before, so traveling a few kays through a tunnel a civilized society had created didn't sound too dangerous.

We followed Frond down a ramp that spiraled beneath the tower. Sunlight didn't reach it so we were forced to use torches that smoked badly. The ramp terminated at the creek below the city. The water flowed through a stone trough, bordered on both sides by a walkway too narrow to travel more than single file. Pipes sticking out of the walls angled into the water. A mechanical resonance was barely discernible beyond the barrage of rushing water.

"There's a turbine down that way," spoke the mayor, pointing in the direction opposite to where we were heading. "It creates enough electricity to run the pumps and heat the water."

"Does the waste water go into the creek?" asked Dinga.

"Gaea forbid. It drops into a pit far below the creek. Here's the gate to Trogdom." The mayor stopped at a corridor perpendicular to the creek. A rusty, thick iron gate blocked access to it. Frond pulled a large silver key from a pocket in her dress. She placed it in the lock, flaking off rust. She turned it with effort. It emitted a hideous scraping squeak. With the key still inside she attempted to swing the gate inward. It didn't budge.

"Let me." With his two mighty hands bulging with strain Centaur attempted to pull the gate towards him. All he accomplished was coating his hands with ochre residue.

"Let me," said Pulp. He wasn't completely unsuccessful. He bent one of the bars.

"Try together," whispered the sticks-and-stones-man. I looked at Frond, expecting her to notice who made the comment. Just minutes away from absconding civilization and Nimbus had to inadvertently give himself away. Apparently she didn't, because

164

she hadn't turned in his direction. The gate budged this time, but just a sim at each grunting surge of strength.

"You may wish to oil this gate," Centaur suggested.

"It hasn't been opened since I became mayor. You are correct, though. It needs to be properly maintained. What would have happened if we had to open it in an emergency? There are contingencies involving the tunnel if Silverton is ever attacked. Maybe if someone else was mayor there wouldn't be this oversight…. No, it's likely they would have forgotten about the tunnel too. I must make a concerted effort to prevent future oversights. By the way, if you return to Silverton through the tunnel ring that bell."

"What bell?" asked Dinga.

"It should be…. There it is, on the ground. The metal hook it was on appears to have rusted through. I'll take care of that too."

I picked up the bell and shook it, hearing one dull strike before the rusted metal bob fell to the ground.

"If you return before it's replaced bang on it with a sword or something. So much to do. Someone checking the water or turbine will eventually hear it. Good luck. If the trogs agree to your request that just might be what Silverton needs to resume communication with them."

I paused as my companions began their descent down the corridor. Frond appeared to want to say something, but kissed me instead. I turned, walking hurriedly to catch up to my companions. In a tender voice that was still able to carry she said, "Dreams last longer than reality. Remember."

Lost in my thoughts, I bumped into Centaur. "If you had been gone any longer, it wouldn't have been me you would have bumped into," he said, smiling.

I declined to reply. I worked my way to the front of the single-file line, snatching Pulp's torch as I passed him. The gent reverted to his swingman position as both ART2 and PROC2. He was more than proficient with both bow and sword, but with him being significantly taller than anyone else he needed to be in the middle of our queue to limit the detriment to our visibility, fore and aft.

"What happened to Nimbus?" I asked.

"He entered the corridor with us," Dinga insisted.

"He's probably just exploring on his own," Pulp conjectured. "Drak are curious folk. And self-absorbed. It would be like one not to tell us where he was going."

"Do you think we might actually be rid of him?" Centaur asked.

"That's a cruel thing to suggest," Dinga retorted.

"I'm not saying it's beneficial that he abandoned us. I was just wondering. We haven't lost our need for a tour guide."

With ease we advanced. Pulp had to crouch a bit, but more a tilting of his neck than a full arching of his back. There weren't any forks or spurs to confuse us. The gate may have built by humans, but the tunnel was definitely of trog construction: the craftsmanship was flawless. Cool, but not cold, the temperature was perfect for moderate, highly encumbered activity. Every step, jingle of metal, and comment echoed oddly. The tone of its reverberation changed two kays into the hike.

We prepared ourselves for the potential danger. Hornet, Dinga, and Pulp drew their bows, Pulp going so far as fitting his with an arrow. Centaur and I raised our weapons, thrusting them in front of us. The axe and sword would enact a heavy penalty if someone charged us precipitously from the torch periphery. We continued forward, but at a slower pace. Still, nothing. We walked even slower. The torches must have been damp. They produced as much smoke as light, concealing us, inadvertently, as efficiently as if in darkness.

Something rushed me, at head level, from the left. I blocked the attack with my torch and countered with an arced slice of my sword. I hit whatever it was, knocking it to the ground. Something else hit me in the head, this time from the right. I was jarred, but undamaged. My attacker wasn't as fortunate. It followed its brethren to the ground with a thud. "BACK!" I shouted. I backpedaled. Nothing else attacked me through the haze of the torch smoke. Finally having the opportunity to examine my surroundings, a tunnel intersecting the one we were in came into focus. It was less regular in dimension, and much smaller: we would have to bend over to enter it, Pulp onto his knees. A steady stream of bats crossed in front of us, a majority of them flying out of the left tunnel into the one on the right.

"The trogs didn't construct that one, did they?" Hornet stood beside me, peering into the new discovery. He was careful not to get in the way of the bats.

"Unlikely," I replied. "The walls aren't as smooth as those of the main corridor. They're scalloped, like something took many small bites out of the stone."

"Should we investigate?" asked Dinga.

"What, the bats?" Centaur questioned. "I'm not that found of guano."

"Let's stay in the main tunnel," Pulp insisted. "Just looking at those small openings is making me claustrophobic."

"Too much adventure for you?" I teased.

"Let's just say I'm done with this one, and ready for another. Do you believe there is anything to gain by swimming upstream through a swarm of bats?"

I didn't. Even a challenge became tedious if it endured.

We darted past the opening, one at a time, between breaks in the persistent, but intermittent stream of bats. Before returning to marching mode we looked behind us, paranoid the bats might be following. They weren't.

An evil foreboding overwhelmed me, so powerful I almost fainted. How was that possible, being so deep in the Positive Frontier? There was a mixing of moralities, usually at the borders, but never such a contrast. After being nearly knocked down by the onslaught I was able to gradual adjust to the perpetual wave of Negativity. It really wasn't that bad. The contrast to what I had been accustomed to is what agitated my psyche. Snow in July is a shock, but not in December. I didn't speak of what I sensed--- uncertain if it was related to being an Octagonal Knight or just having the heebie-jeebies.

167

Two kays past the bats the foreboding began to dissipate. We must be getting closer to Trogdom. What a stupid thing to think. Of course we were getting closer, as long as we were heading in the correct direction. What I meant was we were getting very close, enough for the collective Positively to counter the permeating Negatively.

Something felt wrong again. No, not evil, just wrong---more related to my connection with Limbo than with my moral sensitivity. It was just ahead---but below. I looked down. The floor crumbled beneath me. I scrambled to hold onto something. The only thing within reach was Hornet, who was also falling.

We fell five meters---all of us. Hornet may have been closest, but the others were close enough. We examined each other. No broken bones. Only scrapes and bruises.

There was no obvious escape route. The four walls surrounding us were solid stone, shear without egress. A small pool was the pit's only feature.

"Weren't the trogs supposed to be renowned for their construction prowess?" Hornet commented. "Famous or infamous?"

"I don't think the thin floor was the result of the shoddy workmanship," said Dinga.

"Someone---or thing---set a trap for us," I declared.

"Which doesn't eliminate the trogs ," said Centaur. "They have a reputation for disliking outsiders."

"Unlikely," said Pulp. "Trogs worship truth, and this trap is considerably deceiving. They don't dislike outsiders, just prefer the peacefulness that comes from privacy."

"Then who set this trap?" asked Hornet.

It was time to share my awareness. The ethereal evil may not be the cause of our capture, but it couldn't be ruled-out either.

"And you haven't chosen to share this with us, until now?" asked Centaur.

"My inability to warn you of the trap is a good indicator my abilities as an Octagonal Knight aren't mastered. The evil that I sensed may have just been the bats."

"Bats don't build traps."

"And they aren't inherently evil," added Pulp.

"How are we going to get out of here?" asked Dinga. "If we were intentionally trapped won't our captors eventually want to see what they caught?"

"Unless they just want us to rot down here," said Centaur.

"Climb up on Pulp's shoulders," spoke a familiar voice from beyond the hole in the ceiling.

"Is that you, Nimbus?" asked Dinga. "Where have you been?"

"I'll explain after you free yourself. Too long a delay, the tale becomes moot."

I was first to climb onto Pulp---not easy when one is wearing full armor. It would have been easier if I had removed it and tossed it up, into the tunnel, but I had become accustomed to it, and couldn't see myself parting with it---even temporarily. My first attempt at stretching to the top of the hole brought a shower of debris down upon myself and my companions, as the ceiling crumbled. No one was badly damaged. With Pulp holding onto me tightly I didn't completely fall. Carefully I chipped away at the edge of the hole with a dagger. My companions were wise enough to move to the far side of the pit. The ceiling stopped falling in when I reached the wall. I threw the dagger over the lip, then pulled myself and 15 kilos of gear into the corridor. If it wasn't for the light-weight material my armor was constructed with it would have been a physical impossibility.

The sticks-and-stones-man shook his rocky top. "You wouldn't have survived if that pit was full of sharpened stakes, corrosive acid, poisonous snakes...."

"We get the picture," I snapped.

"OR ALL THREE!" Pulp shouted up to us.

"No, the acid would have dissolved the stakes and snakes long before you were stupid enough to fall into the pit," Nimbus countered dryly.

Next up was Hornet, followed by Dinga. Each additional

person up made the job easier, the extra arms adding leverage. Centaur was last to climb up the gent, due to his bulk. As he gave a last push upward with his legs, Pulp toppled. After the gent recovered I leaned into the hole with Centaur holding my legs. Pulp and I locked arms. Centaur, with Hornet and Dinga's assistance, pulled me up, and consequently, Pulp.

After resting---and Pulp consuming an energy stone---Nimbus shared his excursion. "Sand Golden Prairie requested my prescience. He is the most powerful of us, the Grand Draconian. There is no community or leadership amongst our kind, but there is hierarchy and respect, a respect that's paired with caution, not admiration. Sand requested my prescience for two reasons. The first: I was passing through his domain. A drak must receive permission to do so, even if that drak is more powerful--- which I'm not. The second: subaquans are beginning to impair his solitude. Trogs are good neighbors, but their expansion has displaced some beasts, which in turn caused them to displace others. Xar are worms that consume stone in order to obtain minerals they digest. After stone is pulverized, and nutrients digested, waste must be excreted. Massive amounts of waste. Xar are fastidious, choosing to not defecate where they eat. They release it in remote caverns. Many of the caverns have inhabitants who must flee or be trapped by mineral excrement. The subaquans were one such race displaced. They are fish-like in appearance--- and odor. They are bipedal on land, and swim effortlessly in subterranean lakes and rivers. They are extremely xenophobic, expressed in cruelty when they meet someone of another race. They capture slaves whenever possible, their treatment of them so poor, their ranks require constant replenishment. The xar tunnels have become thoroughfares---to Trogdom. Many clashes have occurred. Many slaves have been taken: trog slaves. There are no subaquans hostages---they fight to the death---considerably more respectable than being imprisoned by inferiors."

"So this Grand Draconian summoned you to act as his...town crier?" asked Centaur.

170

"He kindly asks for your assistance in the resolution of this conflict."

"Why doesn't he do something himself?" asked Hornet.

"He is very much against conflict. So much, he has trouble relating. He is also too large to travel to where these confrontations are occurring."

"So, there are nearly 10,000 trogs, and hundreds, if not thousands, of subaquans, and he thinks the six of us can leap in between them and knock some sense into them?" asked Dinga.

"We don't have to fight them all, just stop the war."

"Isn't there someone with more experience negotiating truces?" suggested Pulp. "None of us are trained in conflict resolution."

"Sand believes the many races you have interacted with in your travels adequately qualify you. Applying such acquired knowledge Sand is confident the trogs and subaquans will find common ground."

I acquiesced. "We can at least speak to the trogs. If we're lucky we'll reach Trogdom before we meet any subaquans."

"I think we almost did," said Hornet. "I've been wondering why that pit didn't have an entrance---except from above. And that wasn't there until we fell through the floor. The subaquans created it. That pool was their door. They chiseled out the pit beneath the tunnel through the pool."

"If that trap is any indication, the subaquans can't be that great of an adversary," Dinga commented. "We escaped easily."

"Not that easily." Pulp stretched with a grimace. "The pit was likely constructed for the much shorter, less limber, trogs. How likely was it for a gent to be captured?"

Cautiously, we closed the distance between us and Trogdom. We were determined to not be ensnared in another trap. I was particularly adamant about notifying my companions the next time I noticed a surge in Negativity.

Our passage terminated, abruptly, at a cave-in. It completely blocked our route. When we thrust our torches at it, hoping to see the light penetrate beyond, all we saw was the lights'

171

reflection off the gray granite boulders.

"We have three choices," spoke Centaur. "We return to Silverton. We clear these stones away---which may take days. Or, we find another route to Trogdom, those bat tunnels likely being the only subterranean option."

"I wish we had some penta to blast our way through," said Dinga.

"And topple the rest of the tunnel down on us," added Nimbus.

I studied our surroundings. "I'm feeling uneasy about being trapped here. There's a reason why they call this a dead-end."

"You sensing something, again?" asked Centaur.

"No, not that. I just don't think it's wise to stay here too long. Unless we plan to clear a path we need to get a move on. If we do decide to clear we need to do so with due haste."

Pulp studied the tunnel clog. "Swimming through a perpetual stream of bats wasn't the adventure I imagined. Maybe they'll keep the subaquans away. I know I want nothing to do with them."

We backtracked silently, but swiftly, pausing for a moment to look into the pit. There still wasn't anyone there, but that didn't mean someone hadn't come and gone already. The hole consumed the entire width of the tunnel, forcing us to leap over it. It was a considerable, but manageable distance, but with a five meter drop below it could be debilitating---we were fortunate no bones were broken when we fell through. Nimbus was our greatest concern. How were those lethargic short legs of his going to make it? Centaur threw him across, without warning, my Octagonal reflexes assisting in catching him.

The bats no longer crossed the central tunnel.

"I hope that means it's no longer their activity period, not that they were frightened away by something," commented Centaur, dryly. He turned to me. "Left or right? What do you sense?"

"Nothing specifically. Negativity permeates this entire area.

172

It isn't stronger in one direction than the other."

I bent over as I entered the right tunnel. I wasn't the type of person to delay once a course of action was decided. If I didn't know the answer, thinking about it a couple of minutes wasn't going to help. I was always the first to finish a test in school. I didn't always receive the best score, but I did have the most free time. Sometimes that got me into trouble.

Pulp was particularly uncomfortable in the confined space. He began on all fours. After becoming uncomfortable he dropped to his knees. Within minutes they became scraped, bruised, and bleeding.

It was impossible to retain battle-readiness. Hornet, Dinga, and Pulp had strapped their bows to their back. Centaur and I still had our weapons drawn, but in the manner our bodies were contorted our leverage was so poor, potential strikes were unlikely to inflict terminal damage.

Light appeared ahead of us, ten minutes into our grueling journey. The tunnel terminated at a natural cave. Light shined down at us through a small opening in the ceiling.

"That must have been where the bats entered," said Dinga.

"Which means the bats will pass through this tunnel, thousands of them, at dusk," I said. "We have until then to find our way out."

"Maybe we can climb through that hole," Hornet suggested. "Do you think it's wide enough?"

"It won't matter unless we can fly," said Centaur.

"DINGA CAN! We could tie a rope to her."

Dinga was less ecstatic. After sending Hornet daggers she punched his shoulder, the force applied exceeding a friendly jab.

"A rope will be too heavy for her."

"A string then, tied to the rope. Back in human form she'll have the strength to pull up the rope."

Since entering the cave Pulp had been constantly stretching, slowly working the kinks out of his muscles. As evidenced by him retaining a tilt, it was a work in process. "Isn't our goal to reach Trogdom, not to escape?" he commented. "If we wished to return

173

to the surface wouldn't going through Silverton be simpler?"

Compared to the tunnel, the cave was enormous, measuring 40 meters across, and almost 20 meters high. Across from where we entered, a xar tunnel began. To our right was a more natural looking tunnel. To our left, a pile of debris. Likely another collapse.

"This entire area is unstable," commented Hornet

"Well, there has been an increase in activity," said Centaur. "Xar chomping through stone must put a strain on the infrastructure."

"The xar were definitely involved," said Dinga, "but I don't think it was due to their digging."

"You don't mean...." Hornet began.

Pulp's eyes became wide, then they sparkled. "This pile of stones and that cave-in at the end of the trog tunnel are...? FEEK!"

"And I touched some of it." Dinga shivered.

"They're just rocks." Hornet smiled. "You'll be touching a lot worst in a few months."

"I won't be the only one touching it."

The smirk faded, to be replaced with more sincere mirth a moment later.

"Let's take the natural tunnel," Pulp suggested. "I don't think my back will hold up much longer. There's a reason gents don't live underground."

Nimbus shook his rocky top, but didn't speak. In the loose manner he did so it was difficult to ascertain its orientation. He didn't choose to elaborate. Affirmation or negation, we would find out soon.

The tunnel narrowed, becoming barely wide enough to squeeze through, then it widened to larger than the cave with the natural sky light. Even when narrow it was tall enough for Pulp to remain standing. His spirits rose. He even became our cheerleader when we became depressed when the tunnel appeared like it wasn't going to end. We stopped briefly to finish the remainder of our bonch and to swallow a couple of swigs of water. Side tunnels and caverns popped up periodically, complicating our route. To simplify the decision-making we chose the largest tunnel each time, aware that didn't guarantee a suitable route. Arriving at a lake, we backtracked to the previous fork, not willing to risk an inadvertent contact.

"I think we may be lost," commented Dinga, after we had spelunked for an additional hour.

"Does anyone have any idea where we are?" asked Centaur.

"Surprisingly, where we want to be, even with all those twists and turns," I answered. "We're still heading in the right direction. A large clustering of...emotions...is getting stronger."

"I didn't think trogs had emotions," Hornet commented.

"Everyone is emotional. Some people just chose not to express it," Pulp clarified. "Or prefer it to overly dictate their life."

"Are we past the xar dung pile?" asked Dinga. "The one that blocked the corridor?"

"I think so," I answered.

With renewed determination we resumed our search. A gorilla-like albino race attacked us. Being caught off guard was caused by a combination of inattentiveness brought on by no recent challenges and the limited visibility of the nocturnal subterranean environment. Some of the beasts carried crudely constructed stone hammers, others used their claws. We got carried away---emotionally, not physically. Defending became attacking, quite violently. The combination of frustration not finding Trogdom, and the discomfort of being cooped up in a labyrinth, drove us. A ring of slain, white bodies surrounded us. The residual two apes fled. Centaur chased after them.

"STOP!" I bellowed through winded breath. "This is wrong. We aren't butchers. They may have just been defending their turf. We need to calm down. These bloodthirsty emotions was the evil I detected. I must have felt them building within myself."

"Maybe that's also the reason THEY attacked," Dinga suggested.

"Was it the claustrophobia that caused us to act this way?" asked Pulp. "I feel soiled---ashamed. Positives don't act this way."

Sometimes emotions initiate extreme behavior, and drugs---

175

particularly alcohol---cause people to act in a manner they're not accustomed. Same say underlying emotions are just brought up to the surface. What if something like that was happening here? Some chemical modified our behavior, changed it, made it more extreme---or drew out what was hidden within? "Could something like elem be influencing us? Emotional/moral radiation from sub-molecular particles? Could what makes a person good or bad be similar to what makes iron hard and helium light?"

"Are you suggesting the trogs dug too deep and struck a vein of Negativity?" Hornet asked.

"If people can be influenced to behave poorly, isn't it as likely they can be influenced to do good? Wouldn't it be wonderful to find some of this Positive elem and inoculate the Negative Frontier?"

"Or infect it," Dinga countered. "Do we have a right to force someone to act a certain way?"

"If it betters society."

"Like birth control in the water supply?"

"Exactly."

"So you don't believe people should have freewill?"

"Look what freewill got me? A life sentence."

Pulp spoke up. "I agree with Dinga."

"I expected you to be the last person to do so."

"I'm a Westerner, but also a Southerner. We do what we think is right. For the most part that means having a good time. We aren't rigid, like Northerners, believing what they believe everyone should believe."

"I thought Octagonal Knights were Neutral?" Hornet questioned.

FEEK! I was allowing external stimuli to influence me again. But what if these external stimuli are within me? External meaning outside the Octagonal dogma. Why was I chosen to be an Octagonal Knight? First I died---made impure---now I had trouble following the basic tenets of my order. I wasn't worthy. Were my imperfections a challenge to master myself?

"I've wondered why morality was such a mixture underground," Hornet continued. "It all makes sense now. Morality elem is subterranean. A particularly Positive pocket will influence Positive intentions. A Negative pocket, Negative ones."

"And those of a specific morality are drawn to a corresponding pocket," said Centaur.

"This area must have a very strong concentration for us to be affected so quickly," said Dinga.

"The sooner we leave this area the sooner our dispositions---our original dispositions---return," Pulp stated.

"What is our original disposition?" I asked, temporarily shelving my self-loathing. "We are constantly evolving."

"Are you implying we may actually be those insane berserkers who instigated that...massacre?" asked Centaur.

"Not if this influence is temporary. The sooner we leave the sooner the Negativity will dissipate from our bodies. What we have been exposed to for most of our lives is more deeply engrained."

"For our souls to retain their authenticity, we must be re-created where the moral elem is concentrated," Pulp stated. "Our souls are nourished by the moral elem we consume. If they don't receive enough fertilizer they wither, mutating in their gasp for survival."

"Negative elem must be heavier than its Positive counterpart," Hornet conjectured. "Being heavier, more dense, it is more strongly attracted to the center of the planet. It explains why the most deadly and evil are the most deep."

As we contemplated the implications of our new discovery we pushed ahead. If morality is essentially a virus, can we be held accountable for our actions? Force of will must also play a part. It must. We can choose to act in a certain manner, in ways that are sometimes against our nature. If we do it often enough wouldn't it be like exercising? Wouldn't our moral muscles grow?

Chapter 29

TROGDOM

We finally found the trogs---in the manner a mouse finds a cat. They were covered, from head to toe, in steel armor, the light from our torches ricocheting off their many battle-scared dimples. Rectangular shields, also of steel, but with splashes of ochre, were held in front of them. They were ridged with spikes, and nearly as large as the men they protected. They were slightly shorter than us, but more broad. In their primary hands they carried steel axes, their heads longer than a woodsman's and curved, like a scythe. They intended to bring them down upon our heads---before a single unintelligible word by Nimbus halted the attack.

The trogs stood their ground, neither moving forward or backing up. "We seek entrance into Trogdom," stated Centaur in a tone confident and steadfast. "We have need of your metallurgy skills. We've been told your people make excellent weapons and armor."

After a moment of silence and inactivity, one of the trogs blurted out groggily through the horizontal slits in his helmet, "I believe King Brick would like to speak to you. Come." The trog's voice was precise, deep---and muffled---a definite downside to an abundance of armor. We waited for all twelve trogs to begin walking before following them. They had other plans, half of them staying behind. It was apparent we were to be thoroughly PROTECTED.

"What did you say to them?" I whispered to Nimbus.

"To cease what they were doing. The command encompasses not only their current action, but all activities. The

178

key was speaking it to them in drak. It hypnotizes them, like a snake's gaze. The distraction, from the influences of the Negative elem, lasted long enough for the berserking to leave them. Basically, I helped them return to their senses."

The trogs were definitely broad, but that may have due more to their armor than to their physiques. They barely fit two abreast down the tunnel of obvious trog construction. One would expect one of them to occasionally brush against the wall, but none wavered more than a sim from their course.

We passed an intersecting xar tunnel, and were immediately waylaid. From both branches of the tunnel, two-meter tall bipedal fish threw spears. The trogs raised their shields, blocking all the missiles. The subaquans---who else could they have been---came next with daggers. They were bound to their webbed arms, giving them the appearance of claws. They attempted to penetrate the gaps between the shields, but the scythe axes were able to slide through and around the shields more efficiently, slicing through arms, relieving them of their daggers---and hands. Before the subaquans could mass enough of their kind to overwhelm the trogs, the steel-clad warriors pushed forward, their shields thrust before them in a jerking, but calculated motion. Subaquans were ripped apart, grated like cheese. Those in back attempted to throw weighted nets over the trogs. The reigning in of the trogs was brief, the nets being easily cut away.

The surviving subaquans fled, leaving the rank odor of dead fish behind. Some of the trogs began to follow them down one of the branches, but were held back by the trog who spoke to us. "We have other business to attend to. Throw the bottom-feeders into the xarway. A cleanup crew will be assigned to seal it."

We resumed our journey to Trogdom. Only the six trogs in front had fought. What mass destruction could the trogs enact if they concentrated all their might?

The end of the tunnel was much different than the one that terminated at Silverton. The door that blocked our passage was a steel plate. The lead trog slid twelve metallic tabs a specific distance. Once the task was completed, he pushed the metal plate.

It silently rotated inward. We followed him into the lit room beyond. The last trog through closed the door behind him. A series of soft snaps was heard, as the locking mechanism reset. Beside the door was an image of the tunnel we had traveled down. A creation of mirrors or lenses---or elem? The latter was unlikely, due to the cost, and duration.

"Extinguish your torches."

We did as we were told. Light remained, but it was dim. Each trog had a small chamber built within his chest plate that glowed through the mesh covering it. Two glowing worms from each were delicately removed and placed inside the mesh cube in the center of the room.

The room we were in was of the same construction as the adjacent tunnel. How were the trogs able to get the stone so smooth? Cubicles were carved into the walls. Most were laden with armor. Shields and scythe axes hung from pegs.

"Place your weapons---all of your weapons---in that empty bin." We did as we were told. What other option did we have? How likely was it to thwart twelve heavily armored, well trained, disciplined warriors?

It was now time for the trogs to lighten their load. Shields and scythe axes were placed on pegs. The removal of armor was more problematic. It required assistance. Being designed to fit tightly, it was constructed in many pieces. Each article was placed precisely into an empty cubicle.

The men beneath the armor were husky, but far from fat. Their chests were broader than mine, nearly as large as Centaur's. Associating trogs with dwarves I was shocked when the long, tangled beards I expected never materialized. I had seen a trog before, but legends must have took precedence in my psyche, because I was still surprised when I saw bald scalps and smooth faces. Removing their steel boots left their wide feet bare. In contrast, their gray underclothes provided unwavering coverage, from shoulder to ankle. The trogs' physical, and emotional, characteristics were so similar the only way to distinguish one from another was by the silver necklaces they wore, laden with beads---the blander the better apparently, the lead trog having three brown beads, and two gray.

"Come," he said. The corridor adjacent to the room we were in---what I considered the foyer---was similar to the one outside the city, except it had glow boxes along its walls. Every 10 meters was a door, each labeled with five beads above it. The corridor was crisscrossed by many others, each with its rows of doors.

"The trog equivalent of suburban hell?" I commented, wryly.

What was odd about all those residences---if that's what they were---was the lack of people entering, or leaving, them. Why so many inactive rooms? Were they not yet occupied, or were the people living, or working, in them somewhere else?

We entered a different region of the city, evident by the diminishing number of doors and side corridors, and---there was no way of putting this delicately---its stink. One of those doors opened, permeating the air with a sewer stench. A trog pushed a cart full of mushrooms. He was soon out of sight, efficiently going about his task.

A remarkable thing was the trogs' lack of communication among their kind. Not a single word was spoken between the food tech and the army patrol. Not a HELLO or even a GOOD DAY. We have been conditioned to recognizing someone verbally, but if we don't does that mean they don't exist, or they're not worthy of our notice? Is the small talk really necessary?

We weren't informed of the origin of the odiferous onslaught. But from the smell I conjectured sewage wasn't wasted. Were the trogs bad hosts for not acknowledging or explaining their odors? Did that confirm we were more prisoners than guests?

The center of Trogdom was reached. More trogs came and went, but all did so in an organized manner. We entered what we believed to be the COMMAND CENTER, or perhaps the WAR ROOM. On the floor was a replica of the city. Each district of every level was intricately detailed on the tiered glass. Connections between levels were shown, as were the locations of surface gates. Silverton

181

was shown, as was the road to it through the Moguls and a portion of the Platinum Mountains. Both were blue. Trogdom was white. Supplementary subterranean zones where either green or red. Red representing danger? The subaquan territories? Conjecture, not assumption. Assumptions could get you killed on Limbo.

A trog with one brown bead and four gray looked up at us as we entered. "Follow." Turning to our escort he said, "Break." They scattered, most of them leaving the war room immediately. Two lingered to glance at the map. Suddenly aware of their impertinence, in un-trog-like fashion they darted off to catch up to their associates.

We followed the high-ranking trog into a room adjacent to the war room. He sat on a stone bench behind a stone desk with an un-trog-like clutter: two pieces of paper lay loosely on it. "Sit." We sat on the two stone benches bookending the door that had shut after the trog had pulled a lever on his desk.

"We haven't had a surface dweller visit us in 19.812 years. Considering your company's unusual assortment of races, professions, and equipment you didn't wander into Trogdom's perimeter arbitrarily."

"We request you cease hostilities with the subaquans," spoke the sticks-and-stones-man, startling us as much---if not more than---the trog.

"You allow a golem to speak for you? Could it be that you are all golems? There have been rumors of flesh automatons."

Flesh automatons? Zombies? Frankenstein monsters? We fought animated skeletons once. Fighting something with flesh, likely rotting, would be worse---much worse. We didn't smell that bad, did we? We were a bit travel weary, but the walking dead?

"I am a sovereign golem," Nimbus declared. "I speak for myself."

"You chose to challenge me with children's tales? Do you perceive me so lacking in discipline to be swayed by amusement? What utility is there in attempting to deceive me with this non-living handyman? The benefits of distraction are offset by the familiarity of one's home."

"I am very much living. A Wizard stole my soul from my true shell. It was transplanted into the golem you see before you."

"Why would a Wizard do such a thing? Gaea forbids corporal manipulation."

"SO, SOMEONE WHO CAN CHANGE HER FORM---A CHANGELING---IS DAMNED!?" Dinga blurted.

"Someone with the ability to change can choose not to."

"When have Wizards started following Gaea's decries instead of their own?" Nimbus inquired. "Something nearly as dastardly as my demise has afflicted the trogs. Possibly also Wizard induced. You have been deceived."

"IMPOSSIBLE! We exist to defend truth. Our lifestyle is regulated by our proactivity. If someone has been successful in committing subterfuge THERE WILL BE WAR!"

"The war is the subterfuge. If you could free yourself from outside influences you would come to realize this war with the subaquans is unnecessary."

"TROGS ARE NOT INFLUENCED, BY ANYONE! We must battle the subaquans, because they battle us."

"Are the subaquans even capable of penetrating the city's defenses? Would they even be attacking you if your expansion hadn't displaced them from their homes?"

"A society must grow if it is to survive and prosper."

"To grow, without change?" Dinga interrupted.

"There have been new arrivals---too great to balance our departures."

"We heard there are more than 10,000 trogs," said Hornet.

"No longer an exaggeration. Our population has doubled in the past five years."

"Doesn't that concern you?" asked Centaur.

"It has been a blessing---a portent that Limbo is becoming more Positive and Ordered."

"Or a method to balance," I added. "But to balance what?"

"Trogs aren't pawns. We can't be manipulated. We battle the subaquans because they are treacherous barbarians. Trogdom must be defended."

"If you were thinking clearly would you be battling a relatively defenseless species? We saw how easy you handle subaquans when a group of them attacked our escort."

"We can't properly train and equip our soldiers? Most of the deceased return to the Platinum Mountains, but not all. Is the cost too great to prevent banishment?"

"Banishment or facilitation to a more suitable lifestyle?" Pulp inquired.

"We don't all view the world through a Chaotic lens. The grass isn't always greener. Routine is more peaceful than whim."

"True, but stagnation can cause decay."

"Our souls are at stake here. We must be diligent, to prevent us from reverting to something re-creationally inferior."

"Trogs have dug below their moral foundation. Negative morality has seeped into Trogdom, progressively modifying your beliefs."

"Absurd."

"What caused the trogs to isolate themselves? Was it your subconscious trying to fight the invading morality from within? Did it require the supplemental peace, and introspection, isolation provides? If you rule out the possibility, then you deceive yourself. Once you distance yourself from the influences that have permeated Trogdom you will perceive the possibility more clearly."

The trog stood motionless, for many minutes. None of us dared speak, or make a sound. The trog had to realize the threat on his own, without any influences.

"I must discuss this with King Brick. Stay." The trog left us--- alone. Even if we wished to escape, how far would we get in the midst of 10,000 of the most well-trained, disciplined warriors on the planet?

"Do you believe your soap box will work?" asked Centaur.

"I spoke the truth. It is the only thing that will persuade the trogs. It all depends on how much the Negative elem has inundated Trogdom. If the trogs are no longer capable of considering the possibility of our contention, there's little hope. It'll be in Gaea's hands then."

"You fear the trogs will extend their expansion?" asked Dinga. "Onto the surface, and...."

"Beyond. It might be the excuse the Wizards need to act, to declare martial law."

"But the Wizards don't rule," Hornet insisted.

"Even after all pledge to them in compensation for defending Limbo from the trog horde?"

"The population growth and moral contamination could be unrelated," Pulp suggested. We all gave him a questioning look, even Nimbus, who at times could portray emotion using a specific arrangement of his sticks and stones. "Their simultaneous occurrence is indicative of a relationship. What I'm suggesting is we might be too hasty in declaring what that relationship is. One could have been created to counter the other."

"Too many trogs and an immoral epidemic. Both sound hazardous to me," Centaur declared.

"It's just a possibility. That's one of the advantages of being chaotic---I'm less likely to jump to conclusions. There is no right or wrong, black or white."

We continued to wait for the trog to return. And wait. And wait. Either the king was a significant distance away, or there was a heated discussion. Likely both.

The trog returned to his office half-an-hour later. He appeared stunned. "King Brick agrees with you. Dismissing accusations---even absurd ones---before examining them is self-deceptive. One of us will escort you to the surface and join you in your journeys, for 100 days or until he becomes confident in this deception you speak of."

"What if it takes longer...?" Centaur attempted to counter.

"You have 100 days to convince me. Yes, I have chosen myself to be that person. There is truth in your declaration of our proficiency. Someone leaving for a fraction of a year---even the general of the trog guard---shouldn't decrease efficiency, not enough to hinder the war effort. My name is Paint Southern Spine.

Please don't get me killed. I enjoy being a trog."

General Paint chose to dress in full battle armor. I looked naked standing next to him. The trogs that intercepted us were impressive---he was imposing: larger and more formidable, augmented brawn with tactical insight, a miniature tank on two legs.

He supplied us with plentiful weaponry and armor, the latter requiring a slight delay. Our superfluous height demanded specific construction. My companions were fitted with lightweight armor, to provide more movement than full battle gear and---possibly---a concession to their relatively weaker constitutions. Helmets were also modified, to provide better visibility. We were supplied with food rations and an assortment of trail supplements. Subterranean cuisine tended to be bland, conforming with the trogs' belief of non-adornment. We intended to trade for something tastier the first opportunity that presented itself. Some surface dwellers may even regard trog food as exotic.

The final item General Paint had to provision himself with before escorting us to the surface was a darkened visor. Trog eyes weren't accustomed to the sun's intensity. His eyes would adjust, but it would take time. It may not be possible for a trog to appear sporty, but General Paint came close.

Chapter 30

ABOVE

We spent the next four days circumnavigating a subterranean wilderness. General Paint apparently knew where he was going: he rarely paused to confirm a route---or take a break. The latter occurred when we---not he---were on the brink of collapse.

"You sure you know where you are going?" Centaur asked the trog, on numerous occasions. His response was consistent: a complete lack of acknowledgement. I understood his reaction. Did you ask a baker if he knew how to bake or a farmer if he could grow crops?

We had discussed our destination without giving too much away. There was much closer access to the surface, but then what? There was no road in the direction we intended to go, not even a narrow, winding trail. This was the most remote corner of Limbo. The trogs' bloated presence discouraged exploitation. Our options were limited to going under, or around. No one wished to backtrack three days.

Centaur's second most asked question was, "Are we safe?" He would have never questioned our abilities above ground, but we were blind down there---metaphorically speaking. We borrowed some of those glowworms for illumination. We didn't know what was around the next bend in a tunnel. What might be there. How many. Subaquans and albino apes were the tip of the subterranean iceberg. Every night as we settled into sleep General Paint would reminisce a battle. TROG LULLIBIES we called them. Centaur would never admit to be scared, but he was concerned. It was not only himself he had worry about it. Dinga could take care of herself, but irrelevant when one considered her to be a daughter, mishaps dispensing a harsher penalty.

That first glimpse of radiant illumination was met with a mixture of adulation and trepidation. It was a exhilarating to see sunlight again, even secondary---it had been so long it was more myth than memory---but it was also a shock to our psyche: the intensity, the precursor to the abandonment of our subterranean womb, the next leg in our journey beginning.

Once fully exposed it took us five minutes for our eyes to adjust enough to walk. Another five before we felt comfortable to travel.

The illumination wasn't the only onslaught. The intense colors made us feel like we had walked onto another world. We went from a linear spectrum to a three-dimensional palette. And there were equally complex textures: of mountains and trees, and sky. Movement. And sounds, not echoing, but layered: birds and flowing water, wind, creaking trees. And warmth. It was also multidimensional, and dynamic: the feel of the sun, and the wind. The contrast between exposure and shadows.

Centaur studied his map. "Where are we---exactly? Closer to Sterling than Silverton, but how close?"

"Fifty kays," the trog responded.

"Fifty kays of bushwhacking," Centaur mumbled.

"There was a trail along that creek." General Paint was referring to the creek at the base of the valley we overlooked.

"Was?"

"The trail likely still exists, but to what extent, I can't confirm. It's been five years since our cartographers have updated this region."

"There isn't a trail on this map."

"Many of the original trails have been abandoned. Their upkeep has been determined to exceed their benefit."

"With all the ore that is mined from the Platinum Mountains each year?"

"By the trogs," said Pulp. "Their efficiency has created a

monopoly."

"True," General Paint confirmed. "There are some small suppliers of ore, but no other conglomerate."

"Was it your intent to run the other miners off?" asked Dinga.

"It was our intent to be efficient. We welcome the solitude of the corollary."

General Paint was fascinated by all he saw: every tree, every bush, every squirrel, every bird. He was scout's second, directly behind me. Initially it was so he could see these wonders. Once we left the Positive Frontier, having a veteran warrior near the front would be invaluable.

Sleeping outdoors made General Paint...uneasy. He had always slept in a tightly enclosed cubicle. We erected a tent for him. That helped. How would he react when we left the close confines of mountains and forests? Some of the plains looked like they went on forever.

The rest of us slept outdoors, wishing to experience in full the scented, chill night breeze. Becoming accustomed to the stale air of the underground didn't mean we enjoyed it. We heard movement in the tent whenever an animal---cricket to wolf---made a sound. General Paint may have just been reacting to unfamiliarity, but some of the murmurs he made sounded more frightened than startled. He slept with his armor on. I have done so on occasion. He was going to wake up stiff in the morning.

The moon brightened the next day, like it did every day, but it was the first time for General Paint. He shrieked, then sliced through the tent to escape. "WHERE ARE THEY?!"

"It's just the sun," Dinga explained calmly. "It does that on its own. No one is attacking the camp. On the surface, morality is fairly consistent. We're still in the Positive Frontier."

General Paint looked back at the tent. "So sorry. Do you mind mending it for me?"

"You are just as capable as I," Dinga replied.

"You're a woman."

189

"And that makes me more capable---and your servant?"

"I didn't imply…. Trog society is very logical in its distribution of work. Men are warriors and laborers. Women do more delicate chores: food preparation, cleaning, and sewing."

"And your women accept this arrangement?"

"It is Gaea's desire for those most fit for a particular job to do it."

"How about I show you how, then you finish the job. Most Limboan's opinion of labor differs from yours. Remember, you are no longer in Trogdom."

"Gaea blesses the humble. I will learn from you."

After camp was broken down and the tent mended, mostly---there was a spot or two one could still see through---we finished our trek through the mountains. Most of it. We didn't reach the Northern Moguls until midway the following day. They were less dry than those southwest of the Platinum Mountains, resulting in more vegetation. The pines were speckled with aspens, and later both were replaced with cottonwoods. Small creeks raced through the stands, making the already pleasant scenery even more so with a more vibrant soundtrack.

General Paint refused to go anywhere near the water, even after seeing us enjoying washing off the dust and sweat we accumulated the past day. The surface was much dirtier than the underworld. He associated bodies of water larger than a wash basin with the subaquans. "Please get out," he pleaded with us. He literally shook from the unpleasantness of the situation.

"Close your eyes," Nimbus suggested. It worked, lessening, but not completely eliminating his anguish.

We were slightly more than halfway through the Moguls when darkness forced us to camp again. Centaur caught a fish for dinner to supplement the fungi. General Paint rushed off after getting a whiff of what reminded him of charred subaquan. Dinga accompanied him.

"Payback mustn't be as sweet in the Positive Frontier," Centaur remarked.

"We might want to bury what we don't eat," Pulp suggested. "I get nauseous when meat is cooked. It must be excruciating for General Paint, with his connection to it."

A quarter later Dinga returned with the trog. The odor was just a fraction of what it was, but still significant, as evidenced by General Paint's pained expression.

"I apologize for abandoning my post," he said. "I accept whatever disciplinary measures such action entails."

"None is necessary," said Centaur. "We should have been more sensitive to your aversions."

"You insult me, sir."

"Centaur's just trying to be accommodating, kind even," Dinga explained.

"Giving me special treatment is not a kindness. FRAILTY?! WEAKNESS?! IS THAT WHAT YOU THINK OF TROGS?! One day you shall see how fragile we are."

We didn't know how to respond. General Paint's tirade was going to escalate into violence. I was confident we could defend ourselves, but not without injury---the greatest harm being done to our relationship with the trogs.

As he had a habit of doing, Nimbus stepped in at the most opportune moment. "Maybe the stench filling your nostrils won't be as strong in Neutrality."

"Out of the mouths of babes," muttered General Paint softly after a moment of reflection. "Or in your case, twigs and gravel. I still don't believe an external agent can modify a trog's disposition, but sometimes individuals can be caught up in the moment. Only Gaea basks in perfection, but we can at least make the attempt. I will challenge my self-discipline."

The holes in the tent became a problem. After mending them the best he could General Paint would lie down for a few minutes, then jerk back up, being unsatisfied with his work. After improving upon the repair the sequence would start over again. He spent half the night becoming increasingly frustrated. Eventually he wore himself out. He was so exhausted in the morning he had trouble waking up. He apologized profusely for his delay, restating his diligence in self-improvement.

The next day we saw a kocra on the horizon. It was flying in tight circles. A young woman shrieked.

"WE MUST SAVE HER!" I demanded. I accelerated my pace, to a velocity that balanced my urgency, endurance, and encumbrance. My companions followed me in the manner their bodies and will allowed. General Paint may have had the shortest stride---excluding the golem---but he was practically on my heels.

The platinum blonde was petite. The ripped silver dress she wore would have been modest if it was in better repair. In the condition it was in it barely covered her.

Upon our approach the kocra screeched. It wasn't pleased that its meal was interrupted.

The young woman intensified her fearful exclamations upon seeing us. The kocra had enough. If flew off. After a couple of more exaggerated expressions and pained utterings, the woman covered her head with her hands and began to whimper.

"Oh, come on," said Nimbus. "Do you think anyone is going to be impressed by that bad acting?"

"The kocra almost had me," the woman said in a soft, girl's voice. "I would have been eaten if I wasn't rescued on the brink...."

"The only way the kocra was going to kill you was you choking on it while YOU ate IT."

"I couldn't eat a fly." Then in a more mature and serious voice she added, "Particularly one from the temple. The buzzing of its companions---kocra are never alone for long---would have become unbearable, almost as unbearable as these constrictions humans wear." The young woman became less encumbered, her clothes falling to the ground. The damsel no longer appeared so helpless and innocent. Our emotions associated with her changed again as her body elongated and mutated.

Dinga was flabbergasted, the rest of us not too far behind. "YOU'RE A DRAK!" We immediately went into defensive mode, scattering and raising shields and weapons. I sensed...amusement.

This creature wasn't completely void of ill intent, but it was seasoned with mischief, not destruction. I relaxed.

Nimbus introduced his FRIEND. "This is Lamprey Western Strait. As you see she is much more than she first appeared to be."

"I am definitely a complex lady."

"Even when you were human you were hardly a lady."

"I was more a woman than you were ever a man."

"Sadly, true."

"But perhaps the form you are in now is the most fitting of all."

For once, Nimbus was speechless. Knowing him as well as we did---likely better---she was taken aback by his out-of-character behavior. Something was wrong. "I am sorry," she continued. "There was a reason you remain in this form. You cannot transform into a drak anymore, can you?"

"Change is inevitable on Limbo. I'll eventually die and be re-created."

"You don't sound too happy about it." Lamprey paused as she pondered the ramifications of what she said. "You fear you won't be re-created into a drak."

"Has anyone before? Of those few who have died have any been re-created as a drak? Being on top of Limbo's evolutionary chain it's inevitable we bumble, stumble, and finally tumble."

"Why did you choose this form by the way? I didn't think you could transform at all. Is this a new ability?"

"It's a long story I don't care to go into---now---perhaps, never. Let's just say I wasn't given an option."

"If you're not currently a drak maybe you won't be subjected to the JUST ONCE A DRAK limitation."

"The longer I'm in this form the more I forget how it feels to be a drak. How can I return to drak form if I no longer feel like a drak?"

"What is a drak?" questioned Pulp. "The true essence of a drak? Or a gent? It can't be our size, because we didn't start out this large."

"Drak exude...confidence," suggested Centaur.

"Nothing seems to sway them," Hornet added. "Society or the environment."

"Will power," I stated. "They are strong believers in self, and their ability to accomplish."

"Are drak overachievers?" Dinga asked. "I'm not implying that their accomplishments are at the limit of the abilities. I'm referring to them being able to maximize their potential. They strive for perfection."

"They are the greatest entrepreneurs the galaxy has ever produced," said Pulp. "Gents are weakened---individually---by our need for companionship. But this sense of community has facilitated the formation of the Brotherhood, making us, compositely, stronger. A drak's solitary nature forces them to try harder, because all they have is themselves."

"What type of person lives underground?" asked General Paint, finally recovering from the shock of his insignificance. A general among trogs is still a trog. No one answered.

"You still playing the damsel in distress game?" Nimbus questioned. "You must be bored. You could join us---a day, or indefinitely."

"You MUST be losing your sense of drakhood if you wish to companion yourself with another of your kind."

"I could use some intellectual conversation." Nimbus turned to look at us. "No offense, but your inane banter---at times--- drives me crazy. Three dimensional thinking is so immature and tiresome."

"I believe it's time to triangulate," spoke Centaur. "If we need to backtrack I would rather do it now than after another 100 kays."

The blue sphere floated about a meter from the green. General Paint was amazed. "Your mission is more than just freeing maidens and finding treasure," he conjectured.

"We thought it wise to not speak so specifically in Trogdom. We couldn't afford to have the spheres confiscated."

"A delay, perhaps, but the spheres would have eventually

194

been returned. Claiming what wasn't ours wouldn't have promoted truth."

"You plan to reconstruct a portal?" asked Lamprey.

"For us to be successful, we must maintain discretion," Centaur responded. "Too many people already know about it, and it is barely a third complete."

"Given enough time we could send an entire army through," suggested General Paint. Unlikely, but I didn't have the verification and gumption to repudiate the statement.

"To do what?" asked Dinga. "It's only natural for those caged to want to escape, but does that give us the right to harm our captors? There was a reason we were imprisoned. Our sins are repaid---are in the process of being repaid. Do we wish to reopen those moral wounds?"

"I apologize. Maybe there is something to that Negative elem affecting me. I'm open to the possibility now."

Direction vectors were drawn on Centaur's map.

"The Twin Hills," spoke Nimbus.

"So we ARE to travel into the Negative Frontier," stated Pulp.

"But just barely," said Dinga.

"That's still hundreds of kays away," said Hornet.

"If only we had a faster means of transportation," I said.

"We could travel by ship."

"You really don't want me to come along, do you?" blurted Dinga.

"We need another means of transportation," stated Centaur

"Could we convince a herd of centaurs to carry us?" I suggested.

"I would rather carry you myself than ask them," said Centaur.

"You could ask Lamprey to take you," Nimbus suggested.

"You truly are non-draconian," spoke Lamprey, "to suggest another drak do anything."

"Would you?" asked Dinga sweetly.

"You would think that one that uses such tactics would be

195

immune to them. What would I agree to do if I was male? All right. I'll carry you to the Negative Frontier---the border of it. I won't invade the territory of a drak of a contradictory morality. There is one problem. I can only carry half of you. Unless Nimbus can return to drak form you'll either have to split up, or strong arm an additional drak."

Centaur smirked. "Is there a local market for such?"

"There is a drak a couple of days away that might be persuaded to join us---temporarily," spoke Nimbus.

"Tsk, tsk," murmured Lamprey. "To invade a second drak's privacy."

"I believe that little game you were playing with the kocra invaded our peace," said Nimbus.

"If we're going to Kenwood I'm going to need to return to human form. Maidens are better received than drak." Lamprey was human again. The torn clothes that had disappeared were back on her.

"You'll want to mend yourself," Nimbus suggested. "Freeing a maiden with torn clothes may be tantalizing, but someone from our own party doing so would be...inconvenient."

The silver dress mended itself, and its hemline lowered. "This is definitely constricting now," Lamprey declared.

"Then don't make it so tight," said Dinga. "Wear traveling clothes, not a cocktail dress."

Lamprey's dress draped now, instead of looking like it was painted on. "I may wish to alter it back when we reach Kenwood. I'm always willing to put up with a little discomfort to create discomfort for others."

Sterling was at the base of the Moguls. It was pristine and quiet. We rented four rooms in the village's lone inn. Few people traveled this far into the Frontier. The only other group in the inn was a married couple who kept to themselves. An hour after retiring for the evening the couple asked to move to a room farther away from us. The only sounds we were making was Pulp snoring---

gents caused a commotion even when sleeping---and Nimbus and Lamprey chatting. They sounded like they were having a slumber party. Drak didn't like each other's company? You wouldn't have been able to deduce it in the manner they were carrying along. It must have been easier to tolerate one another in non-drak form.

We were mildly offended by the couple's abandonment of us. Those living in the Frontier where usually open to differences--- by necessity. Being ordered as Sterling was it wasn't entirely surprising that some people would be uncomfortable with variances from the norm.

After eating an early breakfast in the inn's common room, we set off for Kenwood. As we left Sterling the moon was just beginning to brighten. We continued to follow Mercury Creek. The angle of light hitting it was perfect, reflecting off its surface, giving it the illusion of molten metal. We were determined to make it to Kenwood in one day. We barely did, the sun already dimming as we arrived at the city gates. Fifty-four kays was a considerable distance, even if it consisted of relatively flat, open terrain. We were so close to having this leg of our journey over, we pushed through our fatigue.

Chapter 31

KENWOOD

Kenwood was Limbo's third most populous city, exceeded only by Gulag and Rhinopolis. It was the MOST populous city in the Positive Frontier. The woods that surrounded the city were safe, even at night. Taking a romantic walk in the woods in the dark was quite common, so common in fact that if someone tripped over something in the forest, it was just as likely to be an embraced couple as a fallen log. Five kays from the city the lands bordering the road became manicured. We had been reintroduced to civilization, but gently.

Kenwood's walls were covered in ivy. The city looked as green as its surroundings. The western gate was still raised, although it was substantially past sundim now. A guard reclined on a sofa beside it. He wore a loose-fitting green robe without adornment. He appeared to be asleep.

Being witness to such a dereliction of duty created a fury within the trog. General Paint brought his scythe battle axe down with such a passion that it passed halfway through the sofa, a mere sim from the guard's head. He woke with a start. Before he could call for help or sound the alarm, one look from Lamprey froze him in place.

"You need to teach me that some time," said Dinga.

"I don't think I could. It's like typing: words forming with the placement of my fingers, but I couldn't tell you the order of the keys. When I want someone to do something they just do."

"I forgot mutational elem manipulation is innate."

"We won't harm you," Centaur reassured the guard. "Or the city. We aren't invaders. We seek permission to enter the city---peacefully---nothing else."

The guard looked at the trog, then past him. "No, there isn't a trog army---not yet," stated General Paint. "If you are a fair representative of the city's guard, one trog is all that's required to conquer Kenwood."

"We are weary travelers," Dinga declared.

"Not completely weary." Lamprey's dress was tight again, so tight she was on the verge of bursting out of it.

The guard's lower jaw dropped.

"Would you like to go for a walk?" she asked him.

He didn't respond, verbally, but when she walked off into the woods he followed her.

"Should we just walk in now?" Hornet asked.

"Maybe we should leave a coin or two," I suggested.

"Kenwood doesn't deserve to collect a protection tax," stated General Paint. He boldly walked through the gateway. We followed him.

"Are we going to see Lamprey again?" asked Dinga, concerned.

"She'll be back before we leave Kenwood. She's either losing the guard in the woods, or promoting a romantic liaison. Once a person is mutated into a drak many of their human desires wane, but she might view it as a psychological study."

"That's shameful," I said.

"Not really. He'll get something in return for his participation in the study. Her games are so chaotic I'm confident the next time she dies she'll be re-created in the South."

Kenwood was divided into four Quarters They were formed by the intersection of the Steel River and the Boulevard of Commerce, the road that connected the city's two gates. Clockwise from the northwest they were called the BRAWN, INTELLECT, SOUL, and BLOOD.

The Blood Quarter housed governmental agencies. The civic leaders liked to think they were the life blood of the city. Nearly everyone else believed they acted more like leeches. Most of the city's retail businesses were along the Boulevard of Commerce, more commonly called THE BOULEVARD. The Steel River was sheathed in a green belt. Canals dispersed the water, creating a lattice. They were utilized as often as streets, gondolas serving as taxis.

Vegetation varied. Cottonwoods were prominent along the river. Oaks and maples in the Brawn Quarter. Manicured shrubbery in the Blood. Pines, cedars, and firs in the Intellect, the tallest conifers competing with the 100 meter tall hill that occupied the center of the district. A dwarf forest was predominant in the Soul District, speckled with numerous pools, creeks, and rock gardens, a balanced mix of predetermined design and randomness.

Structures within each quarter were consistent with its

vegetation. The Brawn Quarter had small, uniform buildings tightly clustered together. The Blood, large, low-lying buildings with many wings, with considerable open space between them. The Intellect had narrow high-rises with clusters of single-story structures at their base. Cottages were dominant in the Soul Quarter, many constructed of natural materials in peculiar shapes.

We walked along The Boulevard, in the left corridor, designated for eastward travel. A low-lying blossoming wall separated the two directions of travel. Every intersection with one of the perpendicular avenues created a break in the wall, providing an opportunity to change direction. The Boulevard was alive with activity, in stark contrast to the sedate side streets. The canals complimented the grass and stone walkways. Each waterway was equal distant to its two adjacent avenues. A traveler never had to walk more than a block.

Being sufficiently provisioned, we window shopped as we walked past The Boulevard shops. Our itinerary consisted of finding an inn, then the drak that inhabited the city. Hail Springwood was his name. Having never visited Kenwood, Nimbus was as lost as us. He did suggest we stay in Teton Tower, a high-rise hotel in the Intellect Quarter. It was renowned, a place Hail mentioned to him on many occasions.

Traveling by gondola wasn't fast, but faster than walking--- barely. It took us 10 minutes to reach the Steel River. Teton Tower immediately came into view. The mountain-shaped building was near the base of Cranium Hill. It was 70 meters tall. Its windows were inset, giving them a cave-like appearance. The top of the building had faux snow and bighorn sheep. The gondola let us off meters from the cavernous entrance to the complex, the base being a grotto, refreshed with a cascade.

Two doormen greeted us. They attempted to take our packs. "You wouldn't want to lose that arm, now, would you?" General Paint inquired, smiling wickedly as he detached his axe from its leather sheath.

The doorman relayed an expression simultaneously sour and

laden with trepidation. "Follow me," he finally responded as he led us into the hotel. His nervousness was apparent, but he had the dignity and grace not to turn around to monitor his impending doom. The other doorman followed us, possibly concerned some of us might get lost, but more likely that we were all accounted for.

The interior of the hotel was more four-star hotel than rustic lodge. The one glaring difference: the walls, floor, and ceiling were embellished with the same artificial stone as the exterior. The man at the desk---clearly the manager from his demeanor---looked up at us as we entered. If he was shocked at our group's odd assortment he didn't show it. Living in the Frontier he must interact with such peculiarities daily.

"How many rooms do you wish?" he asked cordially.

"Three should be sufficient," Centaur answered.

"We have a larger bed for the gent, and a smaller one for the trog. I assume that they will room together."

"How did you know?" asked Dinga.

"Decades of repetition have strengthened my analysis of subtle nuances. Everyone falls into a pattern of mutual relationships. Do you wish to dine with us this evening? Our restaurant is below the penthouse. We can also bring supper to your rooms, if you wish."

Centaur looked at us for input before he spoke for us. Hornet yawned, assisting Centaur in his decision.

"You will find menus in your rooms," the manager continued. "Pull the cord when you're ready to order, or need assistance in any manner. Someone will come up to your room immediately. Promptness is guaranteed. How many nights do you plan to spend with us? One gold a night---per room---is our standard rate, with a minimum deposit of one night's stay."

Centaur nearly choked to death, but he did pay up, for just one night's lodging. In the slow, monotonous, precise manner he did so it was like he was cutting away his own flesh and handing it to the manager.

"Checkout is midday. If you leave anything behind you may find it again at 212 North Boulevard. The second hand store sells only quality merchandise. If you don't find what you're looking for it isn't worth buying---especially not a second time." The manager handed us our keys. All the rooms were all on the 14th floor.

We were directed to one of the two elevators. One of the doormen raised the gate for us. After stepping in, he dropped it back into place. Both doormen pulled on the two ropes beside the elevator. In a jerking motion we were lifted off the lobby floor. We rose above the lobby's ceiling to the second floor. Visible were just doors and a foyer. Twelve more stories we climbed in surprisingly rapid and smooth fashion, after that initial rocky start. At the 14th floor the elevator stopped. We had to lift the gate ourselves. Being properly lubricated, it lifted easily. We rushed out, not wanting to be in the elevator during its inevitable free-fall we all predicted.

Dinga scanned the foyer.

"What are you looking for?" I asked her.

"The bathroom."

Hornet smiled.

"A bath is on the itinerary, but I have more urgent concerns."

"You may wish to check your room before you begin wandering," suggested Nimbus.

We did, and were pleasantly surprised. There were only four rooms on each floor due to the size of each room. In addition to a bedroom with a drak-size bed, there was a sitting room overlooking Kenwood, and a fully functioning bathroom: running water---hot and cold. The tub was big enough for a family. The toilet had its own room. It too had water---a first for me on Limbo.

"Where do you think the water comes from?" I asked Centaur.

"A cistern on the roof, or maybe it's pumped up. A gold is lot to spend for a room, but at least it doesn't all go into someone's pocket. It must be very expensive to maintain this hotel."

After washing up the others joined Centaur and me in our room. We ordered a feast, not in quantity, but in price. "Maybe we can drop by the bounty office before we leave Kenwood to recoup some of this," Centaur commented.

"General Paint's people provided us with enough gold to complete this leg of our mission," said Dinga. "Let's try to enjoy ourselves. I imagine we won't have such luxury in the Negative Frontier."

It was quite late when we completed our meal. We agreed our search for Hail Springwood could wait another day. Not sleepy enough to go to bed, I looked down at the city lights below me. The canals and the Steel River glistened from the reflections off them. The Boulevard was still active. I could hear the revelers, or was that my imagination? Centaur had already gone to bed, providing me solitude.

What did it really mean to be an Octagonal Knight? What had I accomplished? Should I even be trying to free myself and my companions from Limbo? If Octagonal Knights are Neutral, should I be going to the Negative Frontier? Having already gone West I'm almost forced to go East, aren't I? I may have the authority to go on a destructive pilgrimage to balance the moralities, but will it really matter, if who---or what---I kill is re-created? Should I encourage them to repent first? Without redemption additional deaths will likely cause their dispositions to become more extreme.

My thoughts were interrupted by a shape in the sky. It was there, but not completely, like it was invisible, or trying to be. My Octagonal senses were attempting to de-cloak it, but they weren't completely successful. It was coming towards me. As I contemplated whether to back into the room or prepare my counterattack its wings angled up and in. Silently it landed on the penthouse roof.

I burst out into the 14th floor foyer, and up the stairwell beside the elevators. The stairs terminated at the 19th floor, at the entrance to the restaurant. A transparent stairway materialized beyond the wall beside me---my heightened Octagonal senses assisting me. I searched the wall and found a spot that I was able to push in. The wall rose. I followed the stairs up one more flight.

I entered a room that occupied the entire 20th floor. Moonlight entered through a large hole in the ceiling. There was no visible means of reaching the aperture 10 meters above me. Large cushions were scattered throughout the penthouse. A sink, toilet, and tub were at one end of the room. I walked across the floor, having to weave around the cushions that were nearly as large as I. My goal was to look through the opening, once I was directly below it.

SOMETHING MOVED! It was on the floor. Was it a rat, or a cat? A dog? Looking more closely I realized the creature that appeared to be less than a meter long, was actually larger: an optical illusion confusing my depth perception. The floor was transparent, and what I had seen was a person in the restaurant below. I looked more closely. There were actually three people in the restaurant. Being as late as it was they were probably servers cleaning up. Looking even more closely I saw that they were setting the tables for breakfast.

I heard a soft thud behind me, so soft that someone without Octagonal senses wouldn't have heard it. I spun around as I drew my sword. A gray drak faced me. It was 10 meters long, from snout to tail---small for its kind. It looked at me inquisitively. "I don't believe I've heard of an Octagonal Knight breaking the law so severely," it said in a deep voice, hollow, like it was whispering.

"I saw a shape outside my window."

"And you came to investigate. How noble. Or perhaps it was just curiosity."

"You wouldn't be Hail Springwood, would you?"

"I have many names. I prefer to be called Professor Springwood." The drak transformed into a middle aged man with a salt-and-pepper beard. He wore a gray suit with steel cufflinks. He had rings---also steel---on all ten of his fingers."

"My friends and I have need of your assistance. Nimbus said we would find you in Kenwood."

At the mention of Nimbus, Professor Springwood's confident, pleasant expression soured. "The next time you see Nimbus...."

"I'll take you to see him immediately, if you wish. He is in this building."

"Another drak is not only in Kenwood, but is staying in MY hotel."

"Actually there are three of you in Kenwood at the moment. Lamprey is also in the city---at least in the general vicinity."

"There hasn't been another drak in Kenwood in 15 years. Now there are supposedly two. It's been well documented that a drak's territory exceeds a million hectares. I'm already beginning to feel claustrophobic."

"You live in a city with over 50,000 inhabitants."

"True, but you're talking about 50,000 humans, plus a few dozen assorted mutes. You wouldn't feel closed-in if there were 50,000 ants surrounding you."

"I would feel much worst if 50,000 ants surrounded me."

"Let's talk to Nimbus. After I convince him he needs to leave---immediately---he can relay that to Lamprey. Where is he? In the lobby? I didn't see him on the roof."

"He's with us on the 14th floor. He's in Pulp and General Paint's room. They are a gent and a trog. We thought he would be more comfortable with mutes."

"A gent and a trog are also in my hotel and I wasn't aware of it? I spend too much time on The Boulevard solving crimes. I need to get my own place in order. Nimbus must have bought a transformation stone. He doesn't have the ability to transform himself. He must have had a good reason to do so. Those innately gifted shun penta."

We took the elevator down to the 14th floor. Hail Springwood didn't knock. The door to Nimbus's room opened without any visible means of assistance. The drak turned golem looked up at Professor Springwood. He looked embarrassed.

"A GOLEM?!" Hail bellowed. "Why not chose a tailless monkey or a flightless bird?" Before Nimbus could explain, Hail hypothesized part of his story. "It wasn't intentional, was it? Either you turned yourself into a golem by mistake, or someone else did. Who would have been powerful enough to do so, and to sustain it? Our resistance to pental manipulation makes it nearly impossible for something like this to happen."

After recovering from his embarrassment, Nimbus told his tale. Hail couldn't believe the audacity of the Wizard. At least the man got what he deserved.

"So you need my help in this mission of yours? The sooner the better to find the remaining pieces of the portal. You probably shouldn't be telling me this, but I see that you didn't have any choice. You fear others might also be seeking the spheres, or you? I'm surprised you haven't met more resistance from the Wizards. Then again, they're likely too conceited to be receptive of the assistance you could offer them. Using what they learned on Limbo they might be able to conquer the galaxy, if they had some means to enter it. I'll help you, but only to the boundary of the Negative Frontier. Nobility runs through my veins---not stupidity. The only way to achieve mutual survival is for us drak to leave each other alone. If I enter an unfriendly drak's territory we'll do more than just talk about it. Time to meet the rest of your party. I may not like spending too much time with others of my own kind, but I enjoy talking to humans."

Dinga was particularly interested in Hail. Nimbus didn't like to talk about the good old days, as he called his life as a drak, and Lamprey was preoccupied with her own agenda. "When you transform into a human do your molecules bunch together, shrinking you? If they did, wouldn't you become very dense, too dense for this floor to support you?"

"You are talking to the right drak. Those who can manipulate penta innately do so without much thought. Not being the type of person who likes to take a passive role I have chosen to study these instinctive manipulations. There are two kinds of matter: active and passive. Active matter performs specific functions, and is of unique composition. Passive matter is filler. It resides between the atoms of active matter. Think of it like air in packaging to increase its rigidity for shipping. Or like a layer of fat between organs and skin. Our size is determined by the quantity of passive matter in our bodies. When I transform from a drak to a human my molecules reconfigure their connections, changing my shape. Most of the passive matter in my body is released, shrinking me."

"Where does it go?"

"Into the air. Each atom of passive matter is extremely small. They rapidly dissipate into their surroundings."

"So dust I pick up on the bottom of my shoes, or breathe in, may have been part of you?"

"Yes...and no. The air we breathe we don't retain long enough to call it our own. Think of passive matter as soil beneath your feet, or energy from the sun warming you. Active matter is who we are, but that isn't entirely true. If anyone can accurately analyze the soul, that would be the true breakthrough."

"Shouldn't there have been a pile of dust in your penthouse, then?" I asked.

"Recently released passive matter can pass through more stable matter---AROUND would be the more accurate way of describing it. When I transformed into a human the majority of my excess passive matter passed through the walls of Teton Tower into the sky. Most of it will eventually settle to the ground. I have often wondered if enough passive matter was released at one time would I be able to seed clouds, causing it to rain. Too little time. Too many experiments.

"I must depart. I need to put my hotel in order before I accompany you. And I need to eat before undertaking such an extensive flight."

"You could eat with us," Dinga suggested, hoping to gain a few more minutes of Professor Springwood's time.

"I could acquire the nutrients I needed eating in human form, but the psychological satisfaction of a draconian hunt wouldn't be achieved. Every two or three weeks I must eat this way."

Pulp was stunned. "You hunt? You slaughter animals, consuming them in a feral blood lust?"

"Not exactly. Not anymore. I transform soy beans into the shape of sheep. I animate them, visually and vocally."

"Tofu porn for drak," I commented, wryly.

"I would appreciate you finding Lamprey by the time I return. I felt much better---for myself and for my city---when I learned Nimbus was a golem. I'll feel even better knowing not a single drak was loose."

Chapter 32

DRAK FLIGHT

The nine of us congregated to the east of Kenwood, in a clearing between the east gate and the forest. Lamprey and Hail transformed back into draks. I tried not to think about the millions of passive atoms that clustered together to form the large beasts. Lamprey, being nearly twice the size of Hail, carried Pulp, Dinga, Hornet, and me. She didn't share the details of her adventures. She appeared to be extremely pleased with herself. Hail carried Centaur, General Paint, and Nimbus. We were strapped to the drak, neither to the riders' or the mounts' liking, but it was necessary.

A drak's mass---made even greater with us on their backs--- required them to glide, whenever possible, to conserve energy. But first they had to climb into the air stream to take advantage of it. I was nearly ripped in two as the harness around my waist tightened as Lamprey pushed off with her legs as her wings flapped profusely. We rose swiftly. Drak don't wish to waste that much energy just hovering. Three kays up the ride became much smoother. The persistent flopping stopped. Lamprey extended her wings, slightly tilted. We headed eastward. Every few minutes she had to flap for a few strokes to gain the slight altitude she lost. The 1200 kay flight took four hours. After our initial trepidation the journey became relaxing---that gentle rocking mimicking a cradle. If we weren't 3000 meters above the ground we may have considered sleeping. The flight was interrupted just once, the penalty of a full bladder being dire for the rider and the mount.

The thrill of flying---the rush of air, the scenery--- compensated for a fear of heights. The one exception was flying over the Northern Spine. We were on a collision course with one of its peaks, but at the last instant the air stream carried us over, with a couple of powerful flaps added just in case. A deep chuckle vibrated below me.

After crossing the mountains we began our descent. As we approached the Negative Frontier I became more unsettled, my skin crawling with invisible insects. It was noticeable when we crossed from Neutrality into the Positive Frontier too, but the sensation was mild---neither pleasant nor unpleasant---just recognizable. Lamprey must have also felt it because she became tense, resulting in the turbulence of landing being more uncomfortable for her passengers. Her rigidity lessened the effectiveness of her intrinsic shock absorbers.

As we glided closer to the ground we decelerated, the heavier air creating stronger resistance. Twenty meters from the ground the drak raised their wings, slowing them considerably. Prior to landing they lowered their legs, slowing them even more. Gravity won in the end. We un-strapped ourselves from our transports, then wished them well.

"You're always welcome at Kenwood," spoke Hail Springwood. "A ten percent discount at Teton Tower---if you come alone." Inferring, without tagalong drak. He pushed off, becoming just a spec in the sky---anonymously innocuous.

Centaur turned to Lamprey. "Are you going to play fair maiden to some Neutral folk before you head home?"

"Gaea, no. Neutrals are less noble than Positives. If I was to play helpless and frightened here I might freeze---or sweat---my tail off before I'm rescued. Good day." Lamprey also flew off, leaving us much less defended.

We looked to the east. It was bleak. An occasional tuft of grass invaded the cracked earth, the contrast rendering our surroundings even more destitute.

"Is there a city nearby?" asked Centaur. "It might be a good idea to rest up before we tackle the Negative Frontier." He spread out his map.

"It looks like Blowing Sand is a good size town," I said. "But it isn't in the direction we need to travel."

"And it's many kays into the Negative Frontier," Hornet added. "We won't get much sleep there."

"We just need to start walking," Nimbus suggested. "The more we delay, the more hesitant we'll become. The sooner we reach the Twin Hills the sooner we'll complete our mission."

"Why begin so late in the day?" asked Dinga. "How far can we go in an hour? Or do you expect us to travel in the dark? Won't that be too dangerous---here?"

"What do you guys think?" Centaur asked Pulp and General Paint. "Being of contrary morality, you two will be most affected once we cross into the Negative Frontier."

"I'd rather get on with it," said Pulp. "My emotions are mixed. I either want to flee from Negativity immediately, or to attack it. Fleeing or attacking, neither can occur unless we start walking."

"I believe the effects of the immoral elem have diminished in me," said General Paint. "I now realize the trogs HAVE been subjected to external influences. I should return to Trogdom so we may seal the corruption that permeates our kingdom. But I'm also committed to this campaign. To free me of this obligation we must complete our mission."

"Your first duty is to your people," Centaur insisted.

"Even if my people still respect me after being derelict in my duty, I won't. I am also a member of THIS company. Let's finish what we set out to do. General Centaur, we are in your hands."

"Bows out and arrows ready. Scouts and procs: undivided

attention. We shall proceed with a steady and determined gait. We'll break every half-hour, to retain our vigilance. More for our mental and emotional wellbeing---I fear---than from being physically tired. Share---immediately---any indication of danger--- be it an inkling, intuition, or a feeling."

Minutes into the hike we passed into the Negative Frontier. There wasn't a sign, a fence, or a boundary marker---we just knew. We weren't the only ones aware. Insects, both crawling and flying, turned around when they came to the virtual border between Neutrality and Negativity. How bad was it going to be if insects didn't want to go?

The sun dimmed about the time we thought it would. The moon was bright enough in the open for us to make our way. I glanced backward. A dusty silhouette of the Northern Spine was still visible. The other three directions retained their barrenness, the Twin Hills not yet perceptible.

"I SEE SOMETHING!" I informed my companions. I wasn't concerned someone—or thing---might hear me. We were obvious to anything within 10---20---kays. We were that exposed. My companions stopped, visually investigating the direction I was pointing. There were three of them. They were big, not as big as a drak, but at least twice the size of Pulp. They walked on four legs. More relevant, they were heading our way.

"Infantry: to the front, with shields raised. Artillery: to the back." Centaur spoke crisply, but with tension in his voice. Nimbus meandered away from us, back, and slightly eschew. His goal: to get a good view of the action without being part of it. "Don't fire until they come close enough to be hit. We don't want them to be chased off to return when we are less prepared."

They were now within 200 meters, still too far away to be hit with arrows, but close enough to distinguish details. They were feline, seven meters long, a third of that tail. They spun around, snapping their tails like whips. Something the size of a small dagger struck my leg, penetrating the metallic mesh. I toppled. My companions had similar misfortune. They lay in a pile, with spikes protruding from them, like a shower of shrapnel had fallen. A second spike hit me, this time safely deflecting off my Octagonal armor. We should have launched our arrows before they attacked---even if most of them went astray. How were we to know their attack included an indiscriminate aerial barrage? They charged. They not only had an injured opponent, but one that was also in shock. They were determined to take advantage of our fleeting inability to act.

Hornet appeared to be the only one uninjured. He launched an arrow. It had a perfect trajectory, striking a feline. The cat toppled, flipping over chaotically as its movement and the arrow's fought for control. A second arrow was launched before the other two cats reached him, but this time its intended target leaped into the air. Bat-like flaps of skin beneath its forelimbs extended its flight. It fell softly on all fours to our right. The third cat leaped, somehow missing Hornet, badly---the combination of Gaea's Grace and his defensive ring saving him. It landed awkwardly behind him.

Those temporarily immobilized began to stir. I leapt to their assistance. As I put weight on my injured leg I crumbled in agony. The spike not only penetrated my flesh, it also shattered my femur. General Paint was first to recover. Being a small target, relative to the rest of us, the daggers had missed him. Pulp wasn't as fortunate. The gent had been struck twice. He fell hard, on top of the trog, knocking the wind out of him.

General Paint picked up his scythe battle axe, striking at the feline that had overshot Hornet. Missing its prey had surprised it so severely it hadn't yet made its second attack. The axe tore through a wing-flap as it struck the creature's flank. It tumbled with a thud. As it picked itself back up General Paint swung at it again, this time directed at its opposite flank. It slumped awkwardly to the ground. Before it could get back up the trog chopped it in two like it was splitting a log. General Paint was in such a berserking fervor that he was only aware of the opponent in front of him. The last living feline leaped at him, its wing-flaps extending its flight to 30 meters. He was pinned to the ground on his stomach. The cat nuzzled his way between the General's helmet and armor, attempting to gnaw his neck.

Something struck the cat from behind. Two small hammers beat at it until it lay unconscious and bloodied. Nimbus? Hornet pulled the feline carcass off the trog. General Paint was badly bruised, but didn't have any lacerations or broken bones. "Couldn't you have knocked the thing off me instead of into me," he said as he pushed himself up. "First a 200 kilo gent falls on me, then a 200 kilo flying fleabag. Few things fell on me in the underworld."

"So, your view was better up close?" spoke Hornet to the golem.

"I don't know what got into me," Nimbus responded. "It was like some instinct took over."

"Maybe you still have some drak in you after all," I uttered from my prone position where I had fallen.

We took inventory of our injuries. Dinga administered the proper tonics. Within the hour most of our injuries were healed, including my leg. As we recovered many beasts investigated us, none of them staying long. To kill the things we did made us too dangerous of an adversary.

We chose to sleep the remainder of the night so we might better recover---those of us who could sleep through the unnerving sounds of the Negative Frontier. They weren't that different from those heard in Neutrality or in the Positive Frontier. There was a slight edge to them: emotional moans and whimpers, residual travesties, perpetual aches so enduring they become isolated in the background. Dingy wallpaper. Cracked mortar. We slept in shifts---attempted to---I don't think any of us got much sleep. To not keep a watch in the Negative Frontier would have been suicide. The night was uneventful---externally.

Chapter 33

MERCENARIES

Another two nights---and three days---in the barren wilds, on the fringe of the Negative Frontier. The fringe of the Negative Frontier. How bleak was it going to be in the heart of the Negative Frontier? And how dangerous? We barely survived the attack of three cats. I enjoyed challenges, but our mission was becoming hopeless. I looked up at the sky. The sun was there somewhere, behind the haze. What was causing it? The dust? Possibly, but it was more than that. Did morality affect the weather? How could it? Maybe it was just our perception of it. I don't think I have ever been so simultaneously on edge and depressed. I believed certain types of people clustered together due to common interests, but if I was bombarded with this malaise every day it would be difficult to not have a sour disposition. Nature or nurture?

The Twin Hills had been visible since our lunch break. Another hour of walking perhaps. We had picked up the pace, the change of scenery providing renewed energy.

Will we have the persistence to reconstruct the portal? I don't know. We were on the precipice of giving up, with not even half of the pieces collected.

Many minutes later, Hornet enthusiastically bellowed, "I SEE A ROAD!" Followed by a less enthusiastic, "I think." It was so murky at times shapes became indistinguishable: bushes becoming men, clouds becoming mountains. It was definitely a road, but which way was Quantum, the Twin Hills' only---human---settlement?

Centaur looked at his map. "The only road within a hundred

214

kays connects Quantum and Blowing Sand. Assuming we're still west of the Twin Hills...."

"With this haze there's no guarantee," I interjected.

"...we head that way." Centaur pointed to the left.

We were still west of the Twin Hills. My Octagonal senses were able to probe through enough of the haze to tell me that. What I needed was them to tell me---exactly---where the next sphere was. The pull their mutual attraction created provided their general direction, and their relative proximity, but no details. Why couldn't we go directly from point A to point B? Why did everything we do have to be so convoluted? Why did it have to be so difficult?

The trail---the single track we followed wasn't wide enough to be considered a road---began to climb---steeply. We had finally reached the Twin Hills. After all that build-up they just appeared---enormous mounds of earth and sporadic vegetation at the perimeter of the haze. And there were more than two of them---many more.

The trail climbed a mound at an angle. Was it going to completely circle this hill before it reached the top? It didn't. After a hundred meters it turned, nearly on top of itself. Switchbacks? I hate switchbacks. "You sure we're heading the right way?"

"The map only showed one road," Centaur answered. "And it went to Quantum."

Up we went, seven switchbacks. We were drenched by the time we reached the top. It wasn't just the excursion, but also the heat, during the warmest part of the day, in one of the warmest regions of Limbo. We had been through so much, and a climb is what almost killed us. Armor was designed to diminish an attack, not conquer a mountain.

Quantum consisted of two dozen stucco buildings strung out loosely, without streets to corral them. Our arrival received a mixed response. Half the village welcomed us: well-armored visitors meant added safety for the duration of our stay. The other half felt dread: arms and armor begetting arms and armor, their isolated universe being overrun by people itching to fight. If so many of them wanted peace and solitude why live in the Negative Frontier?

"Is there a pub here?" Centaur asked. None of the buildings were marked. Through trial and error we would have eventually found one---if one existed---but it was more sociable to ask. We didn't intend to make permanent relationships, but brief, temporary ones could be extremely beneficial.

A man concealed in hair and soot answered. "Parched from climbing the hill? Helps sell beer, but thins the herd. You got a place to stay?"

"Not yet. Is there an inn you would recommend?"

"No inns up here. But I'll rent you my house. I spend more time in the pub."

"We don't have a lot of money."

"A couple of silvers, perhaps?" The man must have thought Centaur's pondering was a negation. He quickly counteroffered with, "A silver, five?"

"Where would you stay?" asked Dinga.

"The pub. Most nights I don't make it home anyway. It's not wise to stumble in the dark, not on top of a hill. A silver, two?"

"Agreed. Now, where is this pub?"

The man pointed to a ten-meter square building 50 meters away. It looked like all the other buildings. There were some city ordinances that limited signage, to protect aesthetics, but this was taking it to the extreme.

"You have an aversion to signs?" I asked.

"Kind of a waste of time when you know where everything is?" Not everyone, but asking did create a business opportunity for someone, albeit a small one.

"And your house?" Centaur asked.

The door of the building beside us was unlatched, then pushed in. The HOME was a single room, 10 square meters of squalor, with a bed, dirtier than the earth floor, which was barely visible beneath discarded bottles and dilapidated strips of cloth and fragments of metal.

"You have quite a collection," I commented.

"Bits of this and that I collected on the battlefields."

"Battlefields?"

"I wait until the combatants are safely disengaged. It's best when they eliminate one another, but I settle for a one-sided eradication. I usually pass when a conflict ends prematurely. Spoils and companion's possessions are retrieved sporadically, over many days, often violently."

"And when there is a victor?"

"They're removed immediately. Celebrations follow, but rarely on the battlefield. Reveling is less enjoyable when there is still work to be done."

"Who is fighting?" asked Centaur.

Our landlord looked confused. "The hobs and gobs, of course. Isn't that why you're here? Why would someone come to Quantum unless it was to profit from the war?"

"Quantum has no other industry?"

"Why does it need any?"

"What happens when the war ends?"

"The hobs and gobs have been fighting for 15 years."

"All wars end."

"Not this one. The sides are balanced."

"What's the dispute?" I asked.

"No one remembers."

"So they're just fighting for the sake of fighting?" asked Pulp. "That's taking Order to the extreme."

"If someone did something to you, wouldn't you want to do something back to them?"

"Not if it harmed me."

"There are reasons they fight, they just keep changing. There's this purple diamond...."

"An amethyst?" Dinga assisted.

"Yeah, that's what some people are calling it. That's what they're now fighting over. They haven't been fond of pretty things before, but all it takes is one side wanting it for the other side to want it more."

217

"What's the shape of this amethyst?" asked Hornet. "Is it round, like a pearl?"

"Possibly. All I heard is it's large and shiny."

Centaur placed our rent in our landlord's hand and began to shoo him without appearing to do so. "Thank you so much for allowing us to borrow your home, and for the information."

"If you're not here to profit from the war...?" Before he could finish his question he was escorted the rest of the way out, and the door shut behind him.

"We may not have to go to the pub after all," I stated.

"There are more details that need to be divulged, but it is a start."

"Why doesn't this make you happy?"

"Learning we have to fight our way through two armies?"

Dinga began moving things and picking up debris.

"What are you doing?"

"Tidying up."

"We're only going to be here one night." He turned towards the others. "What's gotten into her?"

Pulp smiled. "We'll find out in two months."

"Now, everybody OUT." Dinga dropped her hands and waved them like she had a broom.

"Apparently, we have become the clutter," I remarked.

"We might as well head to the pub," said Centaur as he led the charge out.

Half of Quantum must have been in that 100 square meter building. There was a bar---and a lot of tables and chairs. They were so tightly clustered we had difficulty passing through them.

"Maybe just one of us needs to work his way to the bartender?" I suggested.

"Or we could just skip it?" Hornet countered.

"No, we definitely need to drink," Centaur insisted.

"Would that be wise, considering this crowd?"

"I don't mean we need to get drunk. We need to appear sociable in order for the locals to open up to us. And that means doing what they're doing."

"Not everything, I hope." Hornet was referring to the third of the patrons that were either passed out, incoherent, or both. One had a stream of something vile coming out of him. And perhaps not from just his mouth.

"General Paint, would you mind doing us the honor? If you were barreling into me I would certainly get out of your way."

"Trogs don't drink."

"I thought...."

"Stereotypes of fairytales? Drunkenness isn't very orderly." Centaur turned to Pulp.

"No, drinking alcoholic beverages doesn't offend me. It just isn't required to put me in a good mood. Chaotics are able to create their own entertainment. I'll need some money."

"Chaotics don't use money?"

"I don't. I've been living off the land since I moved to the Copper Forest. The environment and the arbols provided all I needed. You think a couple of gold coins will be enough?"

Centaur sighed. "I better go myself."

"No one asked me," commented Nimbus, quietly, without emotion.

"Where did you come from?"

"A half-a-step beyond your perception."

Centaur grumbled as he weaved his way towards the bar.

"Shall we find us a table?" I suggested. Scanning the room, it became apparent the question wasn't rhetorical. "Here we are." Gravity had finally triumphed, relocating two comatose men draped across a table to the floor. We were short two chairs, prompting the trog to acquire two more from patrons not cognizant enough to appreciate them.

Centaur brought four mugs to the table. "You said drinking didn't bother you," he said to Pulp as he set one of them down in front of the gent. "It will look suspicious if too few of us are drinking."

"You think someone will notice?" I said as I scanned the room again.

From the conglomeration of scattered conversations we learned that the gobs had the numerical advantage, but they were smaller, about the height of a trog, but much scrawnier. They had brown, weathered, leathery skin, yellow eyes, and pointy ears. They were cowards, but fought well in large groups. Hobs were our height. They had gray, short-hair hides, red eyes, and walked with a stooped gait. Their long arms dragged on the ground. They weren't bright, but they were fearless fighters. Both races wore a chaotic mix of tattered rags and skins. The latter made from their fallen foes.

"I'm assuming hobs and gobs are both descended from goblins," Hornet commented. "I've heard stories about them, but haven't actually seen one. They were the first mutants, weren't they?"

"Goblin was a term the first inhabitants used to describe anyone who was mutated," Pulp answered. "Some of the mutations were so minor we wouldn't notice them today."

"So there aren't any true goblins, a specific race?"

"It's more a general term, like mute...or demon. Today, some mutant races are more likely to be called goblins than others. It would be very disrespect to refer to a gent as a goblin."

"Or a drak," Nimbus quietly added.

"More comical," spoke General Paint.

"I didn't think trogs had a sense of humor," I said.

"But we are aware of it."

"Why don't the hobs and gobs form a pact?" asked Hornet. "Together they'll be able to not only thoroughly terrorize the Twin Hills, but the entire region."

I answered. "Mutants are like athletes. It's more enjoyable to compete against the best, than become their allies."

"It just seems to me they can accomplish more---a lot more---together than as adversaries."

"Don't even suggest such a thing," said Centaur. "If the nastiest of the nasties ever came together it wouldn't be safe to leave a city. Towns and villages would become ruins. Commerce as we know it would end."

Arms and armor were supplied to both sides. It was a seller's market, resulting in the quality being substantially inferior to the price. Money could be made if you were willing to dance with the devil---two devils. New arms and amour were brought to the region, but more was recycled---a more dangerous vocation, but more lucrative.

Our reconnaissance became less passive. Centaur began to question the pub's patrons about the purple diamond. Nothing lubricates conversation better than another round. It didn't even have to be a very expensive lubrication, after being primed the entire afternoon.

"The amy-thirst diamond exists. I saw it once---from a distance. Something like that you don't want to get too close to. It was in the Quad Depression. I shouldn't have gone that far into the hills, but there were rumors of great treasure there, including the diamond. You find just scraps on the fringes. It was up high, on something like a table."

"Like it was put on display?" Centaur questioned. "Why would someone do that? Something so valuable exposed like that?" Pulp looked concerned. "What is it?"

"Lord Hide lives in the Quad Depression---the last time I visited him."

"A gent?"

"You visit Negative gents?" I asked.

"They are my brothers and sisters."

"There are Negative women?" asked Hornet.

"You've never been married," Centaur commented.

"It's sexist to believe women aren't capable of being as despicable as men," Pulp stated.

"You have also been married?" asked Hornet.

"Let's just say I would have lived a less interesting life on Limbo if one such woman hadn't entered my life."

"You believe Lord Hide is using the amethyst sphere as an incentive---or bait?"

"The only time he isn't looking for a fight is when he's

already in one. He not only chooses to participate in altercations, he enjoys watching them: he's a voyeur. He's lazy---the shabby rags he wears being the most blatant evidence of that. He takes perverse pleasure in watching people kill one another, the more violent and bloody the better. You remember your friend Thumbringer? He had a run in with Lord Tick. Lord Hide practically drooled---literally drooled---as Thumbringer was getting squashed."

"It appeared that Thumbringer recovered," Hornet commented.

"Not only recovered, but won. There was some elemental manipulation involved, but considering the advantages Lord Tick had over Thumbringer, it was a fair fight."

"Lord Tick mustn't have taken the defeat very well," I said. "Gents aren't used to losing."

"Lord Tick is the smallest gent, about halfway between your height and mine. He was accustomed to disappointment, which made him remarkably disagreeable, and always looking for a fight."

"So, let me get this right," General Paint spoke up. "If we fight our way through an army of gobs, then an army of hobs, we'll still have to fight a gent with a bad temperament and bloodlust? You wouldn't mind me returning to Trogdom to bring an army of my own?"

"That wouldn't be too bad of an idea," spoke Nimbus, with less than half the volume as the trog. If there hadn't been dead silence after General Paint's suggestion, we may not have been able to hear him over the din of the pub. It puzzled me how Nimbus was able to think with a stone brain. Apparently, not always. I wasn't the only one that stared at him like he was crazy. "No, not a trog army, but one much closer," he explained. "There's a race of mercenaries that live north of the Northwoods: sumopotts. You'll have to pay them something, but they'll work cheaply. They'll use any excuse to fight. They're very loyal. You won't have to worry about them changing sides on you."

"Even if we pay them to what amounts to minimum wage on Limbo," commented Centaur, "we couldn't afford the size of

222

army we'll need."

"The sumopotts will work on a promissory note. I believe Hail is good for it."

"And Hail doesn't have a problem with you volunteering his money?"

"He'll get something of equal value in return."

"And what will that be?"

"I can't think of everything. You're creative. You'll think of something. You'll likely earn some money one way or another before we see Hail again."

"I've noticed you say YOU instead of US," Hornet commented.

"Drak perceive autonomously."

"You're no longer a drak.... My intention wasn't to belittle. What I mean is you're no longer constrained to act in a particular manner. Being part of a group no longer marginizes your supremacy."

"I'm still a drak---even those times when I forget."

"During one of those times you are welcome to join us," said Centaur.

"Are we done here?" asked General Paint.

"All this sentimentality getting to you?" asked Pulp.

"Trogs are very sentimental, in a very reserved manner. Loyalty, honor, order makes us very emotional. But public displays are Chaotic. As are dozens of people speaking simultaneously, the catalyst for my desire to depart."

Dinga's clothing, including articles specifically female, were spread out on rocks adjacent to the home we rented. They looked like they were wet, but with that warm, dry wind whipping at them it wouldn't take long for them to desiccate.

She greeted us at the door. "After you change into your spare clothes I'll wash the ones you're wearing." Dinga had changed. Domestic would have been the last word I would have used to describe her. She was becoming a mother, the psychological changes apparently occurring before the physical.

Hornet hugged her, then kissed her tenderly. "Lord Hide has the amethyst sphere."

Dinga looked at Pulp. The gent said, "He isn't my MOST cantankerous brother. He's potty trained, but just barely. He's my height, without the good looks."

"We're going to hire an army to get past the hobs and gobs," Hornet continued.

Dinga looked confused.

"You're going fly to the sumopotts to make the arrangements," Nimbus announced.

The rest of us became confused.

"Flying saves us half-a-week," Nimbus explained, "assuming who went survived the journey. It's safer hundreds of feet above the ground."

Dinga didn't say anything. A moment later Hornet said, "You're not really thinking about doing this? Remember what happened in the Pewter Swamp?"

"Remember me finding that hermit cabin?"

"That took just a few minutes."

"This is something I have to do."

"You're...."

"If I don't go someone else will."

"We don't have to construct the portal. We can stay here."

"I AM pregnant. Which means---Gaea willing---what an odd thing to say---I will one day be a mother. I want to provide this child with every opportunity. Which means providing the opportunity to escape Limbo.

"It's much safer if I go. I'm more aware of my surroundings than I used to be. I'm less willing to take risks. I know, it sounds contrary to this discussion, but I am. Where are these sumopotts? I don't have to cross a sea do I?"

"They live in the Mercenary Hills, northeast of the Northwoods." No response from Dinga. "Northwest of here, about 250 kays. The Mercenary Hills aren't as tall as the Twins, but you'll still be able to see them from a distance."

"What do sumopotts look like?"

"Three meter tall bipedal hippos. They wear duckbilled caps, and not much else."

Dinga raised an eyebrow.

"They wear a thong for modesty."

Dinga became quiet again.

Hornet's eyes became brighter. "You're reconsidering."

"I'm calculating how long it will take to fly to the Mercenary Hills."

"Are you going to do this NOW?"

"I guess not. It will be getting dark. But first thing tomorrow morning. An hour there, you think, Nimbus?"

"Less than that for a drak. Maybe an hour-and-a-half for you."

"You don't think I can fly as fast a drak?"

"Nothing flies as fast as a drak."

"I guess we'll see, tomorrow.... Okay, boys. How about those clothes?"

The next morning, after breakfast, Dinga embraced her husband, kissed him tersely, then backed away. "Pick up my clothes for me please after I leave, fold them, and place them in a clean, dry spot. If you gentlemen wouldn't mind, give me a couple of minutes before you walk outdoors."

"How about the people already out there?" I asked.

"I'll be discrete. It doesn't matter as much if someone I don't know sees me."

When we walked outside we saw a black spec in the sky to the northwest that may have been Dinga. Hornet picked up Dinga's clothes.

"What is Dinga going to do when she returns?" I asked. "She won't have anything to wear---readily available."

"I guess we'll have to figure that out after she returns." Centaur smiled.

"You don't appear to be too concerned."

"She isn't my wife."

As we waited for Dinga to return, we revisited the pub. The more we knew about the Twin Hills and its occupants, down to the minutest of details, the greater our prospects for success. Somehow we were going to defeat two armies and a gent. Yes, I was confident. Cor blood wasn't tepid. What gets us into trouble is biting off more than we can chew.

"They don't like each other," someone shared.

"Isn't that obvious?" I responded.

"It's more than just a general animosity. Hobs hate gobs, and gobs hate hobs. They believe their adversary is inferior. So inferior that they should be exterminated, completely eliminated from Limbo."

"Which, of course, is impossible," added someone different, "with people being re-created instead of dying. An ironic twist is those dying are just as likely to return as a gob as a hob, and vice-versa, their mutational gene pools being so similar. Some of the most active combatants probably have changed sides dozens of times."

"Numbers on both sides continue to grow," spoke a third person. "In five years they've doubled. A disproportioned number of people mutate into one of those two races."

"And trogs," Hornet added.

"Could that be why so many trogs have been re-created?" I asked General Paint. "To counter the goblin races?"

"If it is, we'll be ready," he avowed.

"Goblins riled up in the Twin Hills and trogs in the Platinum Mountains," Centaur commented. "How many more races might be affected? How likely is it that the fourth sphere is also in the Negative Frontier? And the fifth and sixth? This isn't the best place to be if there's unrest."

"When is it ever a good place to be?" Pulp questioned.

"You wanted adventure. It looks like you'll get more than you bargained for before we construct the portal."

"Or at least my fill."

"Any regrets?" asked Hornet. "You're far more likely to die

226

out here than in the Copper Forest."

"If I remained in the Copper Forest I may have died from falling off a tree. At times the arbols can become quite distracting. No regrets. If I die I'll eventually return to the Copper Forest."

"Eventually? Not immediately?"

"Sometimes re-creations don't go the way you want them to---or expect."

"There aren't restrictions on gents, are there, like drak? You can be re-created as a gent. But you don't think you will."

"I may not have lived extravagantly enough to sustain my position."

"And that's what it takes to be re-created as a gent?"

"Not guaranteed, but it is a common characteristic."

"Do you have time to change the way you live?"

"Do I wish to?"

Dinga must have really pushed herself, because she returned two hours later.

"Well?" asked Centaur.

"They'll be here in four days."

"That's 60 kays per day."

"Sumopotts are renowned for their promptness," stated Nimbus.

"Will they have anything left in them when they arrive?"

"Their alacrity is guaranteed. Their professionalism prevents them from doing less than their best."

Two sumopott battalions arrived at sundim, on the arranged day. They waited for us at the base of Quantum Hill.

"They expect us to come down to them?" I asked. "Or will they come up to us?" I turned to face Dinga.

"I brought them here," she replied. "It's up to you boys to figure out the rest."

"It looks like they're setting up camp," said Hornet.

"That decides it," said Centaur. "Down we go."

"We?" Stick questioned.

"An Octagonal Knight will create a more potent impression."

"Why are we concerned about impressions? We did the hiring."

"The greatest advantage of power is intimidation," stated Nimbus. "If someone powerful is constantly confirming his advantages nothing is accomplished. Do you think I spent all day terrorizing villagers? It's tiring, and tedious. It's more peaceful when they are so frightened of you they leave you alone."

"Well, I'm definitely coming," said Pulp. "I've never seen a sumopott---up close."

"Come on, Stick," Dinga insisted. "It's not that far down."

"The down part doesn't worry me." I never liked busy work as a child, even the kind that included physical activity. That's why I liked cross country better than track. I hated running around in circles. With cross country you went somewhere. It was a challenge to climb a mountain. But a hill, to return home?---was more toil than trial.

The camp was complete by the time we arrived, the tents in neat rows and columns. I expected there to be cooking odors. It was that time of day. There was the hint of a farm---grain and grass, musk and manure---just a hint---but nothing more. If the wind wasn't blowing in our direction even that odor would have been absent.

From a distance the sight of the sumopotts didn't match the perception. It wasn't their clothes---they weren't wearing any--- nothing substantial. It was their demeanor. They acted very civilized. Mutants always seemed a bit feral to me, even the ones that looked predominantly human, like Pulp. The exception was Dinga, but that was because the form she preferred to be in was human. Up close the sumopotts transformed. Their gray heads were immense, and very leathery, with bulging eyes. Their most impressive feature was their teeth. They had large molars, but they were overshadowed by 5 sim incisors---and 20 sim canines.

By the time we had reached the base of the hill, two sumopotts intercepted us. Each wore a duckbill cap with three chevrons. One of the caps also had the silhouette of 11 felines. The other, 8 fowl.

"Sergeant Leaf, commander of the 11th Battalion, reporting as ordered." He saluted by placing his left hand to the side of his head, palm out.

"Sergeant Needle, commander of the 8th Battalion, reporting as ordered." He also saluted.

"My name is Centaur. I'm the leader of...this group." Centaur then began to name each of us, including Nimbus. "There is a...tribe...of hobs, and another of gobs. We wish you to...not necessarily eliminate... but to tie up...keep them occupied."

"Your goal?" asked Sergeant Leaf.

"To retrieve an artifact in the Quad Depression. It's in the center of...."

"We have studied the region," Sergeant Needle interjected.

"So you wish us to engage a group of gobs, and another of hobs, long enough for you to travel to the Quad Depression, retrieve an artifact, and return safely, to Quantum?"

"Precisely."

"Sumopotts aspire to be precise," stated Sergeant Needle.

"Shall we agree to begin at moonbrighten tomorrow?" asked Sergeant Leaf.

"We'll be ready," Centaur declared.

"We'll have contracts prepared," Sergeant Needle assured us.

"Contracts? We have already agreed on need and compensation."

"But not on the particulars. Completion of the mission is guaranteed---as specified in the contract."

The two battalion commanders saluted us, then returned to their respective camps.

"I suggest you not stray too far from your itinerary," Nimbus suggested. "It will be significantly more difficult returning to Quantum if the sumopotts abandon you."

I looked up at the hill. "Maybe we could join them down here tonight."

"Come on," Centaur insisted. "We've been cooped up for four days. You could use the exercise."

"You exaggerate my impatience. We'll have plenty to do tomorrow."

Chapter 34

DEPRESSION

By the time we reached the base of the hill in the morning the sumopott camp was already broken down. The two battalion commanders greeted us again, each with a parchment.

Centaur read each carefully. It didn't take long. They were detailed, but not verbose, in simple language. And very similar.

"Why, two contracts?" he asked.

"Sumopott battalions are sovereign entities," Sergeant Leaf responded. "We support one another when needed, but we have exclusive missions."

"So, the 11th Battalion will attack the hobs, and the 8th, the gobs?"

"We'll keep them engaged until your return or until sundim tomorrow," Sergeant Needle assured us.

"And if we don't return by then?" asked Hornet.

"Two days gives you sufficient time to accomplish your mission. If you don't return by then we will assume a fatal failure or an alteration in your extraction."

"And what happens if YOU aren't successful?" asked Centaur.

"If this mission wasn't going to succeed we would have

modified our assistance," stated Sergeant Leaf. "Are you ready to begin?"

Each battalion formed three rows, a dozen soldiers deep. So few in number, and without armor---or weapons---how could they possibly succeed? Was it too late for General Paint to summon his army?

The sumopotts left the base of Quantum Hill in parade fashion. Both battalions performed a quarter counter-clockwise turn in unison, the rows becoming columns. The 8th Battalion left first, followed by the 11th exactly twelve paces behind. The 8th began to sing in rhythm to their marching, something about gobs and their mothers. The 11th began singing twelve steps later, about hobs and their fathers. If the sumopotts intent was to surprise their enemies they had an odd way of going about it.

We followed them, but many paces behind. We intended to lunge past them once they engaged the hobs and gobs, but we didn't want to find ourselves in their midst if they got massacred.

We heard fighting before we saw it. Four-dozen gobs fought half that many hobs in the cleft between two of the smaller hills. It was brutal entertainment. Most of the combatants had poorly constructed, rusting weapons. They would have been practically useless on a well-armored opponent. Fortunately the armor they wore was of an equally poor construction. It fell apart as often as it prevented a deadly strike.

The sumopotts separated, the 8th Battalion going left, the 11th right. They continued forward, but at a 10 percent declination, outward. They had flanked their adversaries. The battalions turned a quarter turn clockwise, reforming the columns into rows.

The hobs and gobs, not wishing to become trapped---and not wanting others to interfere in their private war---swarmed the two battalions, the hobs going one way, the gobs going the other. Neither of the degenerative races had a ranged attack, forcing them to come close before engaging the sumopotts.

Each front line of mercenaries began marching towards their adversaries. Twelve paces later the intermediate lines began moving, about the time the hobs and gobs crashed into the first lines. Weapons struck the sumopotts. Instead of ripping flesh, they bounced back, like they had hit dense rubber. The ricochet caused them to slice through their own faces and upper torsos. After the initial strike the sumopotts went into action. They fell onto their opponents, the directed impact and immense weight crushing bones and internal organs. The intermediate line of sumopotts joined the battle. They deflected additional hob and gob blows before falling onto their prey. The final line of sumopotts was cleanup. They took care of the stragglers, then helped their comrades up. They began to search through the pulverized hob and gob corpses for anything of value---which wasn't much.

We stood stunned. Sergeant Leaf shook his head with disappointment. Spoils just weren't what they used to be. He looked in our direction. "You have your diversion."

"More than that," I whispered to myself.

"You better get a move on," said Sergeant Needle. "Our mission isn't complete until yours is."

The sumopotts were very efficient. By the time we had made it past the battlefield they were already on the move again, the 8th Battalion heading into the cleft on the left, the 11th into the one on the right.

The sumopotts had engaged the hobs and gobs so efficiently we reached the Quad Depression without seeing another member of either. We heard fighting, but it remained distant.

The Quad Depression was void of direct light. The four clefts that merged to form the depression were narrow. They were far enough from the center of Limbo that direct sunlight didn't shine into them. A perpetual twilight permeated the area. Shapes could be seen, but unidentified. Bridges, 100 meters above us, appeared to connect the Four Quads. Something large walked on one of them.

"I SEE THE SPHERE!" Hornet shouted. It was in the center of the depression. A tapered marble pedestal rose from a granite prism. The sphere was cradled in the chalice at its crest.

A boulder crashed to the ground, a meter from us. It

crumbled into a thousand pieces, its debris causing minor
abrasions. Pulp looked up, angrily, the first time I have ever seen
him like that. He shouted upwards, loudly, so loud I thought he
might cause an avalanche. "HOW DARE YOU ATTEMPT TO HARM A
FELLOW GENT! ONE MORE ATTACK AND I WILL REPORT YOU TO
THE BROTHERHOOD!"

"IT IS NOT YOU WHO WE ATTACK!" an even more powerful
voice echoed down at us, shaking the fragments of the shattered
boulder.

"There is more than one of them?" asked Dinga.

"Lord Hide is proficient in the royal we," Pulp remarked,
appearing to be mildly amused. Pulp may have been upset with
Lord Hide, but he was his brother. One had to put up with their
relatives' peculiarities---the good and the bad. That's assuming
they had some good qualities. There was a reason a majority of
gents lived in the Negative Frontier.

"SEPARATE YOURSELF FROM THESE INTERLOPERS SO WE
MAY DISPATCH THEM!"

"WE WILL DO WHAT WE CAME HERE TO DO, TOGETHER!"

"VERY WELL, BUT THERE WILL BE CONSEQUENCES. WE WILL
RETAIN THIS FORM FOR MANY MORE YEARS, AS WILL THOSE WE
HAVE A STRONGER ALLIANCE!"

"SO YOU WILL NOT ATTACK US?!"

"WE WILL NOT ATTACK YOU! IT'S MORE ENTERTAINING TO
WATCH!"

More movement above us---enough to release a shower of
scree---then nothing. No activity at all. Utter silence.

Centaur looked up. "I don't see a storm, but I guarantee
you, one is coming."

"You think Lord Hide will send some hobs and gobs our
way?" asked Dinga.

"Considering how quickly the sumopotts are dispatching
them there can't be that many left to send our way," I commented.

"Hide won't be happy about that," said Pulp. "Being orderly,
he doesn't react well to change. It's likely he has a backup. Being
chaotically minded I make-up things as I go. He doesn't have such

luxury. He's proactive, not reactionary."

"We better keep our guard up, then," Centaur suggested. "That sphere is just there for the taking, and its making me awfully uneasy."

We cautiously circled the prism. It was seven meters tall, too high for even Pulp to pull himself up, and too shear to climb. "Pulp, you willing to be used as a ladder again?" asked Centaur. The gent nodded. "Hornet, with that ring of yours and your innate ability to circumvent harm, you should be the one to do the climbing." He also nodded.

The plan almost worked. As Pulp leaned against the pedestal to give himself more support, a shrill dissonance erupted from the top of the prism, causing him to drop Hornet. As we helped Hornet up and examined him for injuries, something sinister came out of the top of the pedestal.

It appeared to be a helium-filled balloon. As it floated above us a gigantic eye was released from its body, the elongated appendage it was attached to making it look like a turtle coming out of its shell. The iris was multi-faceted, resembling a bloodshot sunflower. Additional tendrils were released, smaller, and wiggling like worms---also with eyes.

We became mesmerized. I couldn't move.

Centaur was first to be attacked. One of the tendril-eyes winked at him. He instantaneously turned to stone.

Another looked at me. It took a couple of seconds for it to register, my mind still numb from the enthrallment. I WAS ON FIRE! The pain finally hit me, my nerve endings finally relaying the information to my brain. I was in agony. I never felt such intense pain in my life. It blistered my soul.

I no longer felt pain. I suddenly felt more wonderful than I had ever felt. I didn't exactly feel pleasure. The non-feeling was a welcomed contrast to the pain. A person doesn't really know pleasure until they feel acute pain.

In third-person perspective I saw myself fall to the ground, my flesh burning black. My armor was smudged by the burnt

234

carbon, but it appeared to be undamaged. Spontaneously, it evaporated, like it was water on a hot surface. My charcoaled remains crumbled apart.

My companions were engaged in the fight of their lives. Lightning struck Nimbus, but instead of shattering his wood and stone body, it dissipated, like he had absorbed the energy.

General Paint had gone insane. He randomly struck out, hitting his companions as often as his adversary.

Hornet knocked him unconscious from behind, but not before the trog struck Centaur's stone body, breaking off one of his fingers.

Hornet was spared, none of the orb's attacks against him able to make contact. It would have been a miraculous occurrence if it didn't happen so consistently.

Pulp was struck by a glancing burst of frigid air. His left arm was blackened from the frost bite. The attack disrupted his stupor. He charged the orb.

Dinga hadn't been attacked yet, her less aggressive nature distancing her from the battle.

I felt more than saw what was transpiring. My consciousness hovered above my body, but it didn't stay. With an acceleration comparable to gravity I was forced away from the battle, not aware of its outcome. I moved towards the Northern Spine at an angle. I followed the mountains until they terminated at the forest to their south. By the time I was over a sea I was already decelerating. I was over land again, first above a marsh, then more mountains. As I angled away from the mountains I saw a tower to my left on top of the tallest mountain in the chain. Directly in front of me had to be Gulag. It was much larger than any city I had been to on Limbo. It spread out randomly in all directions. Being the first settlement on Limbo there was no time for planning, and apparently no one had made an attempt to correct its flaws in the more than a century of its existence. Near its center was an octagonal shaped building. It appeared to be constructed of glass. As I slowed to the velocity a man might walk I crashed into the building. Instead of shattering it I passed through, as if it didn't consist of matter.

A vessel the size and shape of a coffin rested in the center of the building. It too was made of what appeared to be glass. I floated into the vessel. A body began to form around me.

*** This concludes Book 3 of the Limbo Chronicles. ***

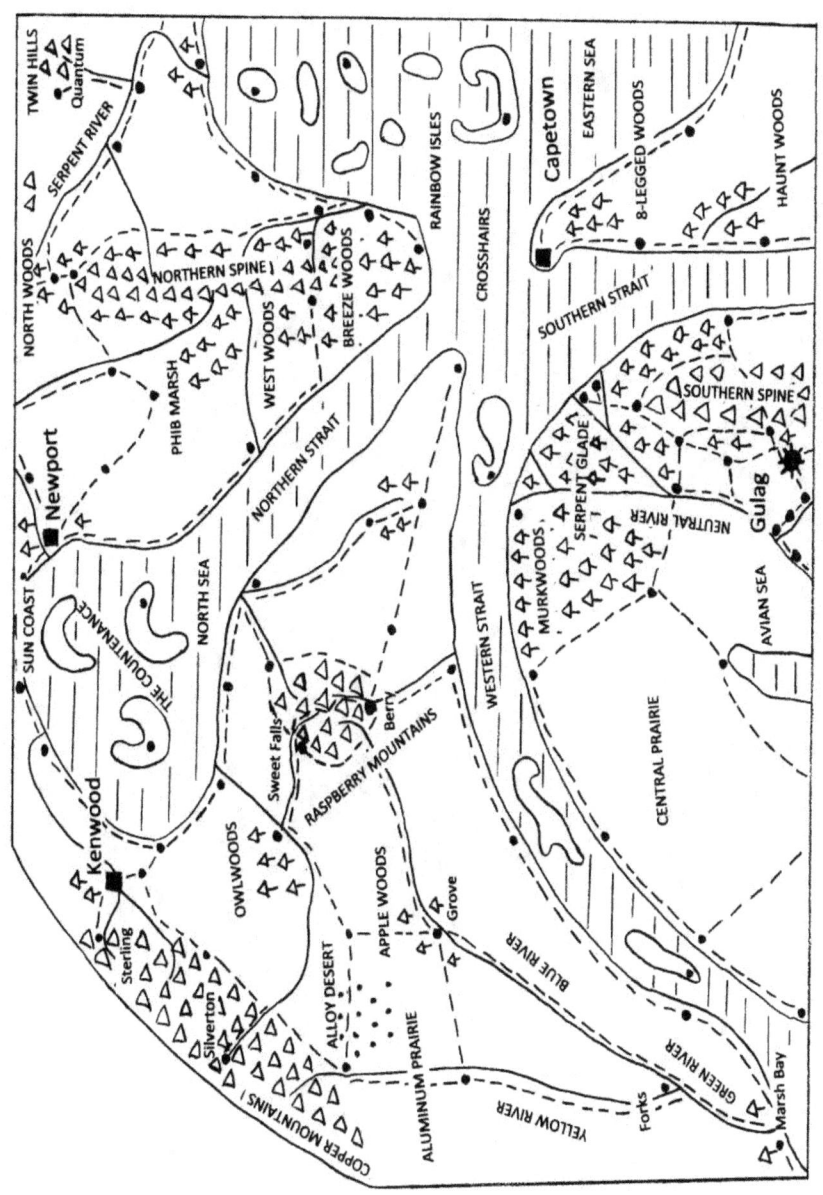

www.ingramcontent.com/pod-product-compliance
Lightning Source LLC
Chambersburg PA
CBHW071901220626
47052CB00002B/160